Angel's
SHARE

Angel's SHARE

KAYTE NUNN

NERO

Published by Nero,
an imprint of Schwartz Publishing Pty Ltd
Level 1, 221 Drummond Street
Carlton VIC 3053, Australia
enquiries@blackincbooks.com
www.nerobooks.com

National Library of Australia Cataloguing-in-Publication entry:
Nunn, Kayte, author.
Angel's share / Kayte Nunn.
9781863959230 (paperback)
9781925435603 (ebook)
Romance fiction.
Man-woman relationships—Fiction.
Australian fiction.
Wineries—Australia—Fiction.

.

Designed and typeset by Tristan Main
Author photo by Jane Earle
Cover image by Olga Danylenko, Shutterstock
Graphic by Ohn Mar, Shutterstock

For Fi – you were so loved.

'Why do you go away? So that you can come back. So that you can see the place you came from with new eyes and extra colors. And the people there see you differently, too. Coming back to where you started is not the same as never leaving.'

Terry Pratchett, *A Hat Full of Sky (Discworld, #32)*

CHAPTER ONE

Matilda Cameron peered through her car windscreen as the wipers sluiced away the water that was bucketing from the heavens. In the gloomy pre-dawn light she could just about make out a long Regency terrace to her right. With its ornate white stucco facade, rectangular windows and black wrought-iron balconies, it reminded her of a soggy wedding cake. To her left lay a pebbled seafront and a grey expanse of what passed for ocean in this part of the world.

She was there, at such a godforsaken hour, an hour when she would normally be in a nice warm bed, because today was the day that they were photographing the stills for a new campaign for DeVere & Soames, one of Britain's most celebrated jewellers. A jeweller with four Royal Warrants, no less, as Jamie Soames, great-great-great-grandson of one of the original founders, had impressed upon her when she'd met with him in his Albemarle Street offices a few weeks earlier.

'I'm sure you realise how important it is that we get this absolutely right,' Soames had said, a tight smile on his patrician features.

'Yes, absolutely right,' she had assured him, trying not to subconsciously mimic his accent. 'You're in the best hands in the country; I know you'll be delighted with our work.' His business was dependent on it. Her job was riding on it.

The weather, however, wasn't cooperating.

She could see Cara, the stylist, parked a few metres away, the back of her station wagon piled high with suit bags, shoe boxes and hats, and there was Paul, Mattie's favourite hair and makeup wizard – 'Honestly, the guy could make a rusty brillo pad look good,' Bianca, her boss at Three Bees, had said when she'd first recommended him – parked next to Cara. There was no sign of the two young models, Cassandra and Jemima, who Mattie had cast last week, nor was the honeywagon anywhere to be seen.

She glanced at Orazio, who was in the passenger's seat beside her, drumming his fingers on the dashboard and looking every bit the temperamental hot young Italian photographer. He was being hailed as the new Demarchelier and was in such high demand in London and New York that she'd been wildly lucky to book him for the dates they needed. She'd only succeeded due to a combination of dogged persistence and major sucking up to his agent. He didn't drive, so she'd picked him up from his Peckham terrace at the excruciatingly early time of 5.30am, loading his camera gear into the back of her car, and they had been sitting, watching the rain on the Brighton seafront, for the past half-hour. She fumbled in her bag for an antacid – her stomach was in knots. She hadn't had time for more than coffee before they'd left and there was nowhere open. Not that she was getting out of the car in this downpour in any case. She ground the chalky tablet between her teeth and then, for something to do besides worry about the weather, consulted the call sheet yet again. She reviewed the plans for the day's shoot, the brief for the photographer, the head shots of the models, the permits that allowed them to shoot, and the contacts for everyone involved, including the absent honey-wagon company. They were also still waiting on DeVere & Soames' security guard with a gazillion quids' worth of diamonds, rubies and emeralds. The reason they were all there in the first place. The success of today's shoot, the whole campaign actually, was in her hands. The buck – as Bianca hadn't failed to remind her – stopped with her. It had been her creative concept, her strategy, and she couldn't afford to bugger it up, not if she wanted to hold onto her job, not to mention get away to her long-awaited holiday on time.

Ten days. Switzerland. With Johnny. Snow-capped mountains, postcard-perfect chalets and romantic log fires. She could almost taste the whipped cream on top of the hot chocolate. Sighing, she got out her phone and punched in a number from the sheet. It was going to be a long day.

As Mattie was dialling, an enormous trailer bearing the fifties-style curling logo 'Sweet As' rumbled around the corner. 'Well, that's one less thing to worry about: the honeywagon's here – at least the girls will have somewhere to change. Now how are we going to get around this weather?' she asked Orazio, keeping her voice upbeat. The shoot had been organised with no time for a proper recce, nor was there an alternative date on which to do it, given Orazio's heavily booked schedule. Not waiting for his answer, she texted Cara. *Any idea what's happened to Cassandra and Jemima?*

Cara's reply pinged back instantly. *Mimi's mum's car died. They're on the 8.30 train.*

Mattie frowned. There wasn't much daylight to work with in winter and this would mean that they were behind before they'd even begun. Hair and makeup alone would take at least an hour. For each girl.

Too impatient to text again, she dialled. Cara answered before the phone even had a chance to ring. 'I'll go and pick them up later,' Mattie said. 'Do you want to get everything out of the car and into the wagon? I'll get Paul to set up and then Orazio and I'll scout a few locations, see if there's anywhere in this godforsaken place that's under cover and out of the rain.'

'No worries, Mats. I'm on it.' Cara was, like Mattie, one of the Aussie advertising mafia, blow-ins from downunder who held the London media world to ransom with their never-say-die attitude and ability to work hard and play even harder. Needless to say, their more laidback, self-deprecating British colleagues couldn't make them out at all.

Mattie had been dazzled and intimidated in equal measure by Cara from the moment she met her. The fashion stylist's petite rear, as round as a peach and clad in shiny copper-coloured jeans, had been sticking out of a cupboard in the Three Bees offices. 'Where the fuck are the new Manolo samples?' she cursed. 'I'll be ropable if anyone's taken them without checking with me first.'

As Cara stood up, Mattie saw that she had long poker-straight platinum-blonde hair and the features of a porcelain doll. With her slim figure and the delicate bones of a prima ballerina, Cara looked like she'd be knocked over in the first gust of wind, but in reality she was a tough operator with a vocabulary saltier than a pirate's. That, combined with the fact that most of the time she dressed as if she were on her way to the Stella McCartney front row, meant that the rest of the office – and their clients – were in equal awe and terror of her. She looked exactly like the kind of precious, high-fashion princess that Mattie had little in common with and even less time for, but she had heard the familiar accent and softened her judgement. 'I think I saw Jasmine with them this morning,' she offered.

'Oh, right,' Cara replied, backing out of the cupboard. 'Thanks, mate. Was about to go off on one there for a minute. Proper dummy spit.'

On the surface the two girls couldn't have appeared more different – Mattie was a spiky-haired tomboy whose preferred mode of dress was jeans and a t-shirt – but after a night out when they discovered an unlikely but shared passion for *Les Mis* and a mutual infatuation with Eddie Redmayne – 'Oh, his cheekbones …' 'No, those sleepy, sexy eyes … God he could totally do me …' – and a fondness for Slippery Nipple cocktails, the friendship was cemented. Never mind that Cara was a city girl who claimed to get dizzy if she saw too much open space and only ever slept under the five stars, and that Mattie was secretly happiest outside under a million of them, the two became firm friends at work and almost inseparable outside of it.

Cara had a cool, left-of-centre aesthetic that was going to be perfect for what Mattie had in mind for the DeVere shoot, and she knew she could rely on her completely, especially if things got tricky. Which it looked like they were going to be. They'd already run through the clothes that Cara had selected to complement the jewels – 'pieces', Jamie Soames had reverently called them when he briefed her – and now all Mattie had to do was scout half a dozen locations in and around Brighton. Not too much of a tall order on any normal day in any normal country, but this was England and today's downpour was making her job almost impossible. She refused to be beaten by anything – let alone the weather – and began to brainstorm alternative locations that would offer some protection from the rain.

'Fierce. But fresh. That's what we're looking for.' Orazio was coaching the two gawky, impossibly skinny, deathly pale teenagers as they sat, hair wound around enormous rollers, having their makeup done. They'd arrived, thank Christ, and Mattie had bundled them down to the seafront and straight into the honeywagon, where Paul was on standby, brushes and tongs at the ready. She'd been alarmed to see that Cassandra had cut a full six inches off her hair since the previous week's casting.

'How many hair extensions did you bring, mate?' she quizzed Paul as her stomach churned with anxiety. 'Cause we're gonna need them all, I reckon.'

Somewhat miraculously, the rain had begun to peter out and Mattie saw a faint hint of brightness on the horizon as a watery sun struggled to break through. The security guard from DeVere had also arrived. Mattie saw Cara's eyes flick over him, taking in his broad chest and solid, rugby-player thighs. She also noticed Cara clocking the handcuffs that bound the bulky briefcase to his wrist and suppressed a smile. She knew exactly what her friend would be thinking and flashed a warning at her with her eyes.

'As if!' Cara protested, getting her meaning. As Mattie laughed, she noticed that the rain had now completely stopped. Thank heavens for small mercies.

Cara gasped when the first of the necklaces was revealed. 'Fucking hell, they are incredible!' she said as she bent over it to get a closer look. Mattie had seen them in the DeVere showroom when she was planning the shoot. They were gorgeous but she could never imagine wearing anything as precious herself. Her budget had never run to jewellery. Even her watch was selected less for its looks than for its ability to withstand careless treatment. In fact, her most prized possessions, should anyone ever ask, would probably be her two pairs of RM Williams boots.

'Great, super, fantastic, *si*, do that … that thing with your eyes, Jemima.' Orazio snapped away furiously as the girls wobbled on spindly heels on the pebbly beach. 'Don't think about the cold; imagine it's a spring morning, and you've got the sun on your face, you're a spring flower, yes, tip your head up like that ... *bellissimo*.'

Mattie studied the two girls, their silk dresses fluttering in the breeze, thin arms blue with cold, jewels flashing like ice in the fading light. An idea came to her.

'How about we pop you up there?' She looked at Orazio, who shrugged.

'Up there' was two metres off the ground on a stone parapet. Both girls looked horrified. 'Really, it'll make a great shot,' she reassured them. 'Look, let me show you what I'm thinking. Orazio, give us a leg-up, will you?' With the photographer's assistance, Mattie sprang up the wall, scrambling with the toes of her boots to get a foothold, and hauled herself onto the ledge. It was narrower than she'd thought, and slippery from the earlier rain, but she stood poised, flinging out her arms and pointing one foot in front of her. 'See, like this.' She had loved gymnastics as a child, and had lost none of the agility that sport demanded.

Up high, she felt as if she could flap her arms and soar right off the narrow stone ledge, floating above the rooftops, over the sea, the pier stretching out like an index finger into the water, pointing the way to France. As she balanced on one leg, looking straight ahead rather than down at the ground, she smiled at the memory of a long-forgotten nickname ... Fearless. That was what Charlie Drummond had called her once, a long time ago. Funny, she hadn't thought about him in years. She could clearly picture his freckled face grinning at her and sending her teenage heart flip-flopping like one of those mood-divining fish that came in Christmas crackers. She shook her head at the memory. Another lifetime. Not one she planned to ever return to.

'You make it seem easy,' said Cassandra, hugging her arms around herself and looking petrified.

'You'll be fine,' said Mattie, reluctantly jumping down and landing in front of her. 'Come on, let me give you a leg-up.'

A few minutes later, Mattie hunched over a tented laptop, where the images appeared as Orazio clicked away. She let out a breath she hadn't realised she'd been holding. She loved this part; everything coming together as she'd seen it in her mind's eye, imagining the shots blown up beyond life-size on bill-boards, or appearing in the pages of glossy magazines. 'I reckon we've got it,' she said to herself. The light was perfect: watery and pale. In contrast, the jewels glowed with barely contained fire. She felt a thrill of achievement. It was something she could feel in her gut; she simply, instinctively knew when she'd pulled off something special. She had been right to insist on Orazio shooting the campaign. In that moment, all of the worry over the weather and the models, all of the late nights of brainstorming and planning leading up to the shoot day were forgotten for this feeling of perfect rightness. She turned to Orazio and gave him a thumbs-up. 'We've nailed it, mate.'

He shrugged. '*Prego.*'

*

'Can you believe tomorrow's nearly here?' Mattie asked her friend as they packed everything away. Cara, together with Johnny's mate Nick, was joining them on the ski trip.

Cara winked. 'One more sleep, mate.' She stopped and rifled through her enormous handbag. 'Bullet?'

'Raspberry? No kidding! You know they're my favourites – bloody hell, where did you get them?'

'Special delivery from Mum. She knows what I'm missing. Thinks it might tempt me home,' she laughed.

'Never!' said Mattie.

She chewed on the white chocolate–coated raspberry sweet and was instantly transported. Cicadas droning. Endless blue skies. Flies driving everyone crazy. Sitting on the back verandah, looking out at the rows of lush vines that stretched as far as the eye could see, the Shingle Hills shadowy in the distance. Her brother, Mark, beside her, doling out the lollies, holding the white paper bag up over her head so she couldn't tell how many were left. He was at least a metre taller than her and ten years older, and she had cursed her lack of height growing up, not least at times like those. She remembered baking-hot days spent chasing the shadows of tall river gums, struggling to stay astride a saddle slick with sweat. Diving into the river – which was always ice cold and ink dark, no matter how hot it was outside – to wash off the dust after a long ride. If she tried hard enough she could almost smell the ripe, equine scent of her beloved Shakira – named after an enduring but ill-advised girl crush on the Colombian-born singer – and feel the comforting solidity of the horse's withers beneath her. Her heart still gave an unexpected pang when she thought of the old mare. Shakira was probably the thing she missed most about home.

Despite her assertion to Cara, she felt a sudden longing for the unrelenting heat and wide horizons, for light so bright you had to screw up your eyes against its glare. It had been more than a decade since she'd got on a plane at Sydney Airport, with nothing but a flimsy portfolio, a place at Central Saint Martins and a burning desire to escape her rural roots. She had deliberately made herself into a different person. The woman who directed million-pound advertising shoots with ease was a far cry from Tilly Cameron, the angry teenager who'd practically scorched the earth in her haste to get away from the Shingle Valley.

CHAPTER TWO

Half a world away, Rose Bennett was having trouble sleeping. She glanced across to Mark, who was spark out next to her, snoring loudly, the covers shuddering with every out-breath. He'd put in nearly fifteen hours at the winery the day before. During the long weeks of vintage he often worked almost around the clock, snatching a few hours' sleep in between shifts, making sure that the pickers knew exactly what they were doing, that the quality of the grapes coming in to the crusher was up to scratch, that the ferment stayed at precisely the right temperature and didn't get stuck or prevent the sugar in the grapes turning to alcohol ... the list of jobs at this time of year was almost never-ending. There was also something else to worry about now, with rumours of a mining company sniffing around the valley.

At this time of year, Rose counted herself fortunate to see him for more than a snatched conversation over a hastily eaten bowl of pasta or a cup of tea. But it was nearly finished, and in two days' time they were taking the kids to the coast. She could hardly wait, and neither could Leo and Luisa, who had also barely seen their father in the last few weeks.

There was just so much to do before they left.

Thoughts swirled around in her head, of Leo, who was eleven and having a few problems at school, of Luisa, delightful and cheeky at nearly five, of Mark's meeting scheduled with the accountant at the end of the week, the work still to be done at her restaurant, Trevelyn's Pantry, and the holiday packing she hadn't even begun…

By the time the alarm went off some four hours later, she was groggy from the interrupted night. Mark spooned her and she felt him warm against her back, familiar and comforting, their bodies slotting together like two inter-locking pieces of a well-made puzzle.

'It's early, do you have to get up just yet?' she whispered, moving her body against his, despite her tiredness.

He groaned. 'Four more days, babe, then I'm all yours.'

After a beat she unwound herself from him reluctantly and slid out from beneath the sheets. 'Okay. Coffee?'

'Legend.'

Rose padded down the wide stairs of Kalkari House and into the sunny kitchen. It was her favourite room in the rambling old house. She loved the pale yellow enamel range that sat in a huge inglenook fireplace, and the scrubbed-oak table that, at the moment, was almost entirely covered by paper, cardboard boxes, glue, sticky tape and felt-tip pens. Leo and Luisa were designing tree houses. Leo had been begging Mark to build him one in the branches of one of the huge liquidambar trees that stood sentinel at the start of the drive, but Mark was too preoccupied with vintage to think seriously about it. Perhaps she ought to take matters into her own hands and find someone local to do it, Rose mused. It didn't have to cost much – well, not unless they incorporated all of Leo's grand plans, she thought as she looked at the latest elaborate construction.

There never seemed to be enough time; she was constantly trying to keep all the balls in the air, running a fledgling business, supporting Mark in his, and trying her best to be a good stepmother. It was exhausting, but she couldn't complain – she loved it all, the whole crazy busyness of her life. Well, apart from the mess, perhaps. She could do with less of that.

Sweeping the models into one corner of the table, Rose waited for the kettle to boil. She heard the sounds of birds cawing their early-morning chorus outside, and over it, the distinctive cock-a-doodle-doo of Nugget, the Kalkari rooster. The sun was rising and it looked set to be another beautiful day. A scorcher, if the forecast was to be believed. It was the school holidays, and Leo loved to hang out in the winery – though he didn't much care for the back-breaking work of picking the grapes, which was where Mark would have preferred his help. Luisa would, Rose knew, be happy to play with her and Astrid in the kitchen, where Rose had not only to prepare lunches for the winery crew and the pickers, but also do some prep for her restaurant, which was a couple of kilometres further along the Shingle Valley. The restaurant had been the home of local grape-growers Vera and Violet Trevelyn before it was gutted by fire a couple of years earlier. Rose's brother, Henry, had bought the property and she had overseen the renovation of the old building, restoring it to its former glory, putting in a commercial kitchen and opening up the downstairs spaces to form a restaurant dining room. It was only open for lunch and dinner Friday through Sunday, but there still seemed to be so much to do every other day of the week, and Rose was anxious to get a head start on things before the weekend rush began.

If she was lucky, she thought, she might squeeze in a quick run before it got too hot and the demands of the day overtook her. She returned upstairs to Mark, mug in hand, tiptoeing past the kids' rooms in order not to wake them.

Mark was already in the shower, so she left his coffee on the bedside table before slipping on a singlet, shorts and shoes and heading downstairs and out the back door.

Kalkari House was still as imposing as when she'd first laid eyes on it, the honey-coloured stone catching the morning light, which also reflected off the panes in the large square windows. Rose never failed to be amazed by the beauty of the place that she now called home, falling in love with it afresh almost every time she stopped to gaze across the wide valley plain. She revelled in the early-morning view of the vineyards spread out across the valley, protected by the steep slopes of the Shingle Hills in the distance.

The air was already warm and fragrant with the honey-suckle that grew along the wall at the side of the house. Rose breathed in, savouring the fresh, sweet scent. She noticed a lone magpie, hopping on the gravel at the front of the house, and looked frantically around for its mate. No joy. She did her best to dismiss the old saying – one for sorrow – from her mind as she gathered her long, dark hair in a ponytail, adjusted her running cap and set off on her favourite loop down the drive and up along the Shingle Road. She soon hit her stride and settled in to a steady pace, cares temporarily forgotten by the time she puffed up the steep hill behind the winery.

Arriving back at the house about forty minutes later, she saw Astrid's car parked at an angle across the drive in front of the house, as if she'd abandoned it in a hurry. The rear passenger door was still open, the hulk of a toddler's car seat visible. Closing the door and coming into the house, Rose found the Austrian nanny in the kitchen, watching as her flaxen-haired, chubby-cheeked son spooned cereal into his mouth.

'Hey, Astrid, how are you? Hello, Maxie!' She ran a tender hand over his fair curls.

Astrid grinned, besotted, at the toddler. 'We're all good here, aren't we, Max?'

Max flung Weetbix on the floor with fat fingers.

'Did you know the car door was open?' asked Rose.

'Oh God, sorry. Max was yelling for his breakfast. I was in such a rush. He's a holy terror when he's starving – a bit like his dad, really.'

Astrid had been nanny to Leo and Luisa for more than three years. When she found herself unexpectedly pregnant to local vigneron Thommo Drummond, Mark had been more than happy for her to come back to work to look after them within a few months of Max's arrival, bringing the baby with her. Luckily for all, and his young mother especially, Max was an easygoing little soul – well, apart from when he was hungry – and Luisa, particularly, doted on him. Rose had first come to Kalkari a few months after Astrid, originally to work as an au pair and cook, and the two women had become friends, united in their mutual dislike of Isabella, Mark's estranged, and now thankfully ex, wife.

'I'll go and see where the other two are and get them to come down for some brekky. I thought we could all go to the river for a swim this afternoon. Looks like it's going to be a hot one. I've got a heap of prep to do at Trevelyn's first though, and I really need to weed the veggie patch over there, as well as make lunches for the picking crew.'

'Sounds good,' Astrid replied. 'I'll take the kids into Eumeralla this morning; Isabella wants me to get their hair cut. The last time, when I did it, she told me they looked worse than refugees and I must have used pruning shears. Pah! What is wrong with using the kitchen scissors anyway?'

Since Isabella had walked out on Mark several years before, she divided her time between the Shingle Valley and her native Spain. She was a constant thorn in Rose's side – not that Astrid fared much better – and Rose was still completely intimidated by her glossy sophistication and cutting comments. Isabella, for her part, looked at Rose like something the cat had brought in. She treated her like an imposter who wouldn't be sticking around for long. Certainly if she had anything to do with it. This made Rose even more tongue-tied around her, and left her feeling like a gauche teenager instead of a grown woman. She did, however, get some small satisfaction from the fact that she was in fact proving Isabella wrong by still being with Mark, nearly three years down the track. Mark did his best to keep the peace, and for her part Rose tried to steer clear of the intractable Spanish woman whenever possible, but it wasn't always easy. She reminded herself that she was going to have to speak to Isabella that morning to see if she would bring over the kids' swimsuits and goggles – she'd turned their rooms upside down before remembering that they'd left them at their mother's the week before. She wasn't looking forward to the call.

CHAPTER THREE

Mattie tugged on the zip of her suitcase, stopping as she heard the distinctive rattle and honk of a black cab outside the window. She glanced around at the shitstorm that was her room. Clothes spilled out of drawers, magazines and books teetered on the bedside table, dirty coffee mugs and plates laid a trail towards the door. The rest of the flat wasn't in a much better state. Cara teased her that she managed to be painstakingly efficient and organised at work, but that her home wasn't fit to keep pigs in. She raced towards the front door, promising herself that she'd sort it all out when she got back.

What lay ahead was far more exciting.

She, Johnny, Cara and Nick were due to meet at the airport in an hour. She was beside herself with excitement; she'd never been to Switzerland and had been captivated by the storybook images she'd seen on the travel websites – like

Heidi come to life. She hadn't had a proper break since starting work at Three Bees almost a year ago, and couldn't wait to escape the unrelenting London grey. Working at one of London's most dynamic ad agencies, with a roster of fashionable, gilt-edged clients, wasn't exactly the career of a fine artist that she'd dreamed of once upon a time, but it more than paid the bills she'd racked up as a student and she loved the creativity of the job, the energy of the people she worked with. She also loved living in a big city, the buzz of being part of such a vibrant place, and nurtured bigger dreams, perhaps at the helm of her own agency one day, or masterminding the revival of a neglected brand. She had a point to prove – to herself and to everything and everyone she'd left behind. The fact that she chewed antacid tablets as if they were breath mints and she couldn't remember the last time she'd woken up without a headache went, in her mind at least, with the territory.

The taxi honked again, and she took a last look around, checking she hadn't forgotten anything essential. Hurrying downstairs, she heaved her suitcase into the cab's boot and climbed in the back. At last she and Johnny would have some uninterrupted time together. And she and her best friend could hang out as well. It couldn't be more perfect.

Mattie had met Johnny just over a year ago. She'd gone out to catch up with a couple of acquaintances on a Sunday night at a pub in Covent Garden. It was a dark, noisy place, thronging with expats and backpackers, their once-familiar broad accents now sounding foreign to her. The bare floorboards were sticky with spilt beer and a booming bass thumped from a speaker above her head. As far as she was concerned it was the bowels of hell, but she'd been in the middle of a meeting at work when the message came through and had been too busy to suggest somewhere better. She eventually spotted the couple she had come to see, but it was impossible to hear even half of what they were saying over the roar of voices and music, and she didn't plan to stay for long. One drink later she was saying her farewells. Promising to catch up with them again soon, she fought her way through the crush to the door. As she pulled on the heavy iron handle to leave, she was nearly sent flying by a tall figure pushing his way in.

'Oh God, I'm terribly sorry, didn't see you there. Are you alright? I didn't do any serious damage, did I? Less haste more speed, hey?'

She craned her neck upwards and saw broad shoulders encased in a striped emerald and white rugby shirt, close-cropped sandy hair and a concerned look in a pair of the clearest blue eyes she'd ever seen. The man spoke with a clipped accent but she had to stand on tiptoes to understand him above the noise in the pub. Taking a closer inventory, she noticed a faint sprinkling of freckles across the bridge of his nose. Broad shoulders and freckles. A killer combination. She wasn't sure what a posh, most likely ex-public schoolboy was doing at The Rouseabout though. It was generally strictly colonials only.

Her voice was husky from shouting over the din. 'Don't worry about it, I'm fine. Honestly, I am.'

'No really, I can't believe I would trip over someone as blindingly gorgeous as you. But maybe that's it,' he continued hopefully, 'perhaps I was knocked senseless by your beauty?'

From anyone else's lips it would have sounded like the world's cheesiest line, but as she looked up at him she couldn't help but be a tiny bit charmed. Still, she doubted the sincerity in his words. Though she'd inherited her fair skin and fine bone structure from her mother and her wide-set, bottle-green eyes and dark brown hair from her father, she knew that she was far from conventionally beautiful – her lips slightly uneven, the lower one fuller and pouting, her nose a little too tilted, her hair too spiky. She was also wearing her favourite faded jeans, RMs and an old t-shirt that had long ago lost its shape – far from a glamorous get-up. Cara would have been horrified.

She leaned closer and yelled in his ear, 'Look, it's fine. I was just leaving.'

'Are you sure I can't buy you a drink? I'm supposed to meet someone here, but I'm rather late, and really,' he peered into the gloom, 'it doesn't look exactly promising, does it? Not surprised you were on your way.' He paused, looking pleadingly at her. 'I know a little place round the corner; we could have a drink there. Please? I'll be forever tormented by my rudeness if you don't let me make it up to you.'

Mattie entertained the idea, taking a good look at him. He was pretty damn cute, she had to admit. And he was trying very hard. On the other hand, she didn't know this guy from a bar of soap.

'I promise I'm not a stalker. Or a nutcase.'

Had he read her mind? Despite herself, she smiled at him. Sensing weakness, he took her arm. 'Come on, just one drink, my little antipodean pixie. Then I'll make sure you get to wherever you need to go. Promise. Cross my heart and hope to die.'

Mattie had allowed herself to be guided out of the pub and down the street.

He had taken her to a quiet wine bar. It was just around the corner but a million miles away in style from The Rouseabout. They sat opposite each other in a candlelit booth, and it felt as if they were in their own private world.

'So do you often pick up strange women in bars?' she asked him with a smile.

'Oh yes,' he said seriously. 'Always the strange ones.'

One drink turned into several, and they chatted easily, like old friends who had years to catch up on instead of strangers who had only just met. He teased her gently, in the same way her brother used to, and she'd forgotten how that could make her feel, as if she was cherished and indulged. She was so used to playing the hard-edged, in-control director at work, that it was nice for someone to see her differently, to take her on face value for a change.

It wasn't until the waiters started flicking the lights on and off that Mattie glanced up and found that they were the last couple in the place. It was time to make her escape before she did something she might regret.

'Sorry, but I really do have to go. I've got to be up early tomorrow – you know, the work thing? But thanks for saving me from a complete dud of an evening.' She stood up, a bit woozy from the red wine they'd shared. Definitely time to head home. He insisted on finding her a cab and she watched his disappearing figure as the cab sped away. A smile curved her lips.

She was even more impressed when Johnny rang her at eight o'clock sharp the next day, as she was striding along Wardour Street on her way to the office, to wish her a good morning.

At first she had been worried that starting a relationship might conflict with her job, which demanded long hours and most of her focus. But things had developed slowly and Johnny turned out to be an old-fashioned romantic. 'I thought they'd become extinct in the last Ice Age,' said Cara as they were discussing him at work one day. He liked to party rather more than Mattie would have liked, and whizzed her around London's hottest nightclubs until she was almost dizzy. No doubt about it, Johnny was energetic and entertaining company and seemed very keen on her, which was extremely flattering. She was hooked, she admitted to Cara in a whispered conversation, swept off her size-five feet.

When Johnny mentioned going skiing, she was ecstatic. They'd never been away for more than a long weekend together, so the prospect of ten days in the Swiss Alps with him by her side was beyond exciting. Actually, Mattie thought, she would have been happy to spend a holiday with him in a tent in a muddy field, but snow-covered mountains, cuckoo clocks and more chocolate than you could chuck a stick at … yep, she could go for that. When he suggested that Cara and his friend Nick might like to join them, Mattie was enthusiastic. She couldn't think of anyone better to spend the holiday with and she could see that a foursome would be fun. And who knew? Cara and Nick might even hit it off.

Mattie begged Bianca for some holiday leave. 'Sara can manage on her own, I know she can,' she said, knowing that her deputy would jump at the chance, but crossing her fingers that she wouldn't do the job too well. Bianca agreed, albeit reluctantly. 'Don't think I haven't noticed that you've worked your arse off since you've been with us,' she said. 'Just get the DeVere shoot done before you go. And make sure you come back in one piece.'

CHAPTER FOUR

The crisp alpine air took everyone's breath away. As the train arrived in Zermatt, Mattie gazed at the view in awe, craning her head to take in the snowcapped peaks towering above her. Dusk was falling and the lights of the village twinkled a welcome as they unloaded their bags. The resort was exactly as she had pictured it, dotted with traditional, sloping-roofed chalets, their lit-up windows glowing golden against the dark sky. She looked at the night sky, indigo now, and pinpricked with millions of stars. The last time she'd seen this many was on a midsummer night in the vineyards. London skies were never dark enough for good stargazing. 'Full moon,' she pointed out, thrilled to see the translucent disc alongside the looming triangular peak of the Matterhorn.

'Ahroohoo,' Nick howled. 'I used to be a werewolf, but I'm alright noooow.'

Johnny groaned. 'Not the werewolf joke again, mate. Give it a rest.'

Nick looked briefly crestfallen but Mattie noticed him perk up as he looked at Cara. Her friend was wearing black stretch pants that clung to every inch of her, topped by a metallic jacket with a fur-lined hood. A beanie was pulled over her platinum hair, and her makeup was as perfectly applied as when they'd left the airport earlier that day. Her eyes sparkled with the same anticipation as Mattie's.

Their hotel only increased their levels of excitement, if that were possible. The large square building had wide, intricately carved wooden balconies along the front and the roof was blanketed by a thick crust of icing-sugar snow, like a Christmas gingerbread house. Inside, it was just as charming, with timber-panelled walls, the smell of something delicious wafting from the kitchens, and in the sitting area a roaring fire and huge sofas that looked like you'd sink into them as effortlessly as a bank of snow.

'This is going to be fifteen different kinds of awesome,' said Mattie, lounging on one of the sofas. She felt better than she had in weeks, the stress of work left far behind.

'Too right, mate,' agreed Cara. 'Just you wait till we get on the slopes tomorrow!'

Once they reached their room, Mattie bounced on the quilted bed.

'Everything to madam's liking?' Johnny enquired, mock-seriously.

'Oh, you bet. Just one thing missing.'

Johnny gave her a look of sudden concern. 'What's that, Mats?'

'You, you goose. I'm waiting for you to join me, right here,' she replied, patting the bed and then stretching her arms wide to invite him in.

They woke early the next morning and headed down to breakfast. Cara and Nick were already tucking in to muesli and soft rolls spread thickly with butter and raspberry jam. There were cups of coffee frothy with milk and sprinkled with bitter chocolate curls, and in one corner a tall-hatted, starched chef was deftly flipping omelettes to order. 'Good morning, chaps,' said Nick, looking up from his iPad. 'Looks like an absolutely smashing day for it.'

Mattie caught Cara's eye. 'Yes, super,' she agreed, keeping a straight face with some effort. Nick was the quintessential Englishman, more so than Johnny even, and it never failed to amuse her. 'Do you want eggs, Johnny?'

'Sure. I'll need plenty of fuel if I'm to keep up with you on the slopes today,' he teased.

'As if! Somehow I reckon I'll be the one trying to catch up.' Mattie had learned to ski on boarding school trips in Australia, but the slopes of Perisher and Thredbo looked like bunny runs compared to the steeps she'd spied from the balcony of their room earlier that morning. 'I didn't even know they got snow in Australia,' Johnny had said incredulously when they first talked about going skiing.

'Too right they do, mate,' she'd assured him.

Johnny, who by all accounts had been popped on a pair of skis as soon as he could stand, had regaled her with his stories of visiting European resorts every winter with his parents, admitting that he had also heli-skied in the Rocky Mountains. Mattie reassured herself that at least the snow looked nice and fluffy. If she was going to stack it, she'd be certain of a soft landing.

'How about you, Cara?'

Cara nodded, the pompoms at her neck bobbing merrily. She was kitted out in head-to-toe current-season Chanel skiwear, gold embroidered double Cs emblazoned on the sleeve of her black one-piece.

'You certainly look the part,' said Mattie, not caring at all that she was dressed in far more pedestrian navy ski pants and a tomato-red parka.

'Thanks, mate,' Cara winked. 'Stylin' it, huh?'

Once the four of them had been fitted with boots, skis and boards, they clomped the few short steps to the gondola, breathing in the crisp, clear mountain air and looking about excitedly at the other skiers and boarders swarming around them. Mattie's heart beat faster, and she knew it wasn't merely from the altitude. She smiled at Johnny.

'Don't you look like the fox that got into the chicken coop,' he said, grinning back at her.

'I still can't believe we've got ten whole days of this. Nine more nights,' she said with a wink. New silk underwear – the only clothing she did love to splurge on – had gone down a treat the night before. 'What could be more perfect?'

'Come on then, let's go and you can show me what you're made of,' he challenged.

'Tough stuff, and don't you know it,' she replied bravely.

'Oh really? Let me sample that tough stuff now, shall I?' he said as he tilted her lips up to his for a kiss. His mouth was warm on hers, a delicious contrast to the chilly air. 'Nope, not tough at all,' he said, releasing her. 'Marshmallow through and through.'

They spent the morning together on the Matterhorn Glacier Paradise. To Mattie it certainly felt like heaven on earth as she swept down the wide pistes, whooping with the fun of it all. It was bliss to forget all about deadlines and demanding clients, and grey, rainy, grubby London. Her ski legs had quickly come back to her, though she wasn't a patch on Johnny in terms of skill or style.

'Did you know you can see Switzerland, France and Italy from up here? It's one of the highest points on the continent,' he said as they stopped to admire the view from the top. The thin air was making Mattie feel light-headed, but she brushed it off, concentrating instead on how deliciously pleasurable the feeling of her skis gliding smoothly over the snow had been as she'd swooped downhill behind her friends.

'Three countries,' she breathed. 'Amazing.'

Johnny hadn't lied when he said he was an expert skier, whizzing down the slopes at breakneck speed, and Nick, Cara and Mattie did their best to keep up with him. He graciously waited for them at the bottom of each run. 'Don't know about you lot, but I could do with some rations,' he said as they stood in the lift line just before noon.

Cara and Mattie nodded in agreement. 'I know just the place' said Cara, who'd done her research before leaving London. 'It's supposed to be awesome.'

'Awesome works for me. Lead on, Cara,' said Johnny.

They tramped into a tiny wooden chalet, which was packed with Gore-Tex-clad skiers. 'Seems like we're not the only ones with the same idea,' said Nick, looking around the room. They found a spot by the fire, squeezed in and began the process of peeling off their layers. 'Ugh, if there's one thing not to like about skiing, it's hat hair,' said Cara, pulling off her helmet and shaking out her platinum-blonde mane. Mattie ran her fingers through her spiky crop. She was having far too much fun to worry about how she looked.

The mountain restaurant was soothingly warm, with heat radiating off the log fire that spat and crackled next to them, and it wasn't long until their cheeks were glowing as they toasted their first morning's adventures with great flagons of ice-cold beer.

'Who's up for some off-piste skiing this afternoon?' asked Johnny.

'Rather,' said Nick enthusiastically.

Mattie was doubtful. 'Are you sure it's safe?'

'We'll be fine. It's as good as it gets out there, plenty of sweet powder stashes still to be had,' Johnny reassured her.

The waitress arrived with their lunch and Mattie didn't have time to worry about it any further. 'Raclette,' the waitress said with a flourish as she unloaded her tray, placing an enormous bowl of molten cheese in the centre of their table, together with a basket of bread, a dish of boiled potatoes and some pickled gherkins and onions. Mattie sighed contentedly; one thing was certain, skiing certainly made a girl hungry.

They demolished their food in no time, and lingered over the last of their drinks until Johnny gathered his gloves and helmet. 'Come on then, chaps. There's a whole mountain of snow waiting for us out there.' Stuffed and a little sleepy from the rich, cheesy lunch, Mattie lumbered outside, Cara and Nick following her. 'Right, everyone ready?' asked Johnny as they clicked their boots back into their bindings, fastened helmets, adjusted goggles and looped their poles over their wrists. Cara and Nick nodded at him.

The cold mountain air had revived Mattie. 'You bet,' she replied.

'Let's go then!'

Mattie followed her boyfriend onto the piste. He led them up to the highest point of the resort, onto the glacier. Mattie felt her stomach plunge into her boots as she contemplated the sheer drop off the side. Grey rock and loose scree poked out from beneath the snow at intervals. Were they really going down there? She gasped, as much from nerves as from the high altitude. They were all a little breathless.

'Not scared, are you?' asked Johnny.

Mattie gulped but shook her head. If he thought it was okay, she trusted him.

'I know you're perfectly capable. I wouldn't have brought you up here if I didn't think you were up for it.'

Mattie wasn't a coward, far from it, but she didn't want Johnny to see that she was just a tiny bit freaked out by the steepness of the slope. *Fearless.* That had been her nickname once. Was it one she still deserved? She looked from Cara to Nick, neither of whom seemed to share her concern. 'No, no, I'm fine, really.'

'You sure?' Cara asked, noticing her expression. 'We don't have to go this way if you don't want to, you know.'

'I can do it if you guys can,' she said, more confidently than she felt.

Nick set off first, ducking under the rope that marked the ski area boundary, followed by Cara, then Mattie, and Johnny brought up the rear. Within seconds they had left all of the other skiers on the mountain behind, and a vast open face of untracked powder snow lay in front of them. It was eerily quiet, with only the low whistle of the wind sounding in their ears.

Mattie came to a halt after a few turns and took in the spectacular scene. 'It's amazing.' She'd forgotten her earlier trepidation and now they were further down the slope her stomach had caught up with the rest of her body.

'Isn't it? I knew you'd love it,' said Johnny, a wide grin showing between his goggles and scarf.

They each took a separate line down the slope, whooping and hollering with joy as their skis carved into the soft, fluffy powder. Reaching the bottom, Mattie found that her thighs were trembling and she was completely out of breath. She wasn't nearly as fit as she once had been. Many years ago she'd been strong from riding horses all day, but working long hours in a city office and never having time to get to the gym had put paid to that.

'Super-de-dooper!' said Nick, coming to a stop behind her and looking up at their S-shaped tracks in the snow.

Mattie bubbled over with laughter at Nick's choice of words and relief that she'd made it down the steep slope. 'That was amazing,' she said. 'There's nothing like that back home, is there, Cara?'

Cara shook her head. 'Un-fucking-real,' she said with a feverish light in her eyes. 'Can we do it again?'

'You betcha,' said Johnny.

This time no one was hesitant about heading back up the mountain.

On their third run of the afternoon they took a slightly different line, traversing the face of the snowfield to reach more untracked powder. Johnny took the lead, followed by Mattie. Nick and Cara had stopped at the top while Cara adjusted the bindings on her skis.

It only took a split second.

Out of nowhere, Mattie felt a huge gust of icy wind and heard a loud crack and then rumble like thunder. She stopped in her tracks and looked behind her. Blinked. She almost couldn't believe her eyes. A vast slab of snow was moving down the mountain above her. She barely had time to register the danger when the snow was upon her, engulfing her. She was swept off her feet, one pole ripped out of her hand and she fell, tumbling down the steep slope. It was like being in a huge washing machine. Her skis had snapped off and she was being tossed around like a rag doll. Her brain registered the word *avalanche*. She tried to scream, but her mouth was immediately filled with snow. A roaring sound filled her ears. Everything was happening so fast but it felt like slow motion. She flailed on the surface of the moving snowpack, swimming with her arms to try to stay on top of it. She knew that if she got buried too deep she'd never be found. Years earlier, a schoolfriend's brother had been caught in an avalanche when he was ski-touring in the Snowies. They hadn't reached him in time. Remembering this now, a sob rose up from Mattie's chest. Scenes from her childhood flashed across her brain. Her mother hanging out the laundry on a windy day; the sun burning bright on her eyelids as she lay back on the grass listening to her heart-beat; playing hide-and-seek in the winery, her brother jumping out from behind a barrel, sending her shrieking out into the yard; galloping along the ridgeline of the Shingle Hills with Charlie Drummond hard on her heels ...

All of a sudden she slammed to a stop, coughing violently from the snow that had forced its way down her throat and up her nose. She felt a moment of sweet relief that the uncontrollable tumbling had stopped. Then she realised that she was completely buried.

She had no idea which way was up. She'd fallen with her hands thrown out and there was a small space in front of her face, a pocket of air. One of her poles was still strapped to her hand; she could feel it pressing into her wrist at an awkward angle. Was it pointing up? Or down? Mattie had no idea. She had stopped coughing, thank God, and desperately tried to slow her breathing. She knew she mustn't, absolutely mustn't panic. She had to do her best to conserve the little air she had and so she made herself take small, shallow breaths. She tried moving but all she could do was wiggle her fingers and toes. Hard as she tried, she couldn't move her body, not an inch. The snow had been so light as she was sliding and tumbling, but it was now set like concrete. Desperate, she clawed her fingers, trying to scrape at the hard-packed snow, trying to make a bigger airhole, but it was hopeless. Realising she was getting nowhere and using up precious oxygen, she stopped. Blood thudded against her temples. She could taste metal. Astonishingly, she couldn't feel any pain, and felt remarkably clear-headed, though she could tell from the way her arm was bent that something wasn't right with it. She could also feel warm dampness creeping along the inside of her ski pants. She had to do *something*. But what?

It took every ounce of strength she had to stop herself from spiralling into hysteria.

Johnny? she asked herself instead. She'd seen him below her and slightly to her left seconds before the avalanche hit. She had no way of knowing if he'd been caught up in it, but didn't see how he could have escaped.

It was eerily quiet. It felt as if she'd been stuck there for hours, but it could only have been minutes. Then, suddenly, she thought she could hear noises, muffled by the snow weighing on her. Or was she just imagining it? None of them had been wearing avalanche beacons. She didn't know if anyone would be able to find her. She did know that she had very little time. Mattie did the only thing she could think of. She began to pray.

Then everything went black.

CHAPTER FIVE

Mattie opened her eyes. The light was blindingly, searingly white and she winced, snapping them shut again. She tried to move her arms and legs but they didn't seem to be working. Where the hell was she? Concentrating really hard, she tried to lift her head up. *Bad idea,* she thought, as a searing pain knifed through her whole body.

She heard a strange voice say something in a language she didn't understand. Footsteps echoed on a hard floor. Mattie opened her eyes again. The light was so bright it made her eyes ache. She couldn't bear to keep them open for long.

'Bloody hell, Mattie, you gave us a fright. How are you doing?'

Cara. Now that was a voice she recognised. She tried to move her lips but no more than a dry moan came out.

'It's okay. Don't try to speak. You've got plenty of time to recover.'

Why did she need to recover? What from? A memory hurled itself back to her. The slide of snow, the tumbling, falling down and down, and then finally stopping, surrounded by darkness. Being unable to move. Was she still buried in the snow? She wasn't cold. 'Www ...' She blew the sound.

'It's all right, babe. You had a fall. We were skiing. Switzerland. Do you remember any of it? Blink if you do.'

Mattie fluttered her eyelids.

'We were above you and saw it all happen. There was nothing we could do to warn you, it happened so fast. The ski patrol was right behind us, thank God. Your pole was sticking up out of the snow, but you were completely buried. They were able to dig you out after only a few minutes. Any longer, and ...' She swallowed. 'Oh Mats, I was so scared. If they hadn't found your pole ... But you're going to be okay, you're alive.' Mattie could hear the barely suppressed emotion in her usually unflappable friend's voice. She remembered now. She'd been so frightened. But where was she?

As if Cara knew what she'd been thinking, she said, 'You're in hospital, down the valley from Zermatt. They're taking really good care of you.' Her voice broke off and Mattie could tell that Cara was trying to collect herself. 'They're going to keep you here for a few more days, and then transfer you back to London.'

Johnny. Mattie wanted to ask about Johnny. Where was he? Shouldn't he be here? She tried to speak again but could barely move her lips. She was so tired. Just a little more sleep ... A grey fog enveloped her and she lost consciousness again.

*

The next time Mattie woke up her head felt a little less hazy. The blinding light had faded and she was able to open her eyes. The room was small and square with sickly yellow walls. She saw curtains with a flowered pattern hanging at the windows, framing an overcast, leaden sky. In the distance loomed the sharp white peaks of mountains. The bed she was lying on crackled underneath her as she tried to shift her weight. *Owww.* She felt like she'd done five rounds with Tyson Fury. She did a mental survey of her body. Her ribs were sore if she even moved a fraction and her right arm was pinned to her chest. She couldn't lift it. Neither could she move her left leg, which was, she could now see, encased in plaster from hip to ankle and suspended above the bed at a 45-degree angle. If she'd been run over by a Mack truck she couldn't have been in a worse state.

'Hello there, how are you feeling?' A nurse with a heavy German accent bent over her, loosening the tightly tucked covers. 'I'm going to take your temperature, just putting this in your ear. Hmm, all good. Now, would you like to try something to eat?'

Mattie nodded, wincing as even that small movement sent a wave of pain through her skull.

The nurse pressed a button and the bedhead inclined slightly. Mattie felt momentarily dizzy and blinked hard, steadying herself against the sensation. The nurse wheeled a table over and picked up a bowl. 'I'm going to help you, until you can manage it yourself. Chicken and dumpling soup. Here you go,' she said, proffering a spoon.

Mattie felt like a baby bird opening its mouth to be fed, and just as weak and helpless. It hurt even to eat, but hunger overcame pain. Once they were finished, she tried to speak. 'Johnny?' she croaked.

But the nurse had bustled away, not hearing her question.

The effort of eating had made Mattie too tired to think, and she listlessly watched the shadows move slowly across the room before falling into a doze. It was several hours before Cara returned, and the sky outside her window had grown dark. This time, Nick was with her.

'Mate, there you are.' Cara bustled into the room carrying an enormous slab of chocolate and a pile of glossy magazines. 'I raided the hospital shop down the hall. They had a few English ones,' she said, placing them on the table next to Mattie. 'How are you feeling?'

'Johnny?' Mattie croaked again. She tensed, waiting for bad news. Lying in her hospital bed, she'd had plenty of time to imagine the worst.

'He's in the ward down the hall,' said Nick. 'He's a bit battered and bruised and they're keeping an eye on him in case of concussion, but apart from that he's fine.'

Mattie exhaled and felt a wave of relief wash over her. Johnny was okay. Her worst fears had been unfounded.

A ruthlessly efficient doctor visited her. 'You have made a bad break of your tibia and fibula. We had to operate and pin the bones back together,' he explained. With clinical detachment, he went on to describe the likely rehabilitation process, saying that she would need to be in a wheelchair for several weeks, perhaps even months, until her shoulder, which had been dislocated by the force of her fall, tearing the ligaments that normally held it in place, had healed sufficiently for her to start to use crutches. After that she could walk in a hard boot. 'Months, not weeks' was his gloomy prognosis.

It would be a while before she was dancing on parapets again then, Mattie thought humourlessly. Had that rainy seaside photoshoot really only been a few days ago? She couldn't quite believe it, but then again, she couldn't believe anything that had happened. She was supposed to be having the time of her life, on holiday with her boyfriend and friends, drinking unfeasibly large glasses of beer, tucking into hearty alpine dinners and snuggling romantically in front of the fire ... She wasn't supposed to be lying in a hospital bed miles from home, unable to walk.

Mattie spent three more days in the Swiss hospital, losing great chunks of time as the painkillers they gave her sent her to oblivion. *They'd be strong enough to tranquillise a stallion*, she thought as she faded out one more time. She was becoming increasingly uncomfortable. Her cast itched like there was a swarm of ants inside it, and every time she moved her ribs screamed in protest. Cara and Nick popped in every day, Cara spending hours by her friend's bedside, painting Mattie's nails a lurid shade of green and feeding her chocolate and gossip in an effort to buoy her spirits. For the first two days there was no sign of Johnny, then on the second afternoon, just as she was at her lowest, she saw him. Her absent boyfriend, fetchingly dressed in a hospital gown, walking slowly towards her.

'Matilda! There you are!' he called out. 'Been looking everywhere for you. Blasted nurses wouldn't tell me a thing, or if they did it was in German so I didn't have a bloody clue what they were on about.' This didn't seem to be much of an excuse. Her nurses all spoke perfect English. She dismissed the thought. It didn't matter. He was here now. 'Oh Christ, Mattie,' he said, reaching her bedside. 'Looks like you got bashed up pretty badly.' She saw the shock register in his eyes, but tried to make a comical face at him. *Ouch.* Even that hurt.

'Ssss ... not too good,' she mumbled.

He stood, body angled away from her as if he could scarcely bear to come any closer, and his eyes darted at her face to take a second look.

He didn't stay long, muttering a lame joke about having to get back to his ward before the SS nurses found him missing. It wasn't until he'd left that she realised he hadn't even kissed her. Mattie was hurt, but not especially surprised. Earlier that morning, a nurse had handed her a mirror and a hairbrush. 'You might like to use this. Don't be too concerned, it looks worse than it is at the moment, and it'll heal quickly. The plastic surgeon can tell you more.'

The words *plastic surgeon* had sent a stab of alarm through her and she put one hand up to her cheek, feeling it puffy and unfamiliar beneath her fingers. Then, just below her eye, she encountered a crusted, swollen mass. She could feel the stringiness of stitches and scabbing. What had the avalanche done to her face? She remembered the taste of blood after she'd fallen. Not wanting to look, but unable to resist, she raised the mirror. A deep purple and black bruise completely circled one eye and her lip was swollen beyond recognition. But worse than that was the cut under her eye – a livid, pulpy red and black slash drawn together by angry-looking stitches. She'd never been one to spend much time primping in front of mirrors, but seeing a freak's reflection looking back at her rocked her to the core. She wasn't surprised that Johnny hardly knew her; she barely recognised herself.

Cara and Nick seemed far less fazed than Johnny had been about her appearance. 'Don't sweat it, babe,' Cara had said when Mattie mentioned her face the next day. 'It's only superficial. You'll have your ugly old mug back in no time.'

'I don't reckon Johnny's quite as convinced,' said Mattie bitterly.

Nick had been in touch with Mattie's travel insurance company (thank God Bianca had insisted she take it out before she left) and made arrangements for her to be medevaced back to hospital in London. Dr Teuton, as Mattie had nicknamed him, said that was likely to be in the next day or two if everything progressed as it should. After Nick had relayed the news, he and Cara said their goodbyes. They wanted to stay to make sure Mattie was going to be okay, but had to get back to their lives. 'I'll come and see you the minute you're back in London,' promised Cara, carefully embracing her battered body.

Johnny slunk in a few hours after they had gone. He told her his mother was flying out the next day to take him home. Mattie was surprised. It hadn't even occurred to her to call her parents; even if they'd been close by she wouldn't have asked for their help.

'But what about me?' she asked.

'Well, er ... you're not exactly able to fly at the moment, are you?' he said, a look of guilt flashing across his perfect features. Anyway, Nick said it was all sorted.'

'Yeah, but ...' Mattie sank back, too exhausted to tell him that she expected he might have done a bit more, might have at least been there for her and stayed until she was safely on her way home too.

'Look, Mats, I'll see you when you get back, hey? Don't expect you'll be up to much for a while anyway.'

Nope, thought Mattie miserably, *you're right there, buddy.*

He squeezed her hand as he left, but Mattie could tell he was doing his best to avoid looking at her black eye and swollen face. Once again, she noticed that he hadn't kissed her hello or goodbye.

As the door closed behind him she felt suddenly more alone than she ever had in all of her thirty-one years. More alone than when she had first landed in London, knowing scarcely a soul. More alone than when Waffle, the family's golden retriever, had died when she was eight. She wanted to howl as she had done then, but the tears didn't come. Mattie knew she should probably call her brother, but every time she thought about what she would have to say, her throat closed up and she put it off. Cara had promised her that she would let Mark know the barest details of the accident, and Mattie couldn't face explaining it to him. She simply wasn't up to it.

Cara had also called Bianca, and within hours of her call an enormous bunch of tiger lilies was sitting in a vase in Mattie's room. Mattie knew that it was going to be a long time before she could return to work. The doctor had talked about months of recovery rather than weeks. There was also the problem of getting up and down the stairs to her third-floor flat. *Cope with one thing at a time*, she told herself, trying not to spiral into a blind panic. The first thing to do was make it back to London. Figuring out the rest would have to come later.

CHAPTER SIX

Rose flopped on the towel that she'd carefully spread out. Feeling the sun's heat almost like a living thing, pressing its way into her oiled limbs, she took in a deep breath, letting it out slowly as she relaxed. The glorious arc of golden sand never failed to both soothe and thrill her. The fact that it had been more than a year since she'd last felt the sand between her toes only added to her pleasure.

'Who's up for a swim?' Mark asked the two cossie-clad kids beside her, both of whom were jumping up and down with wild excitement at the prospect of a day at the beach. 'Sunscreen first though.' Leo and Luisa raced to slather themselves with the thick white lotion, seeing who could finish first.

Rose opened one eye. 'Don't forget the back of your neck, Leo,' she said. 'You three go on ahead. I want to properly warm up first.'

'Come on, Rose, we want you to come in with us,' said Leo, a pleading look in his eyes. 'Please?'

'Yes, Rosie, come and swim,' demanded Luisa.

'Come on, Rose,' said Mark. 'That water looks too good to pass up.'

She squinted at the rolling waves, foaming white at the shore's edge. The ocean did look inviting, a shimmering vista of crystalline blue stretching off into the distance as far as the eye could see. She smiled as she was reminded of the time when Mark had told her he loved her, right on this beach. A time when her heart had leapt for joy at the words she'd thought she would never hear. A time when he had persuaded her to come back to the Shingle Valley and make her life with him.

'Oh, alright then, if I must,' she mock-grumbled.

As she got to her feet she could feel Mark's eyes on her, taking in the skimpy jade-green bikini taut over her breasts and bottom. He took his time checking her out. The local Eumeralla shops didn't run to much in the way of swimwear and so she'd ordered it online, hoping that it would fit. The parcel had only arrived a few days before they left, but thankfully it just about covered her and the colour perfectly set off her long, dark hair and skin that was already turning golden from the sun. A summer of running through the vineyards had kept her in shape and working hard at Trevelyn's meant that she was often too busy to grab more than a slice of baguette smeared with terrine or a chunk of ham for lunch. Once upon a time she'd been overweight and pasty. And miserable. She remembered those days with a shudder. She was never going back there again.

Mark leaned over and ran a lazy hand down her back and across the curve of her hip before playfully flicking the elastic of her bikini bottoms. 'Mmmm ... nice, very nice,' he said approvingly.

'Hey, watch it,' she said, pretending outrage but unable to help laughing at him, happy he had noticed. During the long days of vintage she often felt that he was completely oblivious to her, that he wouldn't care if she was there or had run off with the butcher, his focus was so completely on getting the grapes picked and into the winery at the optimum level of ripeness. It was a welcome change that he now had some time for her, and for Leo and Luisa too. They had spent all morning competing with each other for their father's attention, though the lure of the sea was taking all of their focus just then.

'Want some help with that sunscreen?' he asked, massaging a dollop of it into the small of her back.

'Ohh, that's good,' said Rose, closing her eyes and giving herself up to the feel of his hands, so sure and firm on her skin.

'Turn around and I'll do your front,' he commanded.

As she obliged she gazed into his eyes, seeing that they were almost opaque with lust. Rose noticed that the kids had raced ahead of them, desperate to swim. Mark put down the bottle. 'Come on, gorgeous, we'd better catch up or we'll lose them,' he said, grabbing her hand and pulling her towards the water.

Later, as she lay soaking up the sun's unrelenting heat, Rose watched Mark and Leo shaping a boat out of the wet sand at the water's edge, their two dark heads, so similar, almost touching as they worked. Luisa danced around them, playing with a strand of seaweed she had found, her cloud of curly hair lifted by the ocean breeze. Rose wanted to pinch herself. Nearly three years ago she'd been completely alone, had washed up on the other side of the world with nothing but a backpack and a broken heart. Now, here she was, with a home she loved, her own restaurant and an insta-family. Unreal. She hoped the picture in front of her might, someday soon, include a chubby little olive-skinned, green-eyed baby, scooping up fistfuls of sand next to his or her half-brother and sister ...

That evening, sated by sun and sea air, they trooped into Rustica, the French-style bistro where Rose had once worked.

'*Alors!*' Rose was nearly knocked sideways in an enthusiastic bear hug.

'Philippe!' she cried, embracing him just as joyfully. Philippe had been one of her first friends in Sydney, and he'd gone from being a scruffy barista to a chef and restaurateur with a mini-empire of dining establishments. He had parlayed the success of the original Rustica, with its Provençale fishing village vibe, and opened Petit Rustique, in the Sydney beachside suburb of Manly, and Rustica Cité, which was, as the name implied, in the heart of the city.

Philippe released her and greeted Mark in traditional Gallic fashion, kissing him on both cheeks before leaning down and greeting Leo and Luisa. 'How have you both grown so much, eh? *Attend!* You are so tall! And Rose, *vraiment très belle, toujours.* Mark, you are a very fortunate man to have such a beautiful family.'

Mark grinned. 'They keep me out of trouble.'

'Now, you are here to eat? Of course you are.' With a flourish, Philippe ushered them to a table at the front of the whitewashed timber-clad room, overlooking the beach.

Rose breathed in the delicious aromas of roasting meat, garlic and herbs coming from the kitchen. 'Please, feed us, Philippe. We're famished, aren't we, guys?' she said, looking at Leo and Luisa, who nodded in agreement. 'All that swimming today has given us the most enormous appetites. We could practically eat an elephant, couldn't we, Luisa?' The little girl giggled back at her and then looked doubtful.

'We're not going to have elephant, are we, Rosie?'

'Only kidding, sweetheart. Besides, elephants would probably be too chewy, don't you think? All that tough skin! Ugh!' she said, shuddering.

Rose didn't need to consult a menu; she knew that Philippe would send out a stream of dishes for them to try, together with plenty of shoestring *frites* to keep the kids happy.

Mark handed Philippe a couple of bottles of Assignation shiraz, the Kalkari flagship wine. 'Decant one of these and keep the other for yourself, mate.'

'*Absolument,*' said Philippe and he hurried away to the kitchen.

After they'd eaten their fill of a rich, garlicky bouilla-baisse, chateaubriand, an enormous pile of *frites* and *petit* chocolate and caramel soufflés cooked in miniature copper saucepans, the table was a mess of empty plates and crumpled napkins. Rose tipped her glass to her lips, savouring the last drops of the rich, fruity purple-red wine.

'So how do you think this year's vintage is going to stack up next to this?' she asked Mark, indicating her glass. 'Another Jimmy Watson winner, perhaps?'

'Nah,' he said. 'That sort of gong comes once in a life-time, but I reckon we could get close again this year. Yields have been down but we had almost perfect growing conditions and Jake has done an incredible job getting the vineyards up to scratch, particularly the ones at Trevelyn's. They've produced some of the best fruit I've ever seen in all my years in the valley.'

'Henry will be pleased,' remarked Rose. Her brother Henry owned the vineyards that surrounded Rose's restaurant.

'That reminds me; I should give him a call later with an update.' He consulted his watch. 'It'll be about the right time in the UK now. Anyway, c'mon, you sleepy heads,' he said to the two kids. Luisa had curled up on the banquette seat, resting her head in Rose's lap, and Leo was staring glassy-eyed at his iPad. The early start, the sun and the sea and the long day had worn them out. 'They're so much eas-ier at this age, aren't they?' he said, looking at them fondly. 'When I think of what a nightmare the first few years were – I don't think Leo slept through until he was nearly two ...'

He shook his head as if to dispel the memory. 'Anyway, we really should make a move.'

Saying farewell to Philippe and the rest of the Rustica crew, Mark hoisted Luisa into his arms and he and Rose promised to return again before the end of their holiday.

As Mark put the children to bed, Rose sat on the balcony of their apartment, overlooking the ocean where a full moon was reflected on its dark surface. She breathed a sigh of pure contentment: a perfect day, a delicious meal and for once, the spectre of Isabella banished. She felt as if she had not a care in the world. She wondered where Mark was. He'd been ages. What was he doing? Surely the kids couldn't be playing up? They'd practically had to carry them home from Rustica; they should have both gone out like a light. Just as she was about to go and investigate, Mark appeared.

'Sorry I was so long,' he said, gently sliding the door of the balcony shut and coming to sit beside her.

'That's okay. What's up?' said Rose, not liking the frown of worry that creased his forehead.

He sighed heavily. 'I just got off the phone ...'

Even though it was past ten at night, Mark got calls at all hours, especially when his distributors in England were just waking up. 'Who was it? Not Channings again?' Channings were one of the UK's largest supermarkets, and one of Kalkari's biggest customers, being largely responsible for the profit the winery had made the previous year. Needless to say, they were also one of Mark's most demanding customers.

'No. It's Tilly.'

'Tilly?'

'Yes. Matilda. Seems she was skiing in Switzerland and there was an avalanche.'

Rose's hands flew to her face. 'Oh my God! Is she okay?'

'She's alive, but in a bad way. Dislocated shoulder, fractured leg and a few ribs for good measure. Not to mention a bruiser of a black eye, according to the friend who rang me. She also said that Tilly was adamant that I not let Mum and Dad know about it.'

'Oh no, what is she going to do? I wish we weren't so far away. Where is she now?' Rose had never met Mark's sister, but he had talked of her often and fondly, showing Rose albums of photos taken when they were kids growing up at Lilybells, the Shingle Valley's largest winery. Rose had seen blurry pictures of a tomboyish little kid with a tangle of black hair and bottle-green eyes exactly the same shade as Mark's.

'She's still in Switzerland, according to her friend – um, Cara, I think she said her name was. I should go to her. I've got this sales trip to the US to get out of the way first though. I really can't cancel, it's been months in the planning ...'

'Will you? Go to her, I mean? After your trip?'

Mark ran his hands through his hair, thinking. 'I can't not. And in any case,' he said, 'I can always go and see Channings while I'm there. That at least will make them happy.'

'Will make Alicia happy, you mean,' Rose said. Alicia was Channings' chief wine buyer and she had a massive crush on Mark, finding any excuse to ring him.

'Yeah, well, that too,' he replied.

Rose looked at him glumly. She'd known about Mark's US trip, but him going to England as well would mean they'd hardly see each other again. She'd missed him enough during vintage, and now he'd be gone again, for God only knew how long. She'd known when she met Mark that he travelled a lot, but it didn't stop her missing him dreadfully when he was away.

CHAPTER SEVEN

Opening her eyes, Mattie saw the familiar face of the nurse who'd accompanied her on the flight. She'd been knocked out by some rather good drugs for most of the trip back to London, something she supposed she should feel pleased about, even though she was pretty numb to everything at the moment. 'Hey, sleepyhead,' he said. 'It's all over. You're at St Barts and they'll take good care of you. Now is there anything you need?'

Her eyes rested on an enormous bunch of flowers in a vase by the bed. Gerberas. Her least favourite. Too perfect in their uniform colour and symmetry. The nurse noticed and went over to read the card. 'From someone called Johnny,' he said. 'Boyfriend?'

Mattie closed her eyes. She could hear the nurse rustling with a bag, and then there was silence. She opened her eyes a fraction.

'How about some telly?' he said. 'Not sure that there's much on, but you might find something. I quite like that Phillip Schofield on *This Morning*, even if he has got grey hair now. And Holly, she's nice too.' Mattie couldn't care less, but allowed him to switch on the television and let its babble wash over her. 'There you go, that'll cheer you up.'

She doubted it.

It wasn't long before her new doctor swept in, surrounded by a phalanx of white-coated medical students. 'Well, Miss Cameron, what have we here? A nasty fracture to the left tibia and fibula as well as an anterior dislocation of the humerus from the scapula. A couple of fractured ribs on the left side too. Avalanche, wasn't it? You're lucky to have survived, my dear, let alone not to have suffered a serious spinal injury.'

She knew she had been incredibly lucky, even if she wasn't quite feeling it just then. 'How long will I be here?' she asked.

'Well, that really depends on you. You're also going to need someone to look after you for a few weeks, possibly even months – someone who's at home twenty-four seven. At least until you can get about on crutches. What about your parents? Can you go to them?' he asked.

'Not really. They're in Australia,' she said, her heart sinking as she realised the full extent of her predicament. *And there's no way I'd ask Mum to come and look after me*, she thought to herself. *I don't even want her or Dad to know.*

'Is there anyone else a bit closer?'

Mattie thought of Cara. Her friend had insisted that she stay with her when she was out of hospital. 'Don't worry about a thing,' she had said. 'I've cleared the spare room for you. It'll be fine. I'm actually looking forward to having a roomie.'

But Cara had to work, not to mention maintain her extensive social life, and much as she wanted to stay with her friend, Mattie acknowledged that it probably wasn't the best solution to be left alone for hours on end, barely able to hop to the bathroom. What if she fell and there was no one there to help her up?

'I'm not really sure,' she said eventually. 'I suppose I'll have to figure it out.'

'Well, you're going to be here for at least another couple of weeks, in any case. We want to be sure your tibia heals properly and that the operation you had in Switzerland was up to scratch. Though,' he paused, putting up a couple of X-ray films on a lightbox on the wall at the side of the room, 'it looks like they did a pretty good job. That's some serious metal you've got holding you together now.' The students gathered round the specialist as he pointed out something on the films. He turned back to Mattie. 'You've got your age and fitness on your side but I'll have to warn you, it's not going to be plain sailing.'

Just after six the following evening, she had managed, at the urging of the nurses, to feed herself for the first time. Not that she could really taste the food, but at least it gave her something to do. She was putting her spoon down when she suddenly heard a commotion in the corridor outside her room. There was a loud tip-tap, clop-clop of several pairs of heels, a stifled giggle and a particularly loud voice that echoed off the bare walls. A voice she'd recognise anywhere. It was the one that commanded planning meetings and bawled out the unfortunate junior who had failed to deliver the right coffee or green smoothie order.

'Here she is!' Several heads popped around her door. 'Hello, darling!'

There was silence as they caught sight of her, and a few shocked gasps, but then everyone began speaking at once.

'Oh Mattie, sweetie —'

'Oh you poor thing —'

'Oh my God, what happened to you?'

The last comment was from Bianca — not known for her tact. They tumbled into the room: Becca and Brooke, the other two founders of Three Bees; Bianca, her boss; Arabella, Mattie's assistant; Sara, her deputy art director; and Cara. There was scarcely enough room for them all to squeeze in. They'd obviously come straight from work, judging by the office dress code on show, and looked a little incongruous in the sterile hospital setting, like colourful butterflies in a scientist's bell jar. She could see them taking an inventory of the cast on her leg, her shoulder in a sling, the cut across her cheekbone, not to mention the black eye, which was now spectacular shades of green and yellow. At least the swelling around her mouth had mostly gone down.

'Hey, guys,' Mattie tried to summon up a smile. 'Fancy seeing you here.'

Bianca sat down on the bed, causing Mattie to wince as her leg was jostled. 'That's quite a shiner you've got there, Matilda. But I've got exactly the thing for it,' she said as she foraged through her orange leather tote, pulling out a small jar with a flourish. 'I knew I had some in here. This stuff is supposed to be just the ticket for skin discolouration issues. It should work wonders on that eye, take the bruising away like magic.'

'Just the thing when you've been in an avalanche, hey?' Mattie was unconvinced but politely accepted the jar.

'So, any hunky doctors, Mattie?' asked Sara. 'Is it anything like *Grey's*? Go on, tell me it is.'

Mattie shook her head. 'Sorry to disappoint you. Number of hunky doctors spotted so far is zero.'

'Oh well, anyway, here,' she said, putting an armful of magazines next to Mattie's abandoned supper. 'We got you the latest issues of, oh, absolutely everything, really.' She laughed self-consciously.

'Thanks, and thanks, guys, for coming to see me. Really, I'm very touched,' she managed.

'Nonsense,' said Bianca. 'Our top creative director languishing in the sick bay? Of course, we had to come and cheer you up. Now, is there anything else you need? Anything we can get you?'

'No, thanks, you're all very kind. The doctor says I'm young and healthy and all I need is time to heal. They're not sure about the cut on my face – apparently it might need plastic surgery, and I might end up with a bit of a limp, but all things considered, that's not so bad. The leg was quite a bad break, so they're going to keep me here for a few more weeks, but anyway, let's not talk about me. What's been going on while I've been away?'

The crew needed no more encouragement. Sara launched into a rundown of the Brighton shots – which ones had made the cut for the campaign, the styling and the quality of the light and how honestly you couldn't tell that it had been such a rainy day. Jamie Soames was apparently ecstatic. Mattie listened with only one ear, catching snippets of several conversations going on at once. The intensity of working in a busy agency no longer seemed to matter in the way it once had. She felt suddenly shattered, completely worn out by the noise. She caught Cara's eye.

'Hey, peeps, I think Mattie's had enough now,' said her friend over the din. 'Why don't we let her get her rest, huh?'

'Of course. Now, darling, you give us a bell if you need anything at all.' Bianca bent over to kiss her on her good cheek, unable to hide her grimace at seeing Mattie's scabbed-over cut up close. 'And don't forget to let me know if that cream does the trick.'

It'll take more than cream, thought Mattie glumly as the door closed behind them.

CHAPTER EIGHT

'You've got to eat, love. Get your strength back,' said the nurse as Mattie dispiritedly pushed a lump of greyish meat in congealed gravy around her plate with her left hand. After more than two weeks staring at the same patch of wall, she was getting thoroughly fed up with being in hospital, not to mention totally sick of the bland food that was never more than lukewarm and always served at odd hours. She was therefore hugely relieved when, the next day, the specialist agreed that she was well enough to go home.

'Thank God,' she said on the phone to Cara. 'I was beginning to think they'd never let me leave. I've got to learn to drive a wheelchair, which is going to be interesting, especially as I've only got one working arm. So far I've nearly taken out a student nurse and upended a vase of flowers. Though, come to think of it, that could be why they're so keen to get rid of me. Can you bring me some L-plates?'

The thought of her impending freedom had meant that Mattie was feeling marginally more optimistic than she had in recent weeks, though she still had no idea how she was going to cope without the regular meals and care from the nurses. Would Cara – lovely, fun, but utterly self-absorbed Cara – be up to the job? She seriously doubted it, and hated having to rely on anyone at all. She'd been on her own since she was nineteen, and apart from early help from her brother, who'd paid some of her college fees and sorted her out with a part-time job with a wine merchant when she'd first arrived in London, she'd been totally self-sufficient. She'd never in a million years imagined winding up in this kind of predicament.

The hospital's patient transport dropped her off outside Cara's flat early the next morning. Her friend came out to meet her, and leaned over to give Mattie a careful hug.

'I can't believe you're home. At last. It's all going to be okay now, you'll see. I've been to M&S and stocked up on ready meals so all you have to do is nuke them, and there's plenty of books and mags, and I've set up my laptop in the living room for you.'

Mattie smiled, clocking Cara's sweatshirt with 'I only date cowboys' emblazoned across it. She was so relieved to see her familiar face.

There was one slight problem.

The wheelchair was too wide to go through the front door of the flat. Cara tugged and pulled, pushed and shoved, trying not to upend Mattie in the process. 'Perhaps if I wiggle it … Oh Christ, I don't believe it. It never even occurred to me that it wouldn't fit,' Cara said. Mattie could see that Cara was trying not to show her horror. 'Oh, shit a brick.'

Mattie felt a giggle bubbling up inside her and she began to laugh. The mirth was infectious and soon both girls were clutching their sides. 'Ow, ouch, stop, my ribs, ow …' wailed Mattie, in between giggles. Her sides might ache from the contraction of her sore muscles, but it felt good to laugh.

Cara snorted and wiped away tears. 'Oh mate, what a total fucking nightmare.' She got out her phone. 'Don't worry. I have a plan.' She winked at her friend as she dialled. 'Nick, hey, it's me. I really need a favour. Mattie's with me, and we're outside my apartment. Yeah, I know.' She paused. 'It's just that she's in a wheelchair and the bloody thing is too wide to get through my front door. And we're getting cold stuck out here. Think you might be able to give us a hand?' There was silence. 'Thanks, mate, that'd be great.'

Mattie sat in her wheelchair, shivering, the misery having returned. She felt like a cat that had been put out in the rain, when all she wanted to do was curl up somewhere warm and shut out the world.

Cara went inside and emerged holding a blanket. 'Don't want you to freeze,' she said, tucking it around Mattie's legs. Cara tried to keep Mattie amused with stories of a pop star she'd recently had to style for a magazine shoot, but Mattie found it hard to concentrate on what she was saying. A few minutes later there was the sound of a horn and they looked up to see Nick pulling into the street.

*

Making a hammock of their arms, Nick and Cara lifted Mattie up. They carried her through the front door and into Cara's living room, depositing her gently onto the sofa. 'Thanks, Nick,' said Cara, giving him a wink. You're a lifesaver.'

'Yes, thanks,' echoed Mattie. 'It was really good of you to come over so quickly.'

'Nonsense. I wasn't too far away. Glad to see you out of hospital, Matilda.'

'You and me both,' said Mattie.

'I'll go and get your wheelchair – it folds up, yes?'

Mattie nodded. 'I think so.'

'No sign of Johnny, then?' Nick said when he returned.

'Johnny who?' said Mattie, unable to keep a touch of bitterness out of her voice.

'Oh, I see,' he said, embarrassed. 'Right.' There was a pause. 'I'm sure he'll be over soon,' Nick said, attempting to smooth things over.

How very British of him, thought Mattie. 'I'm not holding my breath.'

Aside from the flowers, she hadn't heard from Johnny since her return to London, and the several messages she'd left had gone unanswered. Even if he was recovering at his parents' place, he still could have called to see how she was getting on.

Cara covered her with another blanket then disappeared into the kitchen. Several minutes later she emerged with a leopard-print hot water bottle. 'This'll help,' she said, placing it carefully on Mattie's lap.

Mattie smiled a weak thanks. She was relieved to be inside and out of the cold.

'I dunno how I'm going to get you off that on my own though,' said Cara, looking uncertainly at the sofa where Mattie was lying.

Mattie wasn't sure either.

She had been staying with Cara for nearly two weeks when Johnny finally bothered to call her, suggesting he come over that evening.

Cara let him in, and then tactfully made herself scarce. Mattie looked up at him from her position on the sofa. 'Hello, stranger,' she said warily.

'Hey, Mattie.' He sounded guarded. Not like the Johnny she thought she'd known. He leaned down to kiss her, landing it awkwardly between her mouth and her unblemished cheek, as if he hadn't been able to decide which to aim for. 'Your face looks better.'

The bruise around her eye was almost gone, and Mattie's swollen mouth had returned to its normal size too, though it still felt sore when she ate. The cut was still a vicious slash across her cheek.

'I suppose it does.' With a sinking feeling, she knew why he'd come. *Nothing like a catastrophic accident to separate the men from the boys*, she thought wretchedly, steeling herself for what he was about to say. From being initially overjoyed that Johnny had survived and was fine, her feelings had turned, curdling like milk left too long out of the fridge.

'How are you doing?' she asked, delaying the inevitable.

'Me?' He looked surprised. 'Oh, fine now, thanks. Nothing that a few days' rest couldn't sort out.' He looked sheepish and rattled the change in his pocket. He perched on the far end of the sofa, as if he knew he wouldn't be staying long. 'Mattie, I do feel bad that you got so terribly hurt. I know I'm partly to blame.'

Mattie was suddenly furious. 'Partly to blame?' She looked at him as if she'd never really seen him clearly before. 'We would never have skied out of bounds if you hadn't insisted on it!'

'Oh come on! I *suggested* it. And you were more than happy to follow me.'

'Johnny.' Her voice was icy. 'You were the experienced skier, the expert. You should have known better.'

'So you do blame me.'

'Actually, if you want to know, I do,' she said angrily, knowing she was being irrational – unfair even – but unable to stop herself lashing out.

'I wasn't exactly twisting your arm, you know.'

'You just don't get it, do you?' At that moment she wondered what it was she'd ever seen in him. 'You could have been there for me – afterwards.'

He shifted uncomfortably. 'Look, Mats,' he said. 'Things just aren't the same, are they? Something got lost while we were in Switzerland —'

'No kidding!' she interrupted. 'How about my whole life? I don't know if I'm even going to have a job to go back to once I'm better. And it's not as if you've been exactly supportive. You know, like a boyfriend is supposed to be. I've barely seen you since the accident.'

'Can I finish?'

She glared at him but remained silent.

'I've tried to get it back, the way I used to feel about you, about us, but it's just not there any more.'

'Why not?' she asked, wanting to make him squirm.

'I just don't see you in the same way.'

'What, because of this?' she pointed to the scar on her cheek.

He had the grace to look shame-faced. 'I'm sorry, Mattie, but I just can't go on pretending everything is back to normal. It's not fair to you. You deserve much better than this.' He shifted awkwardly on the sofa. 'Look, you're an amazing girl. I know the timing is lousy, but I think it's best not to beat about the bush. I can't see a future for us.'

'Is that it?' she said flatly. 'Is that all you've got?'

Johnny looked stunned at her lack of emotion. What had he expected? Tears and hysterics? She wasn't that kind of girl.

'Then we've nothing more to say to each other.' She set her mouth in a grim line. 'Excuse me if I don't get up to see you out.'

'Look after yourself, Mattie,' were the last words he said to her.

That was exactly what she intended to do from now on.

CHAPTER NINE

From a distance, Mattie could hear ringing, but she was floundering, pinned down, unable to move, drowning under a weight of water. She didn't know what the ringing was but it was insistent ... She opened her eyes and the room came into focus. She heard the sound again and saw her phone, lit up next to her. She reached for it with her good arm.

'Ummmnnngh ...' she said, eventually answering.

'Hey, sis. Sorry, did I wake you?'

'Mark!' Her heart leapt at the sound of his familiar voice. 'No, no, don't worry, I don't think it's that early.' Her brother had rung her in Switzerland as soon as he heard the news, and it was only her absolute insistence that she had plenty of help around her that stopped him jumping on a plane right there and then. 'Whassup?'

'What are you doing today?'

Mattie considered his question as she tried to switch

her brain on. 'Most likely staring at the walls of Cara's flat, which is pretty much all I've done over the past week. Tell me what's going on with you; I'm sure it's much more exciting than my life right now.'

'Oh, you know, the usual. Leo's trying to teach Barnsie some new tricks. He almost got him to sit up and beg the other day. Luisa's making mischief, and we've just installed a new bottling line ... same old, same old, really.'

'How's Rose?'

'She's good. Got her hands full with the restaurant, you know how it is. Anyway, speaking of food, how do you think you might feel about lunch today?'

'Oh, ha ha, nice one, Mark. You suggesting we Skype while I eat a microwave Tesco special?'

'Um, not exactly. I was thinking more along the lines of lunch at London House. Rose tells me it's the hottest place in town right now, and it's a stone's throw from you.'

'Yeah, right, very funny. Are you deliberately messing with my head? Cause I could do without that right now, you know. My sense of humour got buried in the avalanche, I reckon.'

'Nup, not messing around.' Mark couldn't keep the glint of satisfaction from his voice. 'I landed half an hour ago. Give me a chance to check in to my hotel and grab a coffee and a shave and I'll be with you.'

'Whaaaat?' Mattie nearly dropped the phone in her excitement. 'No way. You'd better not be kidding me.'

'Swear to God. Now, what's the address?'

*

Mattie's hand was trembling as she hung up. She sat up in bed and swung her legs awkwardly over the side. 'Cara!' she called through the open door. 'Cara!' she shouted again, louder this time. 'Guess what?'

Her friend appeared, rubbing her hair with a towel. 'What? What is it?'

'Mark. My brother. He's here in London. He's coming to take me out for lunch.'

'Oh mate, that's brilliant news. What a fantastic surprise.'

'I know.' Joy welled up in her. It would be so good to see him. She hadn't realised how much she'd missed having family around, especially at a time like this.

'Now, quick, can you help me make myself look at least halfway presentable? I'll need some concealer to cover up my eye.' The bruise had faded to a pale browny yellow, which only made her look tired. There wasn't much she could do about the cut. Though the stitches had been removed, it was still a disfiguring and angry purple-red.

'I think we need to do more than that. Come on, let me at least wash your hair.'

'Is it that bad?' Mattie put a hand to her head, feeling the greasy strands clinging to her forehead.

'Hated to mention it, but yup, it is that bad.'

By noon that day, Mattie was being wheeled into the restaurant. There was a delicious aroma of food cooking, fresh-baked bread and caramelising onions. A warm fug had steamed up the windows, but was welcome after the bitter cold outdoors. It was the first time she'd been out of the apartment since she'd arrived there from hospital, and the sights and sounds of the city had crowded in on her. It was all a bit overwhelming. Thankfully the restaurant was quiet and the starched waitstaff didn't bat an eyelid at her wheelchair, nor her bruised face or tracksuit pants, which were the only thing she could get on over the cast on her leg. Cara had lent her a soft grey cashmere sweater and wound a bright saffron scarf around her neck. This at least added a bit of colour to her pale face. Her normally close-cropped spiky haircut was now more of a shaggy mop, but Cara had done her best to tuck it behind her ears into some semblance of style. No amount of concealer had been able to disguise the scar or the shadows under her eyes, but at least she didn't look as horrific as she had a few weeks earlier.

With a minimum of fuss they showed Mattie and Mark to a corner table where she wouldn't need to be disturbed by other diners wanting to get past.

'So what do the doctors say?' Mark asked after the waiter had taken their orders.

'This' – Mattie knocked on the heavy cast on her leg with her good arm – 'will need to stay on for another six weeks or so. It's going to be a long recovery, with lots of physio. They're going to wait and see if this' – she pointed to her cheek – 'will need surgery to tidy it up. They think it was sliced by the edge of my ski when it came off. It also all still fucking hurts.'

'Oh Tilly, it's been so tough for you.' Concern was written on his face.

'It's Mattie these days, remember,' she said, wrinkling her nose at him. 'Less babyish.'

'Well, you'll always be Tilly to me, I'm afraid,' he said, leaning back as a waiter unfurled his napkin for him. 'Hope they've at least given you some decent painkillers?'

'Actually they make me feel so woozy and confused, I've been trying to wean myself off them,' she confessed.

'You're a tough cookie, kiddo. Do you remember the time you smashed your knee on the cement of the winery floor when you were rollerskating in between the barrels? You got right up again and carried on skating, even though there was blood running down your leg and into your sock. You were only about six at the time.' Mark smiled at the memory.

'Yeah, well, I think this qualifies as a little more serious.'

'Fair call,' he agreed.

'And it does all leave me with a bit of an issue.'

'What?'

'I haven't told my boss yet, but I can't see how I'm going to manage at work with only one arm.'

'Oh?'

'I need both hands for, well, pretty much everything. The computer, driving …'

'Right, I see. That is a problem. Can they hold your job open for you until you're recovered?'

Mattie was saved from answering by the arrival of their starters. She let out an involuntary moan at the sight of a plate of crab tortellini floating in a clear broth before taking a sip of the glass of Puligny-Montrachet that Mark had ordered to go with it. 'Far out, Rose knows how to pick a good restaurant. This looks sensational. A step up from a ready meal, that's for sure.' She was suddenly starving.

Mark reached over and placed a reassuring arm on her shoulder. 'Glad to see you haven't lost your appetite. You always could eat the house down.' He picked up his fork and speared some pasta. 'Now, tell me about Johnny. How is he doing? Your friend – Cara, wasn't it? She mentioned he was hurt too.'

Mattie hesitated. She was embarrassed to tell her brother that Johnny had behaved less than impressively since the accident. 'I, er … he's been spending some time at his parents … in Hampshire.'

'Oh. Was he badly injured?' Mark asked.

'Actually, not so much,' she admitted.

'So he's been to see you?'

'Only once since Switzerland,' she said quietly. 'And that was to break up with me. I don't think he could cope with a less-than-perfect girlfriend.' She pointed to the scar on her face. 'His loss,' she said in a flat tone.

'What?' Mark was incredulous, incensed on his sister's behalf. 'You're kidding? What a total dropkick!'

Mattie chuckled at the expression. It was good to hear those words from someone else and have her innermost feelings confirmed. 'Do you know, I think you might be right,' she said, surprised that she was able to laugh at the whole sorry situation. It felt better than she could have believed possible to have her brother there.

'So,' he said, 'what are your plans now? What are you going to do if you can't go back to work?'

And there was the question that Mattie had been avoiding for the past few weeks. What was she going to do? She only had a few thousand pounds in savings – most of her wages since she'd started working had gone towards repaying her student loans or on simply living – even though she was well paid, London was an expensive city. Bianca had been supportive so far, but Mattie knew she was expecting her back at her desk within a week or so. She'd used up all of her sick days and was now on unpaid leave – not a situation that was sustainable, for her or Three Bees.

'You know you can always come back home, back to Kalkari,' Mark said when she didn't reply. 'It's been a long time since, well … a lot of water under the bridge. Anyway, there's plenty of space, and I know you'd get on with Rose. You haven't seen Luisa since we came over when she was a tiny baby, and Leo's grown so much. We're your family, you know. I want to be there for you, especially at a time like this. I know how much you love your independence, but why not come back, even if it's just for a few months, until you get back on your feet? It's been ten years, Mattie, don't you think it's about time?'

'I know.'

'It's not as if you'd have to stay forever.'

She briefly entertained the thought of returning home, but then instantly dismissed it. The long flight alone would be a nightmare in her present state, even with the benefit of painkillers, she told herself, skirting around the real reason for her reluctance.

'Thanks, but I wouldn't want to be a burden on you. And anyway, my life is here now.' Even as she spoke, she began to wonder, could she really go back? With sudden clarity, she realised that she would need to forgive herself – even more than her parents – in order to do so.

'No burden at all. You'd be doing me a favour.'

Mattie looked at him suspiciously.

'There's a load of admin that needs some attention, and God knows I don't get time for that these days, and I really could do with a proper PA. I'm sure you could manage that even one-handed. I know it's not as glamorous as an advertising creative director, but I'd love to have you there. It's glorious at home at the moment. The sun is shining, skies are blue …' He stabbed his knife at the restaurant window to emphasise his point.

The thought of warm, sunny days and fresh air was almost irresistible. But she shook her head. 'Don't be ridiculous. I'd make a terrible PA, and I haven't been back home for so long. It might be boring after all this.' She looked pointedly around the room, which had filled up with men in dark suits and women with expensive jewellery and salon-perfect hair.

'Yeah, right.' Mark refused to believe her protests. 'I know there's still a country girl hidden underneath that veneer of city sophistication.'

She grimaced. 'City sophistication? Did you clock the trackpants?'

'Isn't that what the fashionable set are wearing these days?' he asked, raising an eyebrow at her. 'Anyway, the offer's there. All you have to do is say the word.'

She smiled gratefully at her brother. 'Okay,' she said. 'I'll give it some serious thought. Now,' she said, eager to move on to safer topics, 'what does Luisa want for her birthday?'

Later, after her brother had dropped her home, Mattie sat in the kitchen, where French doors from the kitchen looked out onto a tiny, bleak garden. She noticed a pair of robins flitting back and forth to their nest, feeding two gawping, bald chicks. She marvelled at their relentless hard work, how they persevered even when a storm almost blew their nest away. As she watched the birds, she rolled the idea of returning to the valley over in her mind, weighing up the possibilities. Could it be a chance to make things right?

It was a conversation with Cara that finally convinced her. Cara, who had surprised her by having infinite patience with her moodiness, and who had curtailed her party-going ways, making sure she was home every night to cook dinner for them both, who brought Mattie books and movies she might like, and who regaled her with stories from the outside world. She could never be grateful enough to her friend for all she had done.

'I reckon you're daft not wanting to go back home, even if it's just for a few months. All that lovely sunshine and wine.'

As Cara spoke, a memory surfaced: Mattie was sitting on the verandah of her parents' house. Heat shimmering off the vineyards. Her family gathered around an outdoor table laden with salads. The smell of barbecuing lamb. Wine bottles beaded with condensation. The echo of laughter in the air. She felt instantly hollow with longing.

'Are you trying to get rid of me?' Mattie half-joked.

'Of course not!' Cara was indignant. 'But from what you've said, it sounds like a great set-up. What's stopping you? Call it an extended holiday. Whatever. Doesn't have to be forever. Get on a plane and see your family, for heaven's sake. Your mum's probably going mental about how you're doing. I know mine would be.'

Mattie didn't bother to explain that her mother still had no idea she'd been in an accident.

CHAPTER TEN

Rose carefully placed the last snowflake on the iced cake and tweaked a carrot nose. Luisa had requested – no, demanded – a *Frozen* theme, and so of course she had obliged. She couldn't refuse the dark-haired little poppet anything very much. She'd crawled into Rose's heart almost from the first day she'd met her.

As she stood back and looked at the large white Olaf snowman cake, she knew Luisa would love it. She wiped her fingers on her apron and placed the cake in the pantry. She didn't want an inquisitive little birthday girl discovering her surprise. Astrid had taken Luisa out for the morning to track down an Elsa dress and was under strict orders not to return until after lunch. Why was it always Elsa and not Anna? Rose wondered. The blonde ice queen, not the spunkier little sister?

Twenty four- and five-year-olds were due to descend on Kalkari at 3pm. Rose still had the party bags to stuff with party favours and sweets and then about a million balloons to blow up. If she was lucky she would have time to put on a clean dress. Isabella was also coming to the party. Well, of course she was – she was Luisa's mother, not that she'd done anything to help prepare for the day. She hadn't even offered. She probably thought her presence was enough, thought Rose sourly.

Rose was already intimidated enough by Isabella without wanting to look like something the cat dragged in, so she'd washed her hair earlier that morning, putting in a burgundy dye to add some shine. For now her hair was all piled up inside a plastic shower cap, but she was planning to rinse it out as soon as she'd finished the party preparations.

Today was also a big day at Kalkari for another reason: Matilda was coming to stay, though for how long Rose wasn't sure. Mark had been vague on the subject, but mentioned that she'd be recuperating for several months at least and was in need of plenty of TLC. He had left the house the day before, staying overnight in Sydney and then was driving to the airport to pick her up that morning. Rose was excited at the prospect of meeting Mark's little sister, and hoped that having her to stay with them would work out. It would certainly be nice to have some more female company about the place.

Rose cleaned up and then headed over to the barn to make sure everything was ready. She wanted to put some fresh flowers in a vase as a welcome. Stealing across to the vines at the left of the long driveway, she used her kitchen scissors to snip a few of the roses blooming there. Roses and vineyards went hand in hand, she'd discovered, with roses acting like the canary in the coalmine, alerting winemakers to signs of disease before anything showed up in the vines. She liked to think that, as her name was Rose, she was also meant to be living surrounded by vineyards. Pretty fanciful, but the thought made her smile nonetheless.

'Oi, what are you doing there?'

Rose looked around in surprise and then her expression changed to one of relief. 'Oh, it's only you. I thought I was in trouble there for a moment,' she laughed. 'I know Jake wouldn't be too thrilled with me stealing his blooms.'

'Hah, nearly got ya,' said Dan, Mark's right-hand man and Kalkari's assistant winemaker. 'Pick away, for all I care. There's plenty more. He won't notice.'

Dan was right. Looking down the rows of vines that stretched into the distance, Rose could see lush velvet-petalled red roses blooming at the end of each one. 'Are you coming over this afternoon? Lulu specially asked me to make sure you were there.'

'Wouldn't risk missing out on one of your cakes. I'll even brave a room full of yummy mummies,' he said, grimacing.

Returning to the barn, Rose looked around with pleasure. No longer the dusty, spider-strewn scene that had greeted her when she had first moved in, the place had been transformed. Mark had called in a local builder to give it a facelift: the plaster walls were snowy with fresh paint, and new windows had replaced the old rotting ones that used to let in a howling draught in winter and the mozzies in summer. Rose had ordered new linen and thick quilted bed-spreads for the two bedrooms, and a couple of large sofas scattered with bright cushions had been positioned either side of a wood-burning stove. Rag rugs in muted tones covered the slate floor. The effect was minimal, but comfortable and welcoming. Placing a glass vase containing the roses on a rough-hewn timber side table, she opened a couple of windows to let in some fresh air, then hurried back to the main house.

'Holy shit!'

Rose looked at herself in the bathroom mirror in absolute horror. She glanced at the packet of hair dye she'd applied earlier that morning.

Much earlier that morning.

Tahitian Sunset. *I'll give you Tahitian freakin' Sunset*, she thought grimly as she squinted to read the instructions again. To say that the dye had somewhat over-delivered on the promise of subtle burgundy highlights was putting it mildly. Her hair was purple. Katy Perry purple. Kelly Osbourne purple. It was definitely not the effect she'd been after. Re-reading the instructions, she discovered that the dye was only supposed to be left on for thirty minutes, not the three and a half hours that had elapsed since she had applied it.

Four scalp-tingling washes later and the colour had barely dimmed. *Nice one.* Just the thing to make her look like a prize idiot in front of Isabella, never mind what Mark's reaction might be when he saw it. Rose groaned inwardly. Scrabbling through her wardrobe, she found an old turquoise scarf. Wannabe pop star or cancer patient? It wasn't much of a choice. She went with the latter, and wrapped the scarf tightly around her temples, tucking her hair up inside it. That covered up the worst of the purple – and at least the scarf matched the party theme.

It was gone two o'clock and Rose was pretty sure she had everything under control. Her cheeks were sore from blowing up what felt like a hundred and one turquoise and white balloons, and they were now bobbing merrily from the trees at the bottom of the Kalkari drive. Lolly bags had been filled with jelly snakes and Caramello Koalas, bread was buttered and scattered with sugary hundreds and thousands – Mrs B, Kalkari's former housekeeper, had impressed upon Rose the importance of fairy bread at a birthday party, though Rose was still not convinced by the multicoloured slices – and a huge piñata in the shape of a snowman dangled from the back verandah. Rose glanced at her watch. She would have expected Mark and Matilda to be back by now. She hoped he would make it in time, not least for Luisa's sake. Hosting twenty sugar-hyped little girls and their mothers didn't faze her in the slightest. But having Isabella there, in the house that used to be hers and without the buffer of Mark's presence, was another thing altogether. Add to that her disastrous purple hair and she felt unease grow like a lump in her throat.

'Ooh, nice scarf,' said Astrid, coming into the kitchen, carrying Max on one hip and trailing Luisa behind her. The little girl was hopping from one foot to the other. She either needed the bathroom or she was excited about the party. With a five-year-old it was hard to tell.

'Rosie, we got a pretty dress. It's so, so beautiful. I love it!' Her eyes danced. 'Did you see all the balloons outside?'

Rose gave her a hug. 'I know, aren't they pretty? What a clever balloon fairy we must have. I can't wait to see your dress.'

'It's an Elsa dress,' she said proudly.

'Oh, it must certainly be very beautiful then.'

The little girl nodded her head emphatically.

'Okay, Miss Lulu, how about we go upstairs and change before everyone arrives, hey?' said Astrid.

A few minutes later, Luisa stepped regally down the stairs, calling to Rose to come and see her. Dressed in a pale turquoise gown, its gauzy overlay embroidered with tiny snowflakes, she was every inch the birthday girl. She wore matching satin shoes, and Astrid had let her wild dark curls tumble down her back. With her rosebud lips, plump cheeks and a plastic silver tiara atop her head, she looked like a little Spanish Infanta.

'Hopefully the Marquesa will approve, no?' said Astrid.

Rose really didn't want to talk about Isabella. She looked at her watch again. Still no word from Mark. 'She thinks she looks beautiful and that's all that really matters.'

CHAPTER ELEVEN

The air hit Mattie like a wall of molasses. Warm and sticky. Her shirt immediately clung to her ribs and beads of sweat formed on her brow. Her hair, lank from nearly twenty-four hours of travel, began to spike in the humidity. Although she had not forgotten the heat, it was something else to be so forcefully reminded of it. And the light. The searing, bright light and cloudless blue sky. She took a deep breath. Even the smell, of eucalypts and, over the pungent whiff of avgas, the faint tang of salt, was comforting and familiar. Despite herself, her spirits lifted. The familiar accent and welcome greeting at passport control had been a good start, and now, at last, she couldn't help but smile. She felt like she'd been living in a world of shadows and had suddenly emerged into the light.

But where was Mark? He'd sounded so happy when she'd called to take him up on his offer of coming to recuperate with him that she'd been convinced she was doing the right thing, despite leaving her London life behind. Bianca had been surprised by her news, but pragmatic. She needed to keep the business going, after all. 'You'll be sadly missed, darling, of course you will, but now you need to go home and heal. You've been through a lot,' she'd said.

Home. She was home. It was almost as if the ten years she'd been away had never happened. It was a disconcerting feeling, especially as there was, at the moment, a welcoming committee of precisely zero. Mark had promised to meet her at the airport, so where was he? Because she was still unable to walk very far, she'd been given the invalid treatment and whisked straight off the plane. An airport minder had helped her through customs with her bags, retrieved her wheelchair from oversize luggage, and been only too happy to wheel her straight outside. 'It's a bonza day,' he'd said cheerfully. It was only at her repeated assurance that she was fine on her own that he'd left her side.

After she'd been sitting there for nearly an hour, Mattie's revived spirits at arriving back in Australia were flagging. The sun was climbing in the sky and the small patch of shade the wheelchair was parked in was rapidly diminishing. She also really needed to pee, not an easy task when she had two large bags next to her. She didn't fancy causing a security alert by abandoning them, but she was fast running out of options. She squinted across to the carpark, suddenly spotting a tall, rangy figure. She'd recognise that long stride anywhere.

'Tilly!' he said, rushing up to her. 'So sorry I'm late. Had to drop off some samples in the city this morning and got stuck in traffic. Then when I eventually did get there, they insisted on sitting down for coffee and having a yarn. I couldn't get away; you know how it is. Anyway, I made it, and more importantly, you made it.' Mark leaned forward and gave her a hug, carefully avoiding the arm in its sling. 'How was your flight? Are you absolutely buggered? You must be.'

'It's Mattie, you boofhead,' she said narkily, angry that he'd made her wait for so long.

'Right, sorry, sis. And sorry again about being late, really I am. Can you forgive me? Are these yours?' he asked, releasing her and pointing to her bags.

'Yep.' Mattie blinked back sudden tears that pricked at her eyelids. Honestly, what did a bit of jet lag and the smell of home do to a girl?

'Aw, come on, it's not as bad as all that, surely?' he said, trying to tease her out of it. 'Listen, I've got one more stop to make before we can head home. There's a new place that's opened in Manly, right on the water, and they're thinking of listing our wines. I promised the distributors I'd pop in and sweet-talk them, help get them over the line. Do you think you're up to it?'

Mattie looked down at her rumpled travelling clothes and ran a hand through her wilting hair. She felt like a hundred kinds of shit, but well ... 'Could I change my shirt first? I'm also busting for a pee.'

'That's the sister I know and love.' Mark grinned at her. 'Up for anything. Come on then, let's get you sorted.'

*

'How about an ice-cream?' Mark asked later as he pushed her along the beachfront in Manly.

'Are you kidding?' Mattie protested. The restaurant, a Spanish-style bodega, had plied them with tapas. She hadn't eaten so much in weeks.

'Not even a Golden Gaytime?' he teased.

'Oh well, if it's a Golden Gaytime, then that's a different matter. Do you remember the time when Mum paid us for helping clean out the winery? I think I must have been about six.'

Mark nodded.

'How you took me to the Eumeralla milk bar? I never thought there could be too much of a good thing until that day. Three Golden Gaytimes later ...' She groaned at the memory.

They found a convenience store and Mark pulled two ice-creams out of the freezer. Wheeling her back across to the beachfront, he solemnly unwrapped them, waiting to gauge her reaction. She took a bite. It was the taste of summer. Of long, dry days schooling Shakira over jumps that Mattie's dad had set up in the paddock – 'Come on, angel, you can do it,' he'd called out, always encouraging her to go higher. Of opening up the big chest freezer that Mum had in the shed and diving into the box of ice-creams kept for treats. 'That's the best thing I've had in ages,' she said giving him a wide grin.

Mark turned to look at the waves that foamed on the sand beyond the path. 'Gorgeous, huh?' he said.

Mattie drank in the view. 'Not too shabby, mate.'

Once they'd finished their ice-creams, Mark turned the wheelchair in the direction of the car. 'Come on then, we'd better get a move on or we'll miss Luisa's birthday and then there'll really be trouble.'

'Oh,' said Mattie, her hand flying to her mouth. 'I haven't had a chance to buy her anything. Can we stop somewhere so I can get her a present?'

'I know the perfect place – a princess and fairy store. We stopped there last time we were all in Sydney – couldn't get her out of the place. It's on the way home.'

Half an hour later, as they drove up the highway, Mattie felt her head lolling on the headrest. She was sitting awkwardly, her broken leg stretched out along the back seat and propped up by pillows, but lack of sleep and the warmth from the sun beating on the windows – not to mention the painkillers she'd taken as they set off – made keeping her eyes open almost impossible. Kalkari was still several hours' drive away.

'Don't fight it, sis,' said Mark, glancing at her in the rearview mirror. 'I'll let you know when we get there.'

She was already spark out.

What seemed like only moments later, Mattie felt her shoulder being gently shaken.

'Wake up, sleepyhead,' said Mark.

The rattle of the car, which had lulled her to sleep, had stopped and all she could hear was the faint hum of distant music, an insistent drumbeat. She blinked, not knowing where she was. Then she saw that they had pulled up at outside the house. Kalkari. Its honeyed sandstone walls glowed in the late afternoon sun and leafy vines stretched either side of it, curving over the hill to the horizon. It was beautiful.

'We're home,' he said.

Mattie thought for a minute, mulling over the word as she took in the view. The Shingle Valley. Home.

Didn't look like it had changed at all.

CHAPTER TWELVE

The doorbell rang and Rose went to answer it. The first of the partygoers had arrived, a harried mother flanked by two identically dressed curly-haired blonde cherubs – both also miniature Elsas. 'Hi, this is Anise and this is Syrah. All right if I leave them with you? I'll be back later to pick them up. Five o'clock, okay?' she said, thrusting a beribboned present at Rose and not giving her a chance to reply. *Christ alive.* Naming your child after a grape variety? Whatever happened to normal names like Anna and Sarah, Rose briefly wondered, ushering the pair into the house.

Soon there was an influx of little girls, all similar incarnations of the ice princess. No sign of Isabella. *Honestly, she'd be late to her own funeral,* thought Rose sourly.

'How about we play pass the parcel, everyone?' suggested Astrid, shouting to make herself heard over the excited chatter and squeals. She turned on some music and the girls obediently formed a circle, all eyes expectantly on the large newspaper-wrapped parcel. Several of the girls' mothers had stayed – 'Is Jake coming later?' asked one carefully made-up thirty-something mother – and Rose was doing her best to keep them fed and watered, topping up glasses of sparkling wine and handing round smoked salmon sandwiches. She sent a silent thanks to Mrs B again for warning her that she'd need to be prepared for the parents as well. The music had paused on Anise, who was attacking the parcel with savage intensity, when Isabella made an entrance. Rose smelled the heavy perfume seconds before she spied the elegant Spaniard. She was dressed to the nines in a cream suit with a tight pencil skirt that stopped several inches above the knee and revealed impossibly long, impossibly smooth brown legs. Scarlet lips, a flawless complexion and clouds of dark hair all added up to an extremely glamorous effect. It wasn't exactly kids' party attire though, Rose thought, touching her head to make sure the scarf was still in place and she wasn't showing too much purple.

'Darling Luisa, there you are,' Isabella said in her strongly accented, husky voice. She sashayed over to where Luisa was sitting cross-legged on the floor and bent down to her, flashing plenty of leg as she did so. 'Mama's here now, my angel.'

Luisa gave her mother a shiny smile, but then waved her away. 'We're playing a game.'

Dismissed but not discouraged, Isabella walked over to where Rose had set out champagne flutes together with several bottles chilling in an ice bucket. Pouring herself a glass, she moved over to talk to some of the parents, who had gathered outside. She didn't acknowledge Astrid or Rose, who were supervising the parcel unwrapping, and proceeded to spend the rest of the party chatting away on the verandah, oblivious to the goings-on inside.

When all the games had been played and party food eaten, Rose fetched the cake. She was beginning to wonder what might have happened to Mark and Mattie. Surely he wasn't going to miss his daughter's birthday party? She was torn between annoyance at his tardiness and worry that something serious might have happened to delay them.

As promised, Dan had made an appearance, bringing Jake over from the winery with him as well. The handsome Kalkari viticulturist had been immediately dragged out to the verandah by one of the mothers, and he now stood surrounded by women who were seemingly drawn to him with the same inevitability as iron filings are to a magnet.

Astrid shushed all of the girls and led them in singing 'Happy Birthday' as Rose carried the Olaf cake into the room. Luisa's eyes were round with wonder.

'Surprise!' Mark's voice boomed across the room as Luisa was about to blow out her candles. The noise from the party had been so loud that Rose hadn't heard his car pull up outside.

Luisa forgot her candles and jumped into her father's arms, clinging tightly to his neck. She was definitely a daddy's girl, thought Rose, relieved to see him at last.

'Daddy! Look at my beautiful cake!'

'I know, sweetheart! Isn't it wonderful?' he replied, mouthing a 'sorry' at Rose. 'Are we going to eat it?'

'First we have to blow out the candles, silly, but then you can have some of his nose.'

'Oh good, I reckon that's the best bit.'

'Uh-huh,' Luisa said seriously.

'C'mon then, give me your best huff and puff.'

Rose peered out into the hallway – where was Matilda?

'She's freshening up in the bathroom,' said Mark, noticing her questioning gaze. 'Ah, here she is now.'

As Mattie wheeled herself slowly into the room, Rose was taken aback by her resemblance to Mark; it was so much more obvious than it had been on their blurry Skype chats. The same creamy skin and deep green eyes, framed by short brown hair. Poor thing, she looked absolutely worn out, and quite frail. Rose went straight over to her. 'How was your flight? It's a hideous one, isn't it? And probably even more uncomfortable with that leg. I do hope they looked after you.'

Mattie gave her a small smile. 'It was pretty grim, but I'm here now, and that's the main thing. It's so good to finally meet you properly. And, oh my goodness, is that Luisa? She's even more beautiful than I realised! And where's Leo?'

'Mrs B said she'd pick him up from a friend's place; he should be here soon. He's grown at least a foot in the last year, I'd say. Now, can I get you a drink? Some water, or bubbles? A sandwich? Astrid's just cutting the cake, if you feel like some of that.'

'Um, just water, thanks. Actually I could murder a cup of tea as well.'

'Matilda, I was so sorry to hear about your accident ...' Isabella breezed over and took her good hand. 'Ay, what a catastrophe.'

'Yes, it was,' said Mattie.

'Of course, if there is anything I can do ... I'm in Eumeralla, well, at least for the next few weeks, then I am back to Spain.'

'Thanks, that's very kind.'

'For how long will you be staying here?'

'I'm really not sure. Until I'm completely better, I guess. I'll have to wait and see. Mark's been so generous to have me.'

'Yes, we all know how generous Mark can be,' said Isabella with a touch of venom in her voice as her gaze found Rose.

'Don't be ridiculous,' said Mark, interrupting as he handed Mattie a glass of water. 'There's always a home here for you, you know that. Now come and say hello to Lulu.'

Luisa was sticky with icing, and she stared dubiously at Mattie's wheelchair.

'Hey, Luisa, remember me? Auntie Mattie?'

The little girl looked up shyly through her eyelashes. 'It's my birthday.'

'I know. How old are you?'

The little girl solemnly held up five fingers.

'Are you having a nice party?'

The little girl nodded. 'What happened to your face?'

Mattie smiled. 'I had a bit of an accident and hurt myself. But I'll be better soon.'

'Okay,' said Luisa, satisfied, and she twirled away back to her plate of cake.

Rose glanced out of the window and saw a familiar figure striding up the path to the back verandah. Sensing a sudden movement next to her, she looked at Mattie and noticed a tense expression cross her face.

'Gorgeous boy!' Thommo exclaimed, scooping Max into his arms and making him shriek with surprise. Rose looked at Mattie again, and saw that she had relaxed. Who had she been expecting?

Most of the guests had gone by just after five and Rose heaved a sigh of relief. Little kids' birthday parties were more exhausting than doing a double shift in a fully booked restaurant. Mrs B had dropped Leo off and he had inhaled the remains of the cake before taking off with Barnsie down the drive. Mattie was out on the verandah, sitting with Mrs B and Mark in a quiet corner. Jake had disappeared, Rose wasn't sure where. Astrid was helping Luisa open her presents, with Isabella looking on, and soon Max was doing his best to tear up the discarded wrapping paper that littered the floor. The place looked like a post-apocalyptic battlefield. Armed with a large plastic garbage bag, Rose swept up paper plates, cups and leftovers, scraping up trodden-in cake crumbs and icing as she went.

'Put that down, Rose, and come and have a drink,'

Mark called from the verandah. 'I'll clear up later. Least I can do after you've organised the whole party.'

Rose didn't need asking twice.

The sparkling wine was icy and delicious and the bubbles fizzed up her nose as she gratefully took a first sip. 'Oh, that's better.' She sat down. 'Phew, what an afternoon! Those girls have got far more energy than I have, that's for sure.'

'Thanks, Rose,' said Mark. 'You did a wonderful job. I really appreciate it.'

'Piece of cake. Ha ha.' She grimaced at the bad joke.

'What's with the hair though? Did you go all out for the party theme?' He raised an eyebrow. Rose's scarf had slipped back on her head, revealing its violet-hued glory.

'Something like that,' she muttered.

'You don't normally have purple hair?' asked Mattie.

'Let's say that next time I'll be more careful to read the packet instructions,' said Rose ruefully.

'Did you know your ears are purple too?'

'Oh God, no! Are they really?' she exclaimed, hands flying to cover them up. 'Bloody hell!'

The two girls laughed together at Rose's predicament. It was good that Mattie could laugh, Rose thought as she took another sip from her glass. 'You must be knackered, you poor thing,' she said. 'I expect Mark ran you ragged all over town, with no thought that you're still recuperating, not to mention having been stuck on a plane for twenty-something hours.'

'I am a bit zonked, even though I slept for most of the flight and then in the car all the way from Sydney,' Mattie admitted. 'My brain hasn't a clue what time it's supposed to be.'

'Why don't I show you to your new home?' Rose offered.

'But I thought I was home.' Mattie looked to Mark in confusion. 'Aren't I staying here?'

'Actually, we've spruced up the barn for you. It's all on one level and there's now a ramp at the front door,' he said. 'I thought you might like a bit of privacy and space, but of course, the main house is yours as well.'

'Believe me, it's far nicer than when I first stayed in there. Wait till you see it,' said Rose. 'I think you'll really like it. And you'll have some peace from the rampaging hordes.' She gestured inside to where Luisa and Max were rolling around on the floor together amid the wrapping paper.

Mark's phone beeped. He glanced at the message and got up, unfolding his long legs from the wicker chair. 'Won't be long. Got one more surprise for Lulu.'

Mattie looked at Rose. 'There's more?'

Rose winked. 'Just wait.'

Soon there was the sound of a loud whinny and the clop-clop of hooves. Rose saw Mark leading a small, round-bellied chestnut pony along the path at the back of the house. Jake was following behind.

'Lulu, come here, darling. Quick!' exclaimed Rose. 'She's been begging us for a pony all year,' she said to Mattie.

The little girl burst through the French doors and ran down the verandah steps to where Mark was standing, holding the bridle. 'A horsey? For me? My own horsey?' she cried, as she caught sight of the pony.

'All yours, sweetheart,' he said. 'His name's Buttons. What do you think? Would you like to go for a ride?'

'Can I? Can I?' The little girl's eyes were practically out on stalks.

'Of course. Look, he's all saddled up and waiting for you.'

'Really, Mark, do you think she's ready for a horse?' asked Isabella, appearing beside him, a frown of disapproval on her face.

'Of course she is. Tilly and I both had our first ponies at four or five, didn't we?'

Mattie nodded. 'I'd fallen off a dozen times before my fifth birthday,' she admitted.

Isabella was unimpressed. 'My little baby ...'

'And anyway, he's not a horse, he's a pony,' Mark said. 'Come on, Lulu, let's get you mounted, shall we? I'll pop this on you first though.'

The little girl needed no further encouragement and stilled as her father put the riding helmet he'd been holding onto her head and clipped it securely under her chin.

'Fits perfectly,' said Mark, satisfied. Luisa eagerly held up her arms to be lifted onto the shiny new saddle.

'See you in a bit. We're going to walk down the drive and back.' Mark waved a hand as they set off, Luisa's short little legs sticking out from under her Elsa dress to each side. *Just like a Thelwell cartoon*, thought Rose fondly.

As Mark led Luisa and Buttons round the side of the house, Jake came over to where the girls were sitting. 'Jake Salmon,' he said, holding out his hand and giving Mattie a winning smile. 'I'm the viticulturist here. You must be Matilda. I was so sorry to hear about your accident.'

Everything about Jake screamed bad boy, from his sleepy blue eyes, which glinted with wickedness, to the dark hair that flopped over his forehead, and cheekbones that would make a supermodel jealous. His skin was tawny from hours spent outdoors in the vineyards, and there was not a spare inch of flesh on his taut frame. An awkwardly mended once-broken nose and a scar over his left eyebrow hinted at a troubled past, but they only added to his gypsy appeal. Despite his almost permanent attire of faded jeans, t-shirts with often more holes than fabric, and muddy work boots, he exuded a roguish glamour. Needless to say, he cut a swathe through the local female population, regardless of age or marital status. His laidback good humour and willingness to buy a round at the pub meant that he managed to be as popular with blokes as with the ladies.

Rose could see it was all lost on Mattie.

'Watch out for Jake,' said Rose, teasing him. 'He's left a trail of broken hearts the length and breadth of the valley since he arrived.'

Jake pretended to be upset by her words. 'All lies. I can't help my devastating charm now, can I? Anyway, I'm sure Matilda can take care of herself.'

Mattie pointed to her leg, encased in its hefty cast. 'You think?'

CHAPTER THIRTEEN

Mattie could barely keep her eyes open. She'd been awake for more hours than her frazzled brain could calculate and was overcome with longing for a soft bed and crisp sheets. She rubbed her hand against the back of her neck. It came away slick with sweat. Her body wasn't coping with the heat at all.

'How about I take you over to the barn and help you get settled?' Rose said as Mattie's head drooped. 'You must be absolutely shattered, and here we are, completely caught up in Luisa's party and her new pony.'

Mark had instructed the builders to put in a ramp from the back door of the house and down to the path that led to the barn, so Rose was able to roll the wheelchair outside without any mishaps. The sun was setting behind the vines that stretched towards the Shingle Hills, colouring the sky crimson and pink. Mattie noticed a huge flock of sulphur-crested cockatoos take off, wheeling high into the sky in balletic formation, squawking like banshees. A cool change was blowing in, tossing the leaves on the gum trees and lowering the temperature by a few degrees.

'Beautiful in the evening, isn't it?' Rose said. 'I think it was this that I fell in love with. Well, and meeting Mark helped too.'

'Yes, it is pretty special,' Mattie admitted, looking afresh at the landscape. She couldn't remember the last time she'd seen so much sky. In London, she was only ever afforded brief glimpses, slices between tall buildings; here the horizon was only capped by the distant hills, their shadowy form a protective arc around the valley. 'Growing up, I guess I took it all for granted. Still feels bloody odd to be back. Almost as if I never left.'

Arriving at the barn, Rose reached forward to open the door. 'Right, Mark's already put your bags in here,' she said as she wheeled Mattie into the living area. Would you like me to find your night things, toothbrush and so on?'

'Thanks, Rose. I'm not used to asking for help, but that would be great.'

'Under the circumstances I'd say you were entitled to plenty of assistance. Now, I'll run a basin of water and then grab your stuff for you. Can you manage in the bathroom or do you want me to stay? I've put down a mat so you won't slip.'

Mattie brushed off her offer of further help. 'I'll be fine. I've gotten pretty good at sponge baths.'

'Okay, sing out if you need anything at all. There should be plenty of towels in there.'

'Thanks, Rose. I mean it. I'm really grateful.'

'Don't be silly. I know Mark's so pleased to have you back, and I'm delighted to get the opportunity to spend some time with you. I'm only sorry that it's taken such a horrible accident to make it happen.'

When Rose had gone, Mattie awkwardly stripped off her clothes and stood, naked, in the small bathroom. Grabbing a washcloth, she dipped in it the basin. The warm water was soothing on her body and she began to feel infinitesimally better. She gave her teeth a thorough brush and then, clad only in a towel, hopped through to her bedroom, where Rose had turned on a lamp and set the ceiling fan lazily turning. Mattie savoured the silence, which was broken only by the rough caw of currawongs as they came home to roost. Sitting against the edge of the bed and raising one hip, she hefted her leg in its cast onto the bed, then lowered herself to the pillows and let out a sigh. The window was open, and carried on the breeze came the sound of Mark's melodious tenor: '*I see trees of green, red roses too, I see them bloom for me and you. And I think to myself, what a wonderful world . . .*' He was singing as he cleared up the remains of the party.

Good as it was to be back with her brother, it didn't feel like much of a wonderful world at the moment. She refused to let herself cry about it though. She closed her eyes, turned her head to the wall and was asleep in an instant.

What felt like moments later, she awoke with a start, her heart thumping almost out of her chest. She'd been dreaming of drowning, floundering in an ocean that wouldn't let her surface, gasping for breath before being dragged back under the icy green water. A cold sweat covered her. It was pitch black. For a moment she thought she was in London, in Cara's flat. It was only a bad dream, she told herself. Just a bad dream. Then she realised where she was. At her brother's. The Shingle Valley. Australia. Gradually her heart slowed. She lay awake, breathing in and out, watching the sheer curtains at the window as they stirred in the faint breeze, before sleep claimed her once more.

Bright sunlight filled the room when she woke again, roused by an insistent knocking at the door. 'Come in,' she called out, awkwardly sitting up in bed.

'You *have* had a good sleep!' Rose called out cheerfully as she walked into the room. 'I'm sure you needed it. The jet lag's pretty hideous, isn't it? Hope you don't mind me disturbing you, but it's gone ten o'clock and I thought you might like a cuppa. It's an English thing, I know, but I always feel so much better if I've started the day with tea in bed. You don't take sugar, do you?'

Mattie shook her head.

'And when you're ready, come over and help yourself to breakfast. I've left out some bread and my special-recipe muesli, and there's eggs from the chooks and some of Mrs B's jam in the fridge.'

'Got any Vegemite?' asked Mattie, attempting to match Rose's sunny mood.

'Ha! You can't keep an Aussie away from that stuff, can you? Of course there is.'

'What's everyone else up to today?'

'Mark's out in the north vineyard – the Assignation block – with Jake. Leo's gone to soccer camp, Luisa is with Isabella and I'm about to head over to the restaurant. I'll be back at lunchtime though, and I'm free this afternoon if you'd like me to take you into Eumeralla.'

Mattie hadn't thought much about how she was going to spend her time once she got to her brother's. All of her energy had been focused on making arrangements for getting back to Australia, organising flights, giving away or packing up her few belongings and clearing out her flat. She really had no idea what came next. It was a deeply unsettling feeling – her diary in London had been chock-full of appointments and client meetings, weekends booked up with drinks, dinners and parties. Now she felt adrift in a place that was familiar but not where she belonged any more. *Treat it as a holiday. Recuperation*, she reminded herself. It wasn't a crime to slow down occasionally.

'Though if you want to take it easy, that's no problem either,' said Rose, interrupting her thoughts.

'No, a trip to Eumeralla would be great. I need to sort out a physio. I'm supposed to check in with a local doc too. Does Doctor Jonas still have a surgery there?'

'No, he retired earlier this year.'

'Oh, that's a shame,' said Mattie. 'I've seen him since I was a kid.'

'Well, don't be too disappointed. His replacement is a bit of a spunk – is that the expression?'

Mattie nodded.

'He's unattached too,' said Rose with a sly grin. 'He's had all the single and even some of the not-so-single women of the valley in a complete tizz. Well, at least those who don't hanker after Jake.'

'Jake?'

'You mean you didn't notice his devastating charm?'

'I'm not exactly in that headspace,' Mattie replied.

'Well, me either,' said Rose blithely, 'but you've got to say, he's pretty easy on the eye. He's a nice guy too – his heart's in the right place, even if he does run a mile from anyone who tries to get serious about him. Anyway, I'll let you wake up properly. Is there anything else you think you might need?'

'No, I'm good, thanks. And thanks for the tea,' said Mattie.

'Least I can do.' Rose waved as she left.

Later, sitting out on the back verandah with Leo's dog, Barnsie, resting his nose on her good foot, Mattie looked out at the valley. Vines stretched for miles, and in the distance she could see the Shingle Road. She knew that further along was Windsong, though she couldn't see it from Kalkari. Her thoughts briefly flickered to Charlie Drummond. When she'd seen Thommo at Luisa's party, she'd thought for a heart-stopping moment that it was his twin. She knew she'd eventually run into him, but reminded herself that after the fiasco with Johnny she'd sworn off getting involved with anyone again; the heartache and the inevitable let-down weren't worth it. Besides, it had been a teenage crush, and those days were long over. He was probably balding with a beer gut by now.

The sky was bluer than she could ever remember seeing it, and the trees dotted across the valley were a soft khaki camouflage. The soothing morning warble of magpies calling to each other was the only sound. It was still shockingly quiet after the constant, all-pervasive rumble of London traffic. A light wind blew through the leaves, dappling the sunlight as it fell on the verandah and bringing with it the spicy scent of eucalyptus. It wasn't too stinking hot yet, but she could already feel the sun's warmth sinking into her bones.

It had taken more energy than she had realised to travel the short distance from the barn to the house. Mark – or probably Rose – had organised a pair of crutches for her, and she'd managed a limping hop with one under her good arm. Somewhat miraculously, she hadn't stacked it on the way there.

Now, sitting in silence with the prospect of endless days of nothing in front of her, she couldn't staunch the feeling of utter desolation. Here she was, back in the place she'd been so anxious to get away from. This wasn't what her life was supposed to look like. She wasn't someone who usually depended on others to help her. She was the strong one, the capable one. She'd managed to keep her thoughts at bay while she was in London, barely able to do more than sleep and get to her doctor's appointments, and dwell on how angry and sad she still was about Johnny. Now the realisation that she had nearly died in the avalanche hit her with full force. Her breathing started to speed up as she relived the sickening tumbling feeling. *Oh Christ.* Was she having a panic attack? *Matilda Cameron, you don't have panic attacks,* she told herself sternly. She tried her best to breathe slowly and calmly and eventually the feeling subsided. Instead, a tear rolled down her face and she dashed it angrily away. 'And you can shut up!' she shouted at a kookaburra, cackling from its perch high in the peppercorn tree above her.

Gazing unseeingly out to the hills, lost in thoughts of the life she'd left behind in London, she didn't notice a figure coming around the side of the house until she heard the sound of boots, heavy on the flagstones.

'Matilda! How're you doing?'

It was Jake. She rubbed her eyes.

'Oh,' he said, catching sight of her miserable expression. 'What's up? Are you in pain? Is your leg hurting?'

'Feeling like a fish out of water, if you must know.' She couldn't believe she was admitting it to him. 'It's pretty bloody strange to be here, actually. It's so familiar, but then it's not. I'm beginning to think I might have made a big mistake coming back.'

'Oh, mate,' he sympathised. 'You've got every right to feel out of sorts, and I'm sure a long flight and turning up here in the middle of a party yesterday didn't help.'

'You don't understand. I *never* cry,' she protested, glaring at him as if he were responsible.

'Okay,' he said slowly.

'Well, that's not strictly true,' she admitted. 'But before all this I hadn't cried since I fell off Shakira and broke my wrist when I was thirteen.'

Jake looked at her, incredulous. 'Shakira? You had a horse named Shakira?'

'I was thirteen!' she said indignantly.

'Oh well, that explains it,' he said, a smirk still on his face. He kneeled down beside her and took her hand, serious again. 'It'll get better. You might not think that right now, but it will. You've just got to take time to heal. Don't rush it.'

'Thanks for the pep talk.' She gave him the semblance of a smile. 'I'm sure you're here for more important things than to cheer up a sad sack like me though. Rose said you and Mark were out in the Assignation block.'

'He needed some records from the winery, and I volunteered to come and collect them. Glad I did,' he said, giving her a grin. 'Listen, some of us are getting together at the pub on Friday – there's a new band on. They're supposed to be halfway bearable. Will you come?' Mattie began to shake her head. 'Come on, I promise you'll enjoy yourself,' he said.

'Oh really? How's that then?'

'I'll tell you when we get to the pub.' His eyes proclaimed innocence, but the mouth was sensuous and knowing. She wasn't born yesterday.

'Nice try,' she retorted.

'I don't know what you're talking about,' he said. 'And I'm not taking no for an answer, I'm afraid. Pick you up at seven.' And with that he jumped off the verandah and loped around the side of the house towards the winery, leaving Mattie mouthing her objections to the kookaburra once more.

CHAPTER FOURTEEN

The pub was buzzing. Friday night in the valley meant that almost everyone of legal drinking age gathered at one or other of Eumeralla's two watering holes to sink a few cold ones, have a yarn and shake the dust off the working week. Jake had been true to his word and turned up on the dot of seven, taking no notice of her protests as he lifted her into his arms as if she weighed little more than a case of wine. 'No hopping for you tonight, sweetheart,' he'd commanded. Mark had raised a concerned eyebrow but Rose had given her an encouraging smile as Jake carried her out the door.

Mattie was feeling marginally less grim than she had when she first arrived. She and Rose had called in at the doctor's surgery earlier in the week and picked up the details of the local physio, and the jet lag was abating. Most afternoons she'd napped on the sofa in the barn and there'd been no more nightmares since her first night home. Really, she thought, as her natural optimism reasserted itself, it was probably lack of sleep as much as anything that had made her quite so blue.

'What'll it be, Mattie?' Jake's voice brought her back to the roar of conversation in the pub.

'Beer, thanks. My round next.'

Astrid was there with Thommo. Apart from briefly spotting him at Luisa's birthday party, Mattie hadn't seen him in more than ten years and was surprised by how much he'd grown up, blurting out as much before she could stop herself.

'Well, becoming a father will do that to you, hey?' Thommo said proudly, giving Astrid a squeeze. 'Have you seen the little man? Isn't he the greatest?'

'Chip off the old block,' she assured him. 'The spitting image.'

Jake returned with their drinks and then introduced her to Deano and Mick, winemakers at Lilybells, the winery that had once belonged to Mattie's parents. It was where she and Mark had grown up. She quizzed the two men on what it was like now, and who lived at the main house.

'Leased to the Davis family, you know, over at Bell-birds. Rumour has it they're going to turn it into some sort of fancy health retreat,' said Deano.

'Yeah, with wine thrown in!' joked Mick.

Mattie looked incredulous.

'No, really, they plan to use the must – the leftover grape skins – as a treatment,' said Deano. 'We're working out how much we can charge 'em for it,' he guffawed.

Mattie grinned back at him. It was good to be out, especially with people who didn't know too much about what had happened to her in the last couple of months. It was also surprisingly enjoyable to be in an Aussie pub for a change, rather than a fancy wine bar. Somehow she felt far more at ease, more like the person she had once been – not the stressed-out, high-powered media maven, but just Mattie, a girl from the valley having a beer with her mates on a Friday night. She'd almost forgotten how that felt.

'So, Jake planning on getting you legless then?' asked Thommo later, while Jake was at the bar again. 'I see he's already made a start – ha, ha!'

She rolled her eyes.

'You'd better watch out for him, you know, Tilly. He's a heartbreaker.' Thommo's tone held a paternal warning.

'Funny, you're not the only one to mention that. And it's Mattie these days, not Tilly,' she said, a sharpness to her voice. She wasn't used to being patronised, however well meaning it was.

Just then she saw another familiar face appear at the door.

Her heart raced, just as it had when she'd thought she'd seen him at Luisa's party.

Charlie.

Thommo had been the reliable brother, the safe bet, but Charlie was the one who made everything seem more exciting merely by being there. Accepter of dares. Breaker of rules. Creator of mayhem and mischief. The boy most likely to get into trouble but equally as likely to charm his way out of it.

Mattie remembered a dance at the Eumeralla town hall the summer she turned fifteen. She'd begged her dad to let her go, and he'd eventually relented. Mark had dropped her off. Mum had persuaded her out of her usual cut-offs and ratty t-shirt and into a dress. She'd brushed her hair until it gleamed like polished silky oak, taming its usual wild tangle. The stiff material of the dress scratched the back of her legs and she felt strangely exposed, though it covered her quite modestly. But she forgot all of that as soon as she laid eyes on Charlie. With his merry smile and happy-go-lucky charm, he was the golden boy in the room, surrounded by a group of girls a few years older and far more sophisticated than her. He looked up as she walked into the room and caught her eye. In the instant he smiled at her, she was lost, head over heels. Not that she'd ever admitted it to anyone.

He'd twirled her around the room in one dance at the end of the evening – probably more out of obligation than anything else, she thought later. She'd never forgotten the feeling of being held in his arms, of his skin, almost burning to the touch, under his shirt, the warm, spicy maleness of him. This sudden and secret passion – she was far too shy to ever approach him and let him know how she felt – was a constant ache, an unfulfilled wanting that accompanied the rest of her teens. No one else had ever come close. Not even Johnny, she realised with a shock.

'Little Tilly Cameron!' Larger than life, he strode across the room and leaned down to plant a kiss on her cheek. She was immediately overwhelmed by the almost forgotten smell of clean earth and cedar, so familiar it made her catch her breath.

'Hello, Charlie.' He'd filled out, his shoulders were broader, his hips still lean, his voice a tone deeper, laughter lines fanning out from eyes as blue as her mother's hydrangeas. The promise of youth had been gloriously realised. No sign of a paunch or receding hairline, dammit. He was even more attractive than she remembered. She gave herself a mental shake. What was she thinking? Zero romantic involvements for the foreseeable future, not even a fling, she reminded herself. In any case, Charlie was most likely married with a couple of kids by now.

'So the rumours were true.' His teeth, strong and white, gleamed as he smiled at her. 'You *are* back in the valley. What happened here then?' he said, pointing to her leg, which was resting on a chair.

'She had a little tussle with an avalanche,' said Jake, moving to stand by her.

'I'd heard something. An avalanche. Bloody oath!' He gave a long whistle. 'You always were fearless, Tilly.'

She felt a small thrill that he remembered her nickname. 'It's actually Mattie these days.'

'Okay, Mattie, then. Well, I'm glad you're still in one piece. The girl who took on an avalanche and won – that's quite a story.'

'Almost one piece,' she replied, indicating her arm in its sling and the cast on her leg.

'You couldn't be in a better place to recuperate, darling. Welcome back.'

'We'll take good care of her,' replied Jake.

Mattie frowned. Why was Jake suddenly behaving like a caveman? He had been so sweet to her earlier in the week, and it was nice of him to take her out, but he needed to tone it down.

Charlie didn't seem to notice. 'Another drink?' he asked, indicating her half-empty glass.

She shook her head. Even half a beer had made her woozy. He wandered off to the bar, hailing a friend across the room, and Mattie, still a little shaken after seeing Charlie for the first time after so long, turned to Thommo. 'So how have things been?' she asked him.

'Oh, pretty good. You know, running Dad's place with him and Charlie has its moments, but for the most part we rub along fairly well. Dad's getting better at taking his hands off the wheel.' He laughed, his golden curls catching the light.

'Are you both still riding?' she asked, remembering again the horse trials they'd often competed in as teenagers.

'Nah. Not really enough time for that these days. Certainly not seriously. Winery takes up most of my energy. I still get out on the weekends though. You should come with me some time. Astrid won't mind.'

Mattie looked at him incredulously and then down at her leg. 'You think?'

'Well, not straight away, obviously. How long will you be in that thing?'

'At least another month. And then I don't think I'll be

up to much after that. I've got to get this scar on my face seen to as well.'

'Yeah, it's a good-un,' said Thommo. The Drummond boys were nothing if not blunt. Mattie didn't mind; actually, she realised, it was refreshing.

'I think I might have lost my taste for adventure somehow,' she added.

'Aw, come on. That's not the Tilly we remember.'

'So how is fatherhood?' she said, not wanting to continue reminiscing.

Thommo's eyes softened. 'Oh, the little bloke? He's a bloody champion. Never thought I'd settle down so quick, but I just love it. Astrid's such a great mum too.'

'I suppose Charlie's married by now?' she asked carefully.

'Nup,' said Thommo. 'Nearly though.' Mattie felt a pang of disappointment. Lucky girl, whoever she was.

'Got pretty serious about a girl last year; they were engaged. French chick by the name of Marie-Claire. Or Murray Cod, as we liked to call her.' He chuckled into his glass.

'Oh,' said Mattie, '*were* engaged?'

'Charlie met her when he was in Bordeaux. Couldn't persuade her to come over here, though I think they're still in touch – I sometimes hear him talking in French late into the night. Took us all by surprise though.'

'What, that it didn't work out?'

'Nah, that he got serious about a girl in the first place – you remember what he's like.'

Jake interrupted their conversation, asking Thommo an obscure question about canopy management, while at the same time putting a proprietary arm around Mattie. She moved slightly away from him; she didn't want him to get the wrong idea. Granted, he was certainly gorgeous, but she wasn't in the slightest bit interested. Men brought nothing but trouble, even Charlie. *Especially Charlie*, she warned herself.

She felt suddenly exhausted, the beginnings of a headache pressing at her temples.

As she was finishing her beer, the band began to tune up. She leaned across to shout in Jake's ear. 'I'm really sorry, but I don't feel like staying. Jet lag's caught up with me.'

He looked crestfallen for a moment but recovered himself quickly. 'Sure. Let me say goodbye to a couple of people first.'

'Oh no, it's alright,' she reassured him. 'You don't have to worry about taking me home. Thommo and Astrid said they were leaving early and have offered me a lift.'

'Are you sure?'

'Yes,' she said firmly.

'Well, let me at least carry you to the car.'

'Oh no, not in front of everyone,' she pleaded.

He gave her a stern look.

'Okay, let me lean on your arm until we get outside. I don't want the whole pub gawping at me,' she relented.

'Whatever you say, princess.'

She caught sight of Charlie across the pub. He appeared to be watching her intently. Noticing her leaving, he gave her a salute, a serious expression on his face. She felt an unexpected heat rise within her and looked away quickly.

Mattie thought back to the last time she'd seen Charlie before she left the valley. She was seventeen and in her final year at school and he was home from uni for the winter holidays. It was the midwinter Eumeralla district horse trials. The ground was frozen solid, the mud in ruts of iron. Rain fell in icy rods. Anyone who came off would be certain of a bruising at the very least, more likely a trip to hospital. There were mutterings as to whether it was even safe to go ahead.

Mattie was chilled to the bone, not sure if her teeth were chattering with nerves or the cold, but Shakira flew over the high fences, though still managing to scare her witless as she hung on for dear life. Astonished that she hadn't fallen off, especially after the last fence, which had loomed ominously over her and Shakira's heads, Mattie galloped to the finish in a near-record time. She barely noticed that her jodhpurs and jacket were sodden and heavy with rain. Anyone who had anything to do with horses in the valley was there, Charlie included. He had started several places before her and was in the collecting ring, gently walking his horse around, its flanks steaming in the frigid air as Mattie came in.

Now the course was behind her, her earlier fear transformed into triumph and she slid down from her saddle and crowed her success. 'I might have even beaten you, Charlie Drummond!' she cried.

He gave her a broad smile. 'You're a little pocket rocket, Tilly. You were completely fearless. I've never seen anything like it. That was a gutsy ride; some of those fences nearly did for Whiskey and me.'

She wasn't sure how she felt at being called a pocket rocket, but glowed at his other compliments. 'You mean you were watching?'

'I might have caught some of it,' he teased.

The presentation confirmed that she'd achieved the fastest women's time, and had come fifth overall, even beating Charlie by nearly thirty seconds. Stepping down from the podium, she was swept up in a bear hug by a boy she barely knew. Everyone wanted to congratulate her.

She looked around in vain for Charlie. She'd wanted to share her pride in winning and show off the silver cup in her hands, but he'd turned away and she watched helplessly as he left the room, his golden head several inches above the crowd. Had he minded losing to her that much?

She never did get the chance to find out. Charlie and Thommo went off to France for vintage a few months later that year, and then to agricultural college in Adelaide the following summer. By the time they came back, Mattie was long gone.

CHAPTER FIFTEEN

'What do you think, darling?' the timid-looking woman asked her willowy blonde daughter, who was standing next to her at Trevelyn's Pantry. Rose had arranged to meet them both that morning to discuss the table layout and possible decorations. Several weeks earlier, Rose had taken on the wedding booking, the first time she'd been asked to organise such a large function. She'd done a few small parties, simple canapés and wine, but as yet had not ventured into the wedding business. She had wanted to get the restaurant well and truly established first, but when a distraught mother of the bride had called her last month, in tears because her daughter's original choice of wedding venue had fallen through, Rose didn't have the heart to turn her down. When Susan mentioned that she and her daughter had loved their lunch at Trevelyn's earlier that year, and that they were only having fifty guests, and it was on a

Friday, and, really, anything she could do would be wonderful, Rose had caved in.

She'd emailed Susan some menu suggestions, and had prepared a couple of main course options for them to taste. She stood to one side, in her starched white chef's jacket, feeling anxious as they looked around. Trevelyn's Pantry was her baby, her dream of a simple, honest country restaurant that respected its setting, but now, looking at it with fresh eyes, she wondered if it scrubbed up well enough for a more formal occasion.

'We-ell …' Gabriella drawled. 'It's not the Grand Hotel ballroom now, is it?'

Susan looked apologetically at Rose. 'I'm sure we can work with it, darling, can't we? Go for a rustic theme instead.'

'It's not like we've exactly been left with a lot of choice,' said Gabriella gracelessly.

A look of relief crossed Susan's face. 'I think it will be even better than we'd originally planned,' she said brightly. 'It'll be relaxed and fun. A real country wedding.'

'Humph. If you say so. At least the food is up to scratch, or it was when we came here last time,' Gabriella said, flopping onto a bentwood chair.

Rose, who had been hovering while they debated with each other, came forward. 'Would you like to try the sample menu I've prepared? The produce is all locally sourced, and the veggies are from our kitchen garden. Then perhaps we can discuss final numbers and anything you'd like to bring in the way of decorations, a cake, and so on, over coffee?'

Susan beamed. 'That would be lovely, thank you, Rose.'

Rose went to get the dishes from the kitchen and placed them in front of the two women, standing back as they picked up their cutlery.

'Not bad,' said Gabriella after she'd tried the main dish. 'Not bad at all.' She took another dainty mouthful of the rare beef and dipped it in horseradish cream. 'Got to get into my dress though,' she said, smoothing her shirt down over a stomach that was as flat as a tack. 'So no more for me.' She pushed the half-eaten plate aside.

'Absolutely delicious, Rose,' said Susan. 'I think we should definitely go with the beef.'

'Lovely,' said Rose. 'So it's chicken liver parfait with sorrel, followed by Shingle Valley fillet of beef with fresh horseradish, roesti potatoes and wilted greens, and then wedding cake. Now, have you thought about wines?'

'Oh well, we want the Assignation shiraz, of course, the one that won the Jimmy Watson the other year. It's from around here, isn't it?' said Gabriella, looking out of the window at the view of the valley.

'I'm not sure how much of that particular wine is left, but I happen to know the owner very well – he's my partner, in fact – so I think we can source some, even if it's a later vintage.'

'Very good,' said Gabriella. 'And you've got proper glasses, I take it?' She looked pointedly at the enamel mugs that Rose had placed on the table in front of them.

'Of course,' Rose assured her. 'Lead crystal.'

'Good. Now, what on earth are we going to do to brighten up this place?'

Rose looked around at the pale cream walls, long timber tables and bentwood chairs. She hated to admit it, but Gabriella was right. It worked very well as a country restaurant, but it was lacking anything that gave it a suitably nuptial feel. 'Not a problem,' she said, thinking quickly. 'I can track down some white linen, and then decorate the tables with flowers, and if the weather's nice we can open the doors to the garden. We can even have the ceremony there if you like. Do you have a colour theme?'

'Pale pink and silver,' said Susan.

'Perfect. How about posies of peonies, pink and cream, in glass vases down the length of the tables, perhaps with silver runners? I can get a quote for you, if you like, unless you want your florist to arrange it.'

Even Gabriella seemed satisfied by this.

Rose left Trevelyn's after her wedding planning meeting and returned to Kalkari. She saw Mattie in her now customary spot on the verandah, laptop open beside her. Mattie had been staying with them for almost two weeks. She was improving every day, and it was good to see that she had a bit more colour in her cheeks. Sitting in the sunshine had helped get rid of the deathly pallor she'd had when she first arrived. She was finally allowed to put weight on her foot and Rose could see that she had become quite adept at hobbling between the barn and the house.

'There you are,' she called. 'I've got a big favour to ask.'

'Oh yes?' Mattie replied. 'I'm not sure I can imagine there's much I can help you with right now, but fire away.'

'I've got a wedding coming up. To be honest, I'm a bit freaked out. It's the biggest function I've done so far at Trevelyn's so I want everything to be perfect. I need to fancy up some menus, and my design skills are absolutely rubbish,' Rose said. 'I know it's way below what you used to do, but do you think you might be able to take a look? Would you have some time to have a play around? Can you manage, you know, with your shoulder?'

'Time?' asked Mattie. 'Yep, time is something I've got plenty of right now.' She grimaced. 'And designing a menu is a no-brainer. Let me have the copy and I'll make it look good. I can just about use a mouse, even with my dodgy shoulder.'

'Oh, that's wonderful!' Rose looked relieved. 'You'll be saving my arse.'

Mattie smiled. 'Really, I could do this with one hand tied behind my back ... Hah. I *will* be doing it with one hand behind by back. Any thoughts about colour? What sort of style are you after? What size do you want it?'

'Oh God, I don't know,' said Rose. 'We're decorating the restaurant with pink and cream peonies, but nothing too old-fashioned or over the top, I think. Clean and modern is best. Is that enough to go on?'

'Leave it with me,' Mattie reassured her. 'When do you need it by?'

'How about yesterday? I need to get the bride to approve it as soon as possible.'

'Best get cracking on it right now then, huh?'

'You're a star, thanks so much, Mattie.'

'Well, it's not like I've got anything more urgent to do,' she said drily. 'But thanks, Rose. It'll be nice to have a creative task again.'

Rose had another surprise for Mattie, something she hoped might cheer her up far more than a small job designing wedding menus. Leo and Luisa had come back from a visit to their old housekeeper, Brenda Butters, or Mrs B, as she was more affectionately known, raving about the litter of kittens her old ginger cat had recently had. 'Rose, she says we can have one if we want. Please, pleeeease can we?' Luisa had begged, looking at her beseechingly.

This information had planted an idea in Rose's head and so she'd stopped in to see the old lady on her way back from the restaurant one afternoon a few days later.

'Hello, love, how are you going? How's everyone up at the house? You'll stay for a cuppa?'

Mrs B's brew was legendary in the valley. The colour of brick dust and so strong you could stand your spoon in it, but Rose didn't dare turn her down.

'Luisa tells me you've got some kittens?' she asked hopefully.

'Aye. Only two more that I've got to find a home for. Why? You're surely not interested? Haven't you got your hands full enough with that menagerie?'

'Well,' said Rose, pausing to take a sip of tea and trying

not to wince at its tannic bitterness. 'I thought it might cheer Mattie up. And Luisa's been on my case, too. So between them both …'

'Right-oh. Would you like to take a look at them now? They're in the back room.' The old lady heaved herself out of the armchair she was sitting in and made her way to the rear of the house.

'Awww.' Rose's heart melted at the sight of the two tiny orange kittens, one with a snowy white chest and paws, and the other completely ginger, each one so small they fitted in the palms of Brenda's roughened hands. 'They're divine! But I'm not sure I could decide between them.'

'Tell you what, these are the last of the litter and I've got to find them a home. Why don't you take them both? I'll go halves with you on the vet bill.'

Rose reached out towards the completely ginger one. 'May I?'

'Of course, love. Here, take them.'

Rose knew Brenda was trying to get her to fall in love with both of them, but nevertheless let her place the two mewling balls of fur in her hands. They were soft as gossamer and, like two little twin turbo engines, they began purring as she gathered them to her chest. She didn't hesitate.

'It's a deal.'

Oh Lord. What was Mark going to say? They already had a dog, a pony and two goldfish. She wasn't sure how he'd react to two more additions to the Kalkari family. As a child she'd been completely dotty about animals, lavishing the family cat with affection. It was the only pet her mother had allowed them to have. She was more than making up for it now.

'Uno!' Leo shouted.

'Not again!' Mattie groaned and folded her hand.

She was sitting in the large, sunny kitchen at Kalkari, playing cards at the scrubbed-oak table, Luisa sitting beside her. Max drummed on his highchair with a plastic spoon as Astrid cooked spaghetti for them all.

Rose crept into the room, a carrying case hidden behind her back. 'Hey, kids, guess what?'

Four pairs of eyes looked curiously at her. Max was still looking at his spoon.

'Ta-da!' she said, revealing the carrying case with a flourish and placing it on the floor.

'Pussy cat? Pussy cat?' said Luisa, hearing the frantic mewling that was coming from the case. 'For me?'

'Well, one is for you, darling, and the other is really for Mattie. I thought she might like some company. Shall we get them out?'

Luisa clapped her hands together in excitement and slid down off her chair. 'Ooof, careful, darling,' said Mattie as Luisa's foot connected with her ankle.

The little girl was oblivious. 'A pussy cat, a pussy cat!'

Rose handed one little ginger kitten over to Luisa. 'Gentle now, sweetheart,' she cautioned. She carefully placed the other into Mattie's good hand. 'Don't they just melt your heart?' she said, hoping Mattie would agree.

'Oh baby, you are so tiny. Aren't you gorgeous, hey? So what are we going to call you?' Mattie held it up to her face. 'Who do you look like, little ginger miss?'

'Oh, she's so soft, Rosie,' said Luisa, her eyes shining with delight.

Rose looked across at the little girl, ecstatically cuddling her fluffy bundle, and down to the kitten mewling in Mattie's arms.

'I'm not sure I'm really ready to be responsible for a cat, if it's all the same to you, Rose,' said Mattie eventually. 'Besides, what happens when I leave here?'

'Let's worry about that later, hey? Why not enjoy her for as long as you like?'

Mattie looked at the little kitten again, holding her up to her face. 'Alright then,' she said, eyeballing her. 'How about Gin for you, and Tonic for Luisa's?'

'Oh, I love it!' said Rose, clapping her hands together. 'Perfect.'

Only Leo looked unimpressed. 'Who needs stupid old cats anyway?' he said to no one in particular. 'And Luisa's got a pony. It's not fair.'

'Come on now, don't forget you've got Barnsie,' said Astrid, trying to console him.

'And he's much better at tricks, in any case,' said Rose.

'Yeah, I suppose,' Leo grumbled, reshuffling the cards.

Mattie stroked her kitten, whose tail was switching like a conductor's baton. 'I mustn't get too attached,' she murmured.

CHAPTER SIXTEEN

'There are vineyards that date back to the 1800s in this valley!' Bob Drayfield roared. 'If the bloody mines start taking over our land, it'll be the end of us. What gives them the right, hey? Hey? It doesn't smell right to me – it's as dodgy as a three-day-old prawn.'

There was a loud cheer of agreement from those who had gathered at Trevelyn's Pantry for a meeting of the valley's winemakers, growers and other business owners. Basically, anyone connected to the valley was there.

'Yeah, what about the salinity? Not to mention the noise.'

'We'll end up with a wasteland,' said another.

'No doubt about it, it'll kill off tourism too,' Amanda Davies, whose parents ran Bellbirds, a B&B further along the valley, chimed in.

Looking out from the kitchen, where she was serving

up refreshments, Rose could see that the room was packed with many familiar faces: Deano and Angie from Lilybells, Bob and his wife, Sadie, Amanda, Thommo and Charlie Drummond, their parents, Bill and Sheree, as well as many others. These people were the lifeblood of the region; their grandfathers and great-grandfathers and their fathers before them had planted the vines that now threaded their way across the valley floor. They were the reason that this area was such a drawcard for visitors, for food, wine and music lovers and why the Shingle Valley had become a renowned wine region not just in Australia, but throughout the world, with bottles flying to all corners of the globe.

'What exactly is fracking anyway?' asked Amanda, who had driven up from the city especially for the meeting.

'It's when they drill at high pressure and inject liquid into the rock to split it – to fracture it,' explained Dan. 'It releases the natural gas in the rock. It uses massive amounts of water, as well as a stack of chemicals, including mercury, lead and uranium. Chemicals that will get into our groundwater. Poison our kids.'

'Not to mention that there'll be trucks going through the valley at all times of the day and night,' said Thommo.

'And the dust that it creates,' added Mark. 'That's potentially poisonous too. How can we be expected to carry on making wine with something like that affecting it? Let alone raise our families here.' There was a lot of grumbling from the crowd. 'Alright,' he said, trying to bring calm to the room. I think we're all agreed that mining would be disastrous for the valley, for the soil, the grapes, our businesses and for tourism. But the question is, how can we stop it happening? What can we do? We need to act, and act quickly.'

The meeting had been called after Mark had been able to confirm that Tarrawenna, a large winery with vineyards at the southern end of the valley, had recently been sold to Tin Pei Resources, a Chinese energy company. The threat of coal seam gas mining had loomed over the valley for years, with only the northern end zoned for tourism and agriculture, but this latest development raised the stakes considerably. Ironically, before he died, the former owner of Tarrawenna had been one of the valley's most outspoken opponents of mining in the area. Everyone agreed that it was a tragedy that this had been allowed to happen, though sadly the clash between mines and vines was not a new one.

'We're not the only ones in the country facing this. I think we should contact other regions and find out what they've done, how they've taken action,' said Bill Drummond.

'Good idea,' replied Mark.

'What about a PR campaign? I can get in touch with the local paper and some of the metro ones,' suggested Amanda. 'We can also get up a petition and go and talk to Jeremy Bell. See what he can do.'

'Good luck with that,' said Charlie. Jeremy Bell was the local MP for the valley, but most people only saw him in the region once or twice a year, when he came to present prizes at the Eumeralla school fete or the local horse show. It was universally acknowledged that he was fairly useless. 'He'd struggle to pour water out of a boot if the instructions were on the heel,' was the oft-quoted saying.

'How about the State Planning Commission?' suggested someone else.

'Right,' said Mark. 'I'll look into that, and try to speak to Jeremy. Anyone else got any other ideas?'

'I reckon we should form an organisation, you know, give ourselves a name. It'll help with the PR,' said Amanda.

'Okay,' agreed Mark. 'Anyone got any suggestions?'

After further discussion, the Shingle Valley Preservation Association was formed.

'They can't simply march in to the valley and start drilling, can they?' Rose asked Mark. 'Don't they have to have licences, approvals?'

'I don't know,' he replied. 'We've no idea yet what the energy company is planning, but let's face it, it's hardly likely that they bought Tarrawenna for its ancient chardonnay vines now, is it? If it comes to it, we might have to take them to court. Though God knows where we'll find the cash for that.'

Rose was worried. They all were. It could mean the end of their way of life, the ruin of their beautiful valley. She felt as if the ground was shifting underneath her.

CHAPTER SEVENTEEN

The next afternoon, as Mattie sat on the verandah putting the finishing touches to the menus, with Gin curled up on a cushion in the sun next to her, Charlie stopped by. 'I was after Mark,' he said as she started in surprise at his sudden appearance, 'but he wasn't at the winery. I've tried calling him, but can't reach him. Any idea where he might be?'

'Have you tried over at Trevelyn's?' she replied. 'I think he said he and Jake were headed that way today. It's a bit of a mobile blackspot there, which might be why you couldn't get hold of him.'

'Oh, right, that makes sense.' He seemed in no hurry to leave, however, and dropped down onto the chair next to her. 'I've been up at our Mudgee vineyards for the past week,' he said, 'or I would have been round to see you sooner.' He scooped up the kitten for a cuddle. Mattie felt a dart of envy shoot through her as she watched him stroke the turbo-purring puss. His hands were square and strong, with neatly clipped nails. Hands that saw plenty of good, honest, physical work. She wondered briefly what they would feel like on her skin, what it would feel like to be held by him ... There was no doubt about it; her attraction to him hadn't faded over the years. If anything it was unaccountably stronger. But it was the last thing she needed, she reminded herself firmly. And he was far from reliable – the larrikin streak in him had always been strong.

'So tell me all about London,' he said. 'What was it like over there?' He seemed genuinely interested, focusing his blue eyes intently on her green ones.

'It all seems almost like another life now,' she replied, despite having had an email from Cara just that morning, with pics from the latest campaign she'd styled. She missed her friend though – it had been harder to say goodbye to her than it had been to break up with Johnny. 'I loved it, despite the pressure, and the people in the industry were good fun – most of the time, anyway. I worked in advertising – creating campaign strategies and beautiful images for clients.' She thought back to her last shoot, how it had all seemed so important at the time. She hadn't even found out how the DeVere campaign turned out. Someone else had taken the images and designed the ads. They'd all moved on without her. It was a fast-paced world where signing a new client, working to impossible deadlines and the response rate to a campaign were an all-consuming preoccupation.

'But you can go back, can't you? When you're better?'

'That's the plan,' said Mattie.

'Was there anyone special there too? Rose mentioned you were skiing with your boyfriend.'

She shook her head. 'He turned out to be pretty bloody useless, actually.' It came out more vehemently than she'd intended.

'So you're off all men?' He chuckled.

'Something like that. What about you?' she asked, making herself bring up the subject of Marie-Claire. 'Thommo said you had a girlfriend – sorry, no, a fiancée, in France? That all sounds very serious.'

'*Had*,' he said. 'The distance was the killer, I guess.' He held her eyes for a long moment, then abruptly got to his feet. She could have sworn there was a wistful look in his gaze, probably because she'd brought up the subject of Marie-Claire, she guessed. 'I'd better track Mark down,' he said, as if he was only just remembering the reason for his visit. 'It's good to have you back, Till ... I mean, Mattie. I hope you'll stick around for a bit.'

As she watched his broad back disappear around the side of the house, she found herself wondering what Marie-Claire was like. She'd have to be pretty special to have caught and held Charlie's attention.

Mattie was still sitting outside several hours later when the phone rang. She limped to the kitchen and picked up the handset.

It was the call she'd been expecting, the call she'd been dreading.

'Hello, Mum.' Her voice, normally strong and confident, was tentative.

After a brief conversation, she ended the call and shouted through to Mark, who had returned from the Trevelyn vineyards and was sitting at his desk in the small study down the hallway.

'Guess who that was?' she said, coming into the room.

He glanced up and she gave him a look that could only mean one thing.

'Yup. They're on their way here.' She'd left a message on her parents' answering machine the previous day, giving her mum the briefest of details about her accident. It was an olive branch of sorts. Now that her daughter was back in Australia, her mother wanted to come down from Queensland to see for herself how she was doing.

Both Mark and Mattie had fallen out with their parents, but each over very different things. Her father had chosen to sell the family winery, Lilybells, when Mark was working overseas, and Mark had never forgiven him for failing to consult him, to ask if he wanted to take it over. For Mattie, it came a few years before, when, at eighteen, she'd announced her intention to go to art school in London. She'd secretly applied, and been thrilled when she was offered a place. Her mother hadn't wanted her to leave the valley, and made her feelings plain. Her father had sided with her mother, and they both refused to help her. They argued that there was a perfectly good college in Eumeralla, Sydney even, and that she would hate London in any case. Not to mention the exorbitant cost of studying overseas.

'And who do you think will pay for that?' her father had asked. 'We're not made of money, you know.'

'I just don't understand why you want to go all the way to London?' her mother said, a note of confusion in her voice. 'It's the other side of the world.'

Mattie knew it would be pointless to try to explain that, as soon as her teacher had mentioned that Saint Martins was the best art school in the world, she'd made up her mind to go there.

'What about your riding?' her father asked.

'And we'd never see you,' her mother chimed in.

Though Mark had backed Mattie up, and she'd pleaded and cajoled, neither of them could change their parents' minds. Mattie stayed at home for a year after school and worked two jobs to save enough for the trip, her course materials and somewhere to live. Her parents probably expected she would change her mind, that it was a passing fancy, but with Mark's help, Mattie had accepted her place on the fine arts course.

Her father's final words to her? 'You're making a big mistake, young lady. And you'll be on your own.'

They hadn't even offered to drive her to the airport. Mark had done that.

As a result, none of them had spoken more than a handful of words to each other in the intervening years. Mattie sent a Christmas card every year with a one-line greeting and her mum sent the occasional letter, but it had been more than ten years since she had seen them.

Mattie had had plenty of time while recovering at Cara's to think back on things, and had come to the conclusion that although her parents had been wrong to try to stop her, they had only done what they thought was best for her. When deciding to return to the Shingle Valley, she had resolved to try to mend the rift between all of them, for everyone's sake.

'Huh.' Mark was unimpressed.

'They said they'd stay at the pub. Didn't want to put you out.'

Mark was silent.

'Come on, Mark. Can we give them a break? Try to mend some fences?'

He sighed heavily. 'Okay, call them back and tell them they can come here. I can't have them staying at the pub when there's plenty of room at Kalkari.'

Rose joined them and Mark relayed the news to her.

'I bet they'll be thrilled to see their grandchildren,' she said to him. 'And don't you think it's time I met them too?'

'I stopped needing their approval a long time ago.'

'You know that's not what I meant,' said Rose, placating him. 'Come on, Mark. It might not be as bad as you think.'

'Want to bet?'

CHAPTER EIGHTEEN

Three days later, Mattie hopped out of the house as a dark sedan trundled up the Kalkari drive. Nerves curdled in her stomach, a mix of trepidation and uncertainty. It could all go horribly wrong.

As her mother emerged from the car, they both hesitated and then met in an awkward embrace. Mattie was enveloped in a familiar smell of roses and sea salt and she found herself clinging to her mother as if for dear life. She was six years old again, being comforted for a grazed knee or a schoolyard slight.

'I'm sorry, Mum.' Those were all the words she had. Incredible that, for so many years, they had been so hard to say.

'No, love, I'm the one who's sorry,' said her mum, rubbing her back gently. 'I just wish you'd told us before … you know, when you were in London. I would have come to you. By the sounds of it, you were lucky to survive – I've read about avalanches; they're fatal more often than not, aren't they? I reckon someone must have been looking out for you on that day – a guardian angel, perhaps?'

Mattie couldn't believe it, but tears welled in her eyes. Stubborn in her determination to make her own decisions, to lead her own life, she hadn't realised how much she'd missed her mother. There was no one like your mum. Ever.

'Dad!' said Mattie looking over her mum's head. She noticed with shock how much he had aged. Mattie reluctantly let go of her mother and embraced her father, blinking to stop the tears that now threatened to brim over. She had completely underestimated the effect of seeing her parents. She'd thought there would be coolness, a wariness on both sides. But seeing their familiar, if more worn, faces broke down any remaining barriers.

'There, there, Tilly darling.' Her mother's voice was soft and soothing. 'Now let's take a look at you. My, you don't look much different at all. As beautiful as ever.' Her mother tactfully ignored the scar on Mattie's cheek.

'Mu-um,' said Mattie, rolling her eyes.

'Hear you took a bit of a tumble, hey, angel?' Her dad's voice was gruff, but there was real emotion hiding there too. Angel had been his nickname for her since she was little. 'Buck up, angel!' he'd yell out when he was schooling her and Shakira over the jumps in the paddock at Lilybells.

'Just a small one,' she said. 'How was the drive?'

'Not too bad. Coupla stops along the way but we made good time.'

'Come on then, let's go inside. I think Rose has some tea for everyone.'

Mattie led them both to the house. Further words weren't necessary; she knew that although there might be a long road ahead, they were beginning to forgive each other. Whether Mark would feel the same remained to be seen.

'You must be Rose,' her father said as Rose came to the front door.

'Right first time.' She smiled warmly. 'It's lovely to meet you at last. I'm afraid Mark's over at a grower's place the other side of Eumeralla. He sends his apologies,' she said. Mattie knew that Mark had actually done no such thing but silently thanked Rose for covering up for him.

'He's promised to be back in time for dinner. Leo and Luisa will be back later this afternoon too. They're dying to see you,' said Rose.

Certainly more than your son, thought Mattie. 'Come in,' she said. 'You must be tired from the long drive.'

Mattie led them through the house and onto the back verandah. As they sat down, she gave them the bare details of the accident, reliving the day her life was turned upside down and inside out. Rose, who had stopped in the kitchen, reappeared, quietly placing a tray of tea and a homemade lemon cake, thick with icing, on the table and leaving them to it.

Half an hour later, Leo and Luisa arrived back with Astrid and flew through the house in search of their grandparents.

Leo remembered his Grandpa Ray and Grandma Ellie, but Luisa had been a newborn the last time they'd met. It hadn't affected the kids' excitement one bit, however, and the four of them were becoming happily reacquainted when Mark returned.

'Dad,' he said, striding out onto the verandah. He bent down to place a brief kiss on his mother's cheek. 'Mum.'

'G'day, son.' Ray's tone was apprehensive.

Mark was saved from replying by Luisa's interruption. 'Daddy, look what Grandma Ellie brought me.' She held out a purple book that was covered in glitter. 'She knew what my favourite colour was!' Luisa was nestled on her grandmother's lap, her cheeks pink and her eyes sparkling with pleasure from the extra attention.

'Fancy that, hey?' Mark's tone was dry, but Mattie could hear a softening in it. 'We're taking good care of her,' he said, indicating Mattie, 'between Rose and me.'

'Of course you are, but we had to come and see for ourselves,' said his mum, laying a placating hand on her husband's arm, as if to stop him from saying anything likely to cause offence. 'Even though she always was an independent young woman.'

'Not that there's anything wrong with that now, is there?' said Mark curtly.

Mattie mentally crossed her fingers, hoping that they might all be able to bury their differences after so long. She'd certainly made up her mind to. She felt an enormous relief that they'd taken the first step; it was like a weight lifting from her.

'Perhaps you'd like to show me the winery, son?' Ray asked, a conciliatory note in his voice.

'Sure,' said Mark. 'We're just about to bottle the cabernet. Come and see what you think. We went with all-new French oak, the full Rolls Royce treatment.' The pair headed out, Mark explaining his methodology as they walked.

'Now, Luisa, why don't we go and help Rose?' said Eleanor, glancing at Rose, who had rejoined them, for confirmation that her suggestion was welcome.

'What a great idea,' Rose said. 'Leo, do you think you could go and see if there are any eggs? I need a few for the custard to go with pudding.'

Mattie was grateful for the peace as everyone departed to their various jobs. She'd been more wound up about her parents' visit than she'd realised, and although she was feeling stronger every day, she still tired easily.

'So what's happening to Tarrawenna?' said Mark's father as they sat at dinner that night. 'I heard that old man Wilkins died.'

Mark's mouth set grimly. 'That's right. His kids sold it off to the highest bidder.'

'Oh yes?'

'Which just happened to be Tin Pei Resources.'

'Tin who?'

'Tin Pei. They're a Chinese mining company.'

'Oh good God,' said Ray. 'We all know what happens next.'

'Yep,' said Mark. 'Potentially coal seam gas mining and everything toxic that that brings with it. The dust, the damage to the water table ... it could threaten everyone's livelihood here, not to mention destroy such a beautiful valley.'

'So what are you doing about it?'

'Well, for a start we're going to see if there's anything that can legally stop them.'

'Too right,' said Ray. 'I remember years ago, must have been when Tilly was only a little tacker' – he looked wistfully at Mattie, sitting across from him – 'there was a South American mob that bought up a huge parcel of land the other side of Eumeralla. Wanted to strip mine the place. We had a helluva fight on our hands. But fight we did – every last one of us.'

Mark looked at him, surprised. 'I don't remember that.'

'You'd have been pretty young. There was no sense worrying you kids about that stuff then,' he said. 'Looks like the valley's got another battle on its hands.'

Mattie smiled to see her father and brother finding common ground again, even if it was over something that posed such a threat to the valley.

'It most certainly does,' said Mark. 'We've formed an action group, and I've been trying to reach Jeremy Bell, but I'm not having much luck there.'

'Jeremy? Lord, I'd forgotten about him. He and I go way back. Let me see if I can get in his ear, son.'

'That'd be good, Dad. We need to pull in every favour we can.'

*

Mattie's parents were still around a few days later, when Mattie was due to go into New Bridgeton to have the cast on her leg removed. Her mum offered to drive her over for the procedure and Mattie readily agreed – the journey would give them some time alone to catch up, to properly clear the air.

'How are you feeling, being back?' her mum asked as they hurtled along the Eumeralla Road.

Mattie shrugged. 'It's a bit early to tell, really. I had a great life in London, a really great life.' Her chin stuck out defiantly. 'It feels as if I've gone backwards, literally limping back here.'

'I'm so sorry, darling. So sorry you feel that way about the valley. I'd always hoped you'd love it as much as the rest of us did. You certainly seemed to when you were younger.'

'It's not that I didn't – don't – love it, Mum,' said Mattie, feeling exasperated. 'I just had bigger dreams. I needed to see the world, to explore, to find my place.'

'And did you?'

'I thought I had.'

Her mother nodded. 'It was different in my day. I would never have dreamed of travelling so far from home. Do you plan to go back? To London?'

Mattie turned and looked her mother in the eye. 'Of course.'

'Well, you should do what you think is best.'

It was as close to an apology as she could hope for. 'Thanks, Mum,' she said simply. 'It means a lot to hear you say that. But I'm sorry too ... for how I behaved. I could have tried to find a compromise somehow, been less of a bull at a gate about it all.'

Her mother sighed. 'How many years have we wasted?'

Mattie was silent.

'Some of us wear our scars on the outside; for others they are less visible,' her mum murmured softly.

They checked in at the outpatients' surgery and took their place in the crowded waiting room. Forty minutes later, they were still there. 'I'll go and get us some coffee, shall I?' Eleanor suggested.

Only a few seconds after she had disappeared in search of the cafeteria, Mattie's name was called. She got to her feet and swung her way through to the consulting room. Hopping onto the narrow bed, she braced herself for the whine of the saw. She remembered its spine-chilling pitch from having broken her wrist as a teenager. She closed her eyes as the nurse started up the saw and got to work. Over the noise, she heard the door open and looked up to find her mum holding two cups of coffee. Eleanor hastily put them down and went to her daughter's side. Mattie noticed her mother stumble slightly as she came towards her. Eleanor recovered herself and Mattie grasped her hand and closed her eyes again.

Eventually the high-pitched whine from the saw stopped and the nurse used a metal spreader to ease the cast off. Mattie looked on in shock as the protective stocking was cut away and she saw her lower leg emerge. It was pale and hairy, and the calf muscle had wasted away. It didn't look like it belonged to her at all.

'I'm glad you're here, Mum.'

'I'm only sorry I wasn't there for you before,' her mother replied.

'You're here now.'

CHAPTER NINETEEN

'Do you think that'll do it?' The chippy took a break and stood, fists on hips, admiring his handiwork.

'Yeah, I reckon. The little tacker'll be stoked when he sees this,' said Mark. 'You've done a great job, mate. Perhaps he might stop moping around so much too.'

'Oh, come on, Mark,' said Rose. 'This will make all the difference, you'll see.'

Leo had been glum ever since Luisa's birthday pony surprise, and the arrival of the kittens had only made it worse. He'd seemed to perk up while his grandparents were visiting, Rose had noticed, but since their departure the previous week, he'd become quiet and withdrawn once more, preferring to spend time playing in his room on his iPad rather than out with his friends. Rose had been relieved that Mark's parents' visit had gone well; both he and Mattie had spent time with them, and though the atmosphere had been strained at times, the children had helped deflect any tension. They departed with promises on both sides to visit more often.

When Mark had suggested building Leo the treehouse he wanted, Rose was delighted.

Mark had enlisted Mattie's help, and, after searching for designs on the internet, Mattie sketched a rough plan and he took it to the carpenter who had built the ramps for them.

Now here it was, the pale timber from the platform catching the afternoon light. Short, thick planks had been nailed crosswise to the trunk as a makeshift ladder, and there was a rope attached to a basket that could be raised and lowered to transport anything a boy might need up there. Large open windows had been cut into two sides of the treehouse and sealed with clear plastic sheeting, and Rob, the chippy, had scavenged a cast-off length of corrugated tin roofing, cutting and fitting a skylight into one side of it. 'It'll be pretty weather-tight, I reckon,' he assured them. The door was fastened with a hook and Mattie, who had the use of her arm back, had painted a sign, complete with a roaring lion that proclaimed it 'Leo's Lair'.

Rob had built most of the treehouse at his workshop, so that Leo wouldn't figure out that something was going on. He'd arrived at Kalkari that morning to construct it and had finished just as Astrid was heading off to pick Leo up from school in the afternoon.

Rose scaled the ladder to hang the sign. She furnished the inside of the treehouse with a couple of beanbags, an old telescope she'd found in an op shop in New Bridgeton and added an old fruit crate containing some of Leo's favourite books and games. She looked at her watch. Any minute now and Astrid would come chugging up the road with the kids. She couldn't wait to see his reaction.

'Really? A treehouse? All for me? Nobody allowed in unless I say so?' Leo was more animated than Rose had seen him in weeks. 'Oh man, this is awesome. I can't believe it. Cool! It's gonna be great. I can't wait to tell my friends all about it. Can I go in now?' Leo hopped with joy. 'Yes!' he cried exultantly as he scampered up the tree trunk, agile as a squirrel. 'Coo-eee!' he called down at everyone below. 'Hey, I can see forever from here, all the way to Eumeralla practically.'

Luisa looked up at her brother. 'Me too?' she asked Astrid.

'No, honey, this is just for Leo.'

Luisa stuck out her lower lip.

'How about we go and find some carrots for Buttons?' said Astrid.

The little girl immediately brightened.

'Now you be careful, Leo, okay? Don't go taking any risks.' Mark was serious, but a smile played about his face. 'You were right; he loves it,' he said, turning to Rose. 'Come on, let's go and have a cuppa and leave Leo to it. I've a feeling he won't be down for a while.'

'Mattie, do you want a lift back up the drive?' Astrid offered. Mattie had limped down to be there for the big reveal, not wanting to miss out.

'Thanks, but I'm doing okay,' said Mattie. 'The physio says I can walk as much as I like on it now, and it'll help me get stronger.'

'Go easy on yourself, sis, you've got a lot of recuperating still to do. You can't expect to bounce straight back from injuries like yours,' Mark said.

'I know, but it's bloody slow going,' Mattie grumbled. 'Still no word on whether I'll be able to run again. Certainly no cartwheels in the near future.'

'That's great, Mattie,' Rose encouraged her. 'You're making brilliant progress. Come on, I'll walk back to the house with you. There's plum cake in the kitchen.'

'Then I definitely am going to have to start some exercise.' Mattie pinched an invisible roll from above her waistband.

'Yeah, right,' said Rose as she linked arms with Mattie. 'I don't know where you put it – there's nothing to you.'

'She always did eat like a trencherman. Even gave me a run for my money when I was a teenager,' laughed Mark.

'Hey, buddy, how are you going up there?' Mark called to Leo. It was getting dark and he and Rose had walked down to collect him. 'Dinner's nearly ready.'

The boy's face appeared at the treehouse window. 'Hang on a sec, Dad.'

'So you like your new pad?' said Mark as Leo scrambled down the tree.

'I reckon. The telescope is awesome too. I could see the Southern Cross super clear.'

'I'm glad you like it.'

'Did you build it?' Leo asked.

'No, Rob did that, and Rose and Mattie designed it. So you should thank them as well.'

'How do they know about treehouses?'

'Well, you might not believe it, but they were both your age once. In fact, Auntie Mattie was the biggest tomboy you could imagine. When she was ten she cut her hair short and refused to wear skirts for years. Spent most of her time covered in mud, fishing for yabbies in the dam at Lilybells.'

'No way!'

'True story. But things were different when she went away to art school; London changed her. I don't think there's much of the tomboy left there any more,' Mark said wistfully. 'We were the best of pals, even though there's quite a few years between us. There weren't any other kids close by, so we had to rely on each other, make our own fun. We played endless games together outside. Half the time, Mum never knew where we were. Mattie tagged along after me, even as a tiny tacker. We'd come in absolutely filthy and starving. Mum said it was like feeding two wild animals. We even nicknamed ourselves the Ferocious Fearless Beasts.' Mark ruffled the boy's hair. 'Come on now, it's time to get back. Race you both to the front door!'

The three of them took off up the drive, their shoes scattering gravel as they ran, Leo easily keeping pace.

'Auntie Mattie, is it true?' Leo panted as he came into the house. 'Were you once a Ferocious Fearless Beast?'

Mattie looked startled, then laughed. 'What kind of stories has your dad been telling you?'

CHAPTER TWENTY

Rose had planned to wake extra early on the day of the wedding to make sure she had everything under control but she'd had a late one the night before, giving the restaurant a final clean, and had slept heavily. Which meant she was now groggily staring at the clock, trying to make sense of the glowing green numbers.

'Bugger,' she said as they registered in her brain. 'Mark,' she wailed, shaking the sleeping form next to her. 'It's 8.15. How on earth could we have overslept? Why didn't the alarm go off?'

Mark grumbled and turned over. Since vintage had finished he'd taken his foot off the accelerator. He'd had a late wine dinner in New Bridgeton the previous night and Rose hadn't even heard him come in. She was surprised the kids hadn't woken her either, but as they got older they were getting better at creeping downstairs and putting the TV on before Astrid arrived.

She tried to rouse him. 'Did you arrange for the wine to be delivered?'

'Mmmmn hmmn.'

Rose took that as a yes. She leapt out of bed and raced to the shower, frantically running through the day's plans in her head. The ceremony was at noon, and the two extra staff she'd hired to help out were due at Trevelyn's at 8.30. The restaurant was only five minutes' drive away, which gave her about ten minutes to shower and dress. Breakfast would have to wait.

Hair dripping from a hurried shower – it *still* had a stubborn tinge of purple about it – she bolted out the door, pausing only to say a hurried good morning to Astrid and the children, who were having breakfast in the kitchen. Max blew a gobbet of cereal at Rose as she waved at him. Her phone beeped. A text message from Gabriella, checking all was on track and asking if the cake, which was being delivered from Amazing Cakes, confectioner of choice of the Sydney social set, had arrived.

Rose made a mental note to check on it as soon as she arrived at Trevelyn's.

Thankfully, calm prevailed for the rest of the morning. Jen and Lesley, two of the mums from Leo's school who'd come over from Eumeralla to help out, got started on the entrée while Rose trimmed the beef fillets. The florist had arrived, the back of his van filled with hothouse peonies, and he was sculpting table arrangements out in the restaurant. Rose's phone beeped. Gabriella checking on the cake again. Rose's hand flew to her forehead. *Bugger.* She'd forgotten to chase it up. She glanced at her phone. Ten o'clock. They were cutting it fine. She knew that the cake wasn't really her problem – Gabriella had organised it herself, but it wasn't a wedding without a cake and it was a point of personal pride for Rose that there should be no last-minute dramas.

Noon arrived. The cake still hadn't, though Rose had been assured that the driver was on his way. She covered for them, texting Gabriella to say that all was under control. The last thing any bride needed was to worry about that on her wedding day.

Unlike the cake, the groom had arrived and was standing awkwardly in the gardens, flanked by two best men, all in dark suits, shoes polished to a high shine. Peering out from the open kitchen, Rose could also see Gabriella's mother, Susan, with an attractive redheaded woman who looked to be in her early forties, wearing a flowered tea dress and clutching a clipboard to her chest. She must be the celebrant.

'All set?' Rose looked at her two extra kitchen staff, who nodded their agreement. Lesley's eldest daughter, Olivia, had agreed to help out the regular waitstaff, and was making adjustments to the place settings. The glassware sparkled and the flowers perfumed the room. Rose was satisfied. Or at least she would be if the damned cake had arrived. She had no idea how she was going to conjure one up out of thin air with only minutes to go. She looked in vain in the cool-room. At a push, she could send out a fruit salad, but she knew that wouldn't impress the bride one tiny bit.

*

A classical guitarist played a ballad under the verandah and guests – there were no more than fifty of them, Susan had assured her – had begun to arrive, spilling out onto the verandah and into the garden. Rose caught sight of a few familiar faces, including Jake. She hadn't realised that he was a friend of Gabriella's, but then she shouldn't have been surprised. He seemed to know most of the women between eighteen and eighty in the valley and beyond.

Only the bride was left to make her appearance. And the wretched cake.

Rose's mobile trilled again. The delivery van was in Eumeralla and would be there within half an hour. Rose breathed a sigh of relief. Going to the front of the restaurant, she saw Gabriella approaching on the arm of an older man – her father, Rose presumed. She was wrapped in a swathe of white satin and lace and clutching an enormous bouquet of peonies. Rose saw her frown and tug the back of her dress, which had caught on the steps to the restaurant.

'Here, let me help you,' said Rose, rushing forward before she tore the fine satin.

'Oh Christ, I haven't ruined it, have I?' Gabriella fussed nervously.

Rose unhooked the gown and stood back. 'It's fine. No damage done. You look stunning.'

Rose, who always cried at weddings, even at those of people she didn't know very well, teared up. She thought of herself in white, surrounded by the people she loved most in the world, gazing up into Mark's eyes ... *Get a grip*, she scolded herself, dashing away a tear. Mark had already been down that path and it hadn't ended well for him. She couldn't see him being in a hurry to repeat the experience. She knew she should be content that they were so happy together the way things were, but a part of her still wanted the fantasy, the special day wearing a beautiful dress with all of their friends gathered around ...

She raced back to the kitchen to oversee the final preparations.

'Love's young dream, huh? I give it less than five years,' said Lesley, chewing on a piece of leftover baguette as they surreptitiously watched the ceremony taking place out in the garden. 'My Damo knew her at school. Queen Bee, she thought she was. It'll take a stronger man than David Bale to stand up to her.'

'Aw, don't be so negative, Les,' said Rose. 'You never can tell.'

'Yeah, well, a leopard doesn't change its spots, does it?' said Lesley. 'You're a hopeless romantic, you are, Rose.'

'They're knocking back the wine quick enough,' said Olivia later, coming into the kitchen with an armful of empty plates. The conversation had risen from a gentle hum to a full-blown roar, the noise level increasing with the amount of wine being drunk by the guests.

'I'll get another case from the coolroom,' said Rose, wiping her hands on a cloth. On her way out, Rose heard a frantic knocking coming from the bathrooms.

'Hey. Hey! Hallo! Can anyone hear me?'

The voice hovered between annoyed and exasperated. Rose hurried over to see what was going on. Swinging open the door to the Ladies, she was assaulted by a waft of Shalimar. The same perfume her mother used to wear. She was knocked sideways by a sudden longing for England, her family. Perhaps she should go back for a visit next time Mark had a trip there? It had been too long. She wondered if Astrid could move in and look after the kids while they were gone …

But there was no time for nostalgia. It seemed the celebrant had got stuck in a stall. Rose could see her wide-eyed face peeking out between the top of the door and the ceiling. She must have been standing on the loo. Rose glanced down at the floor. A pair of dark trousers crumpled over well-polished shoes were clearly visible. *Ohhh-kay*, she thought, taking a moment to assess the scene.

'Oh, thank goodness. I, um, we … seem to be stuck.' The woman was trying to maintain a vestige of dignity.

Rose suppressed the giggle that threatened to bubble up. 'I see. Have you tried the catch?'

'Yes, of course we have. It's jammed.'

'I'll be right back.'

'What? You're not leaving us here?'

'Just for a sec. I've got to get something to undo the lock.'

'Well hurry, please!'

Rose returned bearing a couple of screwdrivers of different sizes, forcing herself to keep a straight face. 'Don't worry. I'll unscrew it from this side and we'll have you out in a jiffy.' Rose was able to remove the screws and wiggle the lock apart.

'Oh, thank you so much,' the celebrant said, holding the door firmly as Rose freed it. 'But we'll take it from here. We're just fixing up a pair of trousers.'

I bet you are, Rose thought.

The man inside the cubicle had been silent the entire time. Clearly whoever it was didn't want his identity to be discovered. Rose needed to get back to the kitchen so she left them to it, chuckling to herself. More went on in the sleepy Shingle Valley than she sometimes gave it credit for. It wasn't until she was back in the kitchen and looked out into the busy restaurant that she noticed who else was missing from the room.

Jake Salmon.

She smirked. It wasn't exactly surprising.

Five minutes before the cake was due to be cut, and after several panicked phone calls from Rose, Amazing Cakes finally arrived, screeching to a halt outside the restaurant. Rose and Lesley raced out to meet them. 'Couldn't bloody find the place,' the driver offered without an apology.

Amazing Cakes certainly lived up to its name, Rose grudgingly admitted, admiring the three-tiered confection studded with pale pink icing-sugar peonies. A tiny, sugar-paste bride and groom, flanked somewhat incongruously by two miniature penguins, sat atop the final tier. Apparently the happy couple had met in Antarctica, according to the delivery driver.

As Rose wheeled the cake out to a chorus of 'aahs' from the guests, a voice rang out, loud enough to stop traffic – or at least the hubbub of conversation in the room. 'What's with the freakin' penguins?'

Gabriella had got stuck into the champagne, alright.

Susan's eyes widened at Rose and she frantically shook her head.

Uh-oh. Rose did a swift about-turn with the trolley, returned to the kitchen and pulled the offending sea birds off the top of the cake. Perhaps they hadn't met in Antarctica after all.

CHAPTER TWENTY-ONE

Eight weeks, three days, nine hours and thirty-odd minutes.

That was how long it had been since the avalanche that had turned her life on its head. Mattie sat on the verandah, drinking a cup of strong coffee and slowly raising and straightening her leg, obeying the physio's instructions. She cared about the look of her leg far more than the scar on her face, and hated its weak, withered state. Gin and Tonic lay curled up on the seat beside her, basking in a patch of sunlight, and the day stretched ahead of her as a vast expanse of nothing, as empty as the cloudless sky overhead. Not unlike so many of the days at Kalkari. Autumn was in full swing in the valley and had turned the vine leaves russet and crimson. Mornings were cool and misty before the sun burned through. It had always been one of her favourite times of the year, with the beauty of the valley at its peak.

But sometimes even the most beautiful place could be a prison, she thought wretchedly. There was nothing for her to do, nothing to take her mind off what might have been if they hadn't chosen to take that last run. If they hadn't gone quite so far along the ridge ... well, she'd be back in London, at work, laughing with Cara, stressing about whatever impossible task Bianca had set, and looking forward to dinner out in the evening, most likely with Johnny. She cringed as she remembered his reaction to her battered face and the cowardly way he'd left her on her own. Well, at least one good thing had come out of the accident – he'd shown his true colours and she was well out of it. It didn't stop her thinking about him though, and wondering how her judgement could have been so far off the mark. She wasn't used to getting things so badly wrong.

Wishing she'd done just one thing different that day also wouldn't change the fact that here she was, virtually marooned on a remote vineyard on the other side of the world from her old life. A life that she wasn't certain existed for her any longer.

A few days earlier, she'd emailed Bianca, asking if there was any chance of her job back. She'd received a brief and breezy reply: *Sooo glad to hear you're on the mend, babe. We're all jealous of you sunning yourself downunder. Unfortunately, business is a bit slow at the moment. Not sure if we could find anything for you – Annabel, your replacement, has turned out to be such a gem. I can't do her out of a job.*

Mattie was incensed. And then despondent. And then incensed again. She had been so easily replaced. She had thought Bianca relied on her, couldn't manage without her. Well, that turned out to be another lie. She felt a physical ache when she thought of life in London – riding on the top of a double-decker bus, picnics and concerts on Hampstead Heath, walking with Cara through Hyde Park on a lazy Sunday, nights out with the Three Bees crew, laughing till tears ran down their faces ... Now the world seemed stripped of anything exciting. There was no longer any need for her to leap out of bed in the morning, to greet the day with enthusiasm.

'Hey there, Mattie, how are you doing?' Rose was at the screen door. 'Oh!' she cried, seeing the bleak look on Mattie's face. 'Sweetheart, you poor thing. What's up?'

'Nothing much.' She was determined not to be caught feeling sorry for herself. 'It hits me every now and then. I sometimes feel like I'm reliving that day over and over.' She tried to laugh it off. 'Don't worry, I'll be okay.' She was too proud to admit to Rose that she'd asked for her old job back and been rejected.

'You've got to take it easy on yourself.' Rose came to sit next to her. 'It's still only been a couple of months. You're bound to be a bit traumatised by it. I know I would be. Especially with things not working out with Johnny.'

'Yeah, that.'

Rose looked thoughtful. 'When was his birthday?'

'His birthday? Why on earth is that important?'

Rose stared at her, not backing down.

'Um, October, I think – yes, the end of October, just before Halloween.'

165

'Your birthday is February the third, right?'

'Uh-huh.'

'There you have it – Scorpio and Aquarius. Two of the least compatible signs of the zodiac. It would never have worked out.'

'Rose,' said Mattie seriously. 'You know that's a load of complete crap, don't you?'

'Don't be too ready to write it off. Now, take Charlie for instance ...' She looked slyly at Mattie, judging her response.

'For instance?'

'I happen to know that Charlie's a Sagittarius —'

'And?'

'Match made in heaven.' Rose grinned.

Mattie rolled her eyes. 'Give me a break!'

'Come on, he's single, and he seems pretty keen on you, from what I've heard.'

'What exactly have you heard?'

Rose tapped the side of her nose. 'You know how Astrid likes to chat ... Apparently Charlie told Thommo that he was really happy to see you back in the valley.'

Mattie instantly dismissed it. 'That could mean anything. Anyway, I'm not interested. My focus is on getting better so that I can get on with my life again.'

They sat in silence, contemplating the chickens scratching at the end of the yard. 'I'm sorry that this awful thing brought you to Kalkari, but we're all so happy you're here,' said Rose, taking her hand. 'Including Charlie.' She winked. 'The kids love having their auntie nearby, and Mark's thrilled too. I know how close you are. He's been so pleased to be able to show off everything he's been doing.'

Mattie knew Rose was doing her best to cheer her up and was thankful for it. She was right – it was good be around family for a change, even if they were busy with their own lives. 'He took me over to the winery yesterday for some barrel sampling,' Mattie said. 'He's done amazing things. I knew he was good, but I had no idea he was quite so talented.'

'Clearly it runs in the family – Gabriella was really pleased with the menus. And I heard that Bellbirds are looking to update their logo and signage. I had a chat with Amanda Davis when I saw her the other day and suggested you might be the person for the job. Not that I think you should be rushing back into work, you're here to rest and recover, but I thought I'd pass it on in case you're interested.'

Mattie brightened. She had loved doing logo and branding work, understanding the essence of a client's business and encapsulating that into a perfect image and design. 'Actually, that sounds as though it might be interesting. God knows I could do with something to take my mind off things.'

'Oh good. I've got to go over to Trevelyn's for a few hours, but how about we head to Eumeralla this afternoon? Amanda's up from Sydney at the moment – she spends most weeks down there – so we can pop into Bellbirds on the way home, if you like.'

'That would be great,' Mattie said. As Rose went back inside, she found herself wondering just what Charlie had meant by being happy that she was back. Was it merely a passing comment, or should she read more into it? She was almost afraid to find out.

'Oh, darling, I heard about your dreadful misfortune.' The immaculately groomed blonde's tone was patronising and Mattie could see she was trying not to wince as she took note of the scar on her face.

'Amanda. I didn't realise it was you,' Mattie replied. 'Rose said Amanda Davis …' She and Amanda had been in the same year at primary school.

'Oh yes,' Amanda trilled, holding a sparkling diamond in front of Mattie's face.

At least two carats, Mattie thought, remembering her lesson from Jamie Soames.

'Three years now. Jonathan and I live in Sydney. He's in banking, you know.' The smugness in her voice set Mattie's teeth on edge, but she tried to smile at Amanda pleasantly. Mattie wanted the work, no matter how far beneath her experience it was. 'But we try to get up here as often as we can.' Amanda's smile didn't reach her eyes. 'Darling, you must look us up next time you're in town. We've got a gorgeous little place in Bellevue Hill, and I run my own PR firm. The Davis Agency. You might have heard of us?'

Mattie gave a slight shake of her head.

'Well, anyway, let's get on, shall we? I'd be so pleased if I can find someone local to do the job – support the community, you know? Rose tells me you're quite the design whizz these days. This is our current logo.' Amanda held a brochure in one perfectly manicured hand. 'It hasn't changed since Mum and Dad started the business thirty years ago, so it's long overdue for an overhaul, if you see what I mean.'

Mattie did indeed. The brochure showed some very dated, dark photography together with a curlicued font and cream background. It was a world apart from the charming old brick farmhouse that sat at the foothills of the Shingle Hills, with its stripped-back beams, white walls and lush gardens planted with flowering shrubs and delicate maples. Amanda showed them through the house, and Mattie popped her head into a bedroom. Waffle-weave towels, plump pillows and a linen-upholstered bedhead spoke of a much more contemporary, but still charmingly rustic, look.

'We've just about finished with the interiors – the repainting's done and we've replaced all the bedding and put in new furniture. This is much more what people expect these days.'

Mattie nodded. She could already see a new logo and layout forming in her mind. 'You're right. The current brochure doesn't reflect this at all. How about something a lot cleaner and simpler?' Mattie looked around at the room. 'And for the logo, well, I was thinking something like this ...' She sketched as she spoke. 'It's very rough, and I'm not quite sure of the colour palette yet, but you see where I'm going ...'

'Mmm,' said Amanda, considering it. 'Yes, I think that might do.'

She wasn't exactly raving, but Mattie decided to push for more while she was there. She had nothing to lose. 'Why don't I take a look at your website at the same time? Overhaul the whole brand?'

'Oh yes, I suppose that would be a good idea. I've been meaning to get one of my girls onto it, but we've just been so busy. I've won more accounts than ever this year.' Mattie gritted her teeth at the self-satisfied tone in Amanda's voice.

'Okay,' said Mattie. 'How about I start with some preliminary ideas and get back to you in a week or so?'

'If you could make it next week, that would work. You don't exactly have much on at the moment, do you?'

Ouch. 'You're right.' Mattie smiled saccharine-sweetly. 'I can give this my full attention.'

They spoke briefly about payment and then Rose and Mattie headed back to the car.

'I'm sorry she was so patronising,' said Rose. 'I've only spoken to her a few times and I had no idea —'

'Don't even worry about it,' said Mattie. 'I've dealt with far trickier clients than her, believe me.'

As they drove back, she looked out of the window at the patchwork of vines that stretched to the horizon, noticing sprays of water coming up from the dams. She spied a group of horses in a paddock lazily flicking their tails at flies, saw signs pointing invitingly towards cellar doors and country restaurants. As the shadows lengthened, she saw it all afresh and a sense of peace crept over her. How could she have so easily left all this behind? Was it the prospect of some work, regardless of how simple it might be, that was responsible? Or could the valley be stealing its way back into her heart?

CHAPTER TWENTY-TWO

Mattie's body was healing well, and the physio from New Bridgeton was very pleased with her patient. 'I don't think you'll need to see me much longer,' she said, watching Mattie walk up and down. 'Wear a surgical boot on longer walks, but you can take it off now and let those muscles get stronger on their own. You're making great progress. And if you do the exercises I've given you the limp should disappear eventually.'

'When will I be able to drive?' Mattie had been starting to get antsy, being stuck at Kalkari, miles from anywhere and completely reliant on Rose or Mark to give her lifts.

'I reckon you're fine to drive now, when you're not wearing a boot.'

'That's the best news I've heard in ages!' Mattie nearly hugged her. If she could have skipped out of the clinic she would have, but as it was she had to make do with a hobble.

'You look happy,' said Rose as she came to collect her. 'What did she say?'

'She's cleared me to drive, and I only need to wear this boot occasionally. All I need now is to sort out some wheels and you won't have to keep ferrying me around.'

'That's great, Mattie. But I haven't minded it, you know.'

In the few months that she had been staying with them, Mattie had come to realise what a sweetheart Rose was. She couldn't have been more different than Isabella. Mattie hoped her brother understood what a good thing he had.

'I know,' Mattie replied, 'and you've been amazing. But like I said, I'm not used to being dependent on anyone.'

It was Charlie who came to Mattie's aid. She'd mentioned she was on the lookout for a cheap runabout to Rose. Even if she was only going to be staying for another six months or so, a car would mean she was free to come and go as she pleased, not having to rely on Rose and Mark for lifts. Rose had mentioned it to Astrid, who'd mentioned it to Thommo, who'd mentioned it to his brother ... That was the way things worked in the valley – news and gossip travelled like wildfire, whether you liked it or not. Charlie rang her one morning, just as she was getting out of the shower.

'Fearless!' he cried. 'Heard you're in need of some wheels? I've got a mate, Crash, who's getting rid of an old

Corolla. Not sure what sort of state it's in, but I'll give him a bell and find out. Leave it with me.'

'Seriously? You want me to buy a car off a bloke called Crash?'

'Should I tell you how he got his nickname?'

'Probably best not to.'

One lunchtime later that week, he gave her a lift over to the other side of Eumeralla to have a look at the car. Sitting beside him, she felt unnervingly close, his denim-clad thighs mere inches from hers. His hands were steady and sure on the steering wheel, his forearms strongly muscled. And when he looked at her Mattie felt something inside her melt clean away. She shifted uneasily in her seat and stared out of the window. She wasn't looking for any kind of romantic relationship anytime in, ooh ... the next decade at least.

Charlie didn't appear to have noticed the rising tension in the car, and effortlessly swung the vehicle onto the Eumeralla Road. 'So,' he said, breaking the silence, 'how does it feel to be back in the valley, now you've been here a few months? Think you'll stick around for a bit longer? 'Specially once you've got a set of wheels?'

She turned to look at him, noticing again his strong profile, square chin and the unruly golden hair that curled into the collar of his shirt ... the broad shoulders and lean hips, the legs so close to hers ... he radiated virile good health and try as she might, she couldn't help being attracted to him. She wondered what it would feel like to kiss him, to

press her lips to his, to feel his strong arms around her ...
She lost herself in the fantasy.

'Mattie? Are you with me?'

She dragged her mind back to his question. 'Sorry, miles away.' She swallowed and tried to refocus. Hooking up with Charlie would be a terrible idea. 'Um, well – Mark's been very kind to let me stay as long as I want, but I do have to go back to London at some point.'

'Really? Why? Don't you think you could make a life here? It might not be the bright lights of the city, but it's not a bad place to call home.'

'I know that,' she said. 'I'm just not sure if it's really where I belong.'

'You could,' he said, turning to smile at her. 'You just have to want to. It's as simple and as hard as that. I should know.'

'Don't take this the wrong way,' she said. 'But I feel like I've failed. Returning here in this state' – she indicated her face, where the scar was still raised on her cheek – 'with very little to show for all my time away ... A few successful ad campaigns don't really add up to much, do they? If you must know, I feel like a big fat loser.' She bit her lip and turned her face to look out of the window.

Mattie felt the ute slow down and there was a scrunch of gravel as Charlie pulled the car onto the side of the road. She turned to look at him, surprised that he had stopped in the middle of nowhere.

'Now listen here, Matilda Cameron. There is no way that anyone thinks you're a loser, just because you've come home and need some time to get well again, so get that straight. It isn't as if you stayed here and never left, never did anything with yourself. You'll always carry those years with you, no matter where you are in the world. Anyway, a girl who could face one of the gnarliest cross-country courses I've ever seen and finish with a smile on her face isn't a loser. Not in my book, not in anyone else's, okay?'

She gave him a weak smile. 'Okay.'

'I learnt a valuable lesson once, when I was in France. We'd gone out sailing for the day, with Marie-Claire's family.' Mattie tried not to wince as she heard the name. 'As we were sailing back to port, a huge storm blew up. I was at the helm, and pretty keen to impress her father. I battled away for a good half an hour, getting absolutely nowhere. Eventually, when I could see that we'd never make it back to the mooring before dark, I turned the yacht nor'east and made for land further up the coast where we stopped in a sweet little port until the storm had passed.'

'Is there a point to this story?' asked Mattie.

'Look, what I'm trying to say is that sometimes, when the wind isn't blowing your way, you have to adjust your sails, and that it's not the end of the world. Actually, it can even turn out better than you'd expected.'

Mattie looked at him curiously. 'Charlie Drummond. Are you getting wise in your old age?'

He threw his head back and laughed. Mattie looked hungrily again at the full parted lips, the strong white teeth. He looked so vital and strong, his zest for life practically radiating off his skin. It was exciting just to be around him;

the air he moved through seemed somehow clearer, charged with possibility.

'I'm doing my best not to,' he said, once his mirth was under control. 'Come on then. Let's go and find you some wheels.'

A few minutes later they pulled up outside a dilapidated weatherboard cottage. There were a number of cars in various states of disrepair parked in the paddock behind it. Were they on a fool's errand? The used car market in the Shingle Valley wasn't exactly extensive, but this didn't look at all promising. She hoped Charlie knew what he was doing.

Crash appeared at the front door and ambled over to meet them. He indicated a silver hatchback that − *thank God*, Mattie thought − at least had four inflated tyres and no signs of rust. Charlie popped the bonnet, umming and ahhing as he checked the engine over. Mattie peered inside, though truth be told she didn't know exactly what to look for. After Charlie had finished his inspection and seemed to be satisfied, she took it for a test drive up and down the Eumeralla Road. The engine ran smoothly and she couldn't see anything obviously wrong with it.

'What did you say you wanted for it, mate?' asked Charlie when they returned.

'Five grand,' said Crash, rubbing the goatee on his chin.

'That's a shame.'

'How do you figure that then?'

'We've only got four to spend.'

Mattie blinked. She could have stretched to five and a half and Charlie knew that; they'd discussed it on the way there.

Crash looked reluctant. 'Look, I'm only selling it 'cause Mum doesn't drive it any more.' He paused, considering the offer. 'Okay, because it's you, Charlie, and seeing it's for your girlfriend. Done.'

Charlie looked at Mattie, his eyes silently warning her not to contradict Crash's assumption. 'Sweet,' he said. 'Right, Mattie, do you want to drive it home?'

'You bet!' She was itching to get behind the wheel of a car again.

Once they'd sorted out the paperwork and she'd handed over a cheque, Mattie prepared to leave. She buckled up, pleased to see that the petrol gauge was showing three-quarters full. She'd burned through most of her meagre savings when she was in hospital in London, and buying the car pretty much cleaned her out. Back in London, she'd been too busy having fun, eating at expensive restaurants with Johnny, enjoying her first taste of financial freedom after years as an impoverished student, to think too much about her future. Now she was forced to think carefully about every purchase. It might not have been the smartest move to spend her last few thousand on a car, but somehow it felt like the right one.

'I'll follow you back to Kalkari,' Charlie said. 'Just in case.'

'In case of what? Do you think the car won't make it?'

He shrugged his shoulders. 'We'll soon see.'

He might be gorgeous, but his laidback attitude was infuriating sometimes. 'I'll hold you responsible if it doesn't,' she said, smiling to show she was only partly serious. 'But thanks,' she added. 'For saving me a grand when you knew I could have paid more.'

'Crash has been trying to sell this thing for months. And he also owed me a favour.'

'Well, thanks anyway. I appreciate it.'

'At your service, madam,' he said with a mock bow and a wink, smiling at her so winningly that Mattie felt butterflies mass in her stomach.

Impulsively, she reached over and kissed him on the cheek, inhaling as she got close to him. 'You're a mate, Charlie,' she said, doing her best not to let him see her blush.

A beat of silence.

'Don't suppose you fancy catching up for dinner on Saturday?' he said, sounding uncharacteristically hesitant. 'There's a new place I've been meaning to try out.'

Heat really did flame her cheeks this time. She needed to get a grip – she was behaving like a nervous schoolgirl. Was he asking her out? On a date? Something very like happiness flared through her, chased by uncertainty as she remembered her resolve to steer clear of anything remotely romantic. He was probably being kind, feeling sorry for her.

'Um, yeah, sure, that'd be nice,' she was surprised to hear herself saying. 'I'll shout you a beer for helping me with this.'

'Absolutely unnecessary, but okey doke. I'll pick you up at seven. Now, let's get going before my brother notices how long I've been away.' He sauntered over to his car, whistling a tune. She could have sworn he had even more of a spring in his step than usual.

The drive home was uneventful. Charlie followed her as far as Kalkari, and Mattie waved a hand in farewell as she turned up the drive. She spent the rest of the afternoon in the barn, determinedly putting thoughts of their prospective dinner out of her head. She was working on the logo for Bellbirds, refining the design she'd sketched up for Amanda, and was about to email her the files for approval when she saw a new message in her inbox.

Cara.

She'd heard from her friend only occasionally in the weeks since she'd been in Australia and had missed her terribly – no one else could make her snort with laughter the way Cara did. It seemed she had been up to her ears in shoots for a fashion client and was complaining that Bianca expected the impossible. *Six girls, two guys and eight different locations – can you even believe it?* she wrote to Mattie. To add to her stress, Cara's assistant had quit a week into the project, leaving Cara no time to find a replacement. *She said she couldn't cope. And wasn't available to work past 6pm. Bloody Gen Y slacker.* Mattie could practically hear steam coming from Cara's ears through the email. Now was perhaps not the time to remind her that she was almost of Gen Y vintage herself. Cara also said that the new creative director, Mattie's replacement, was on the ball and helping to make things run smoothly.

Cara's news gave Mattie another pang of longing for her old life. She'd been feeling more positive than she had in weeks, what with her new car, having a bit of creative work to focus on, and even the prospect of going out on a date with Charlie, though she was still in two minds as to whether it was a good idea or not. But hearing from her friend and all the goings-on in London took some of the wind out of her sails.

Mattie heard her mum's voice in her head. *No use crying over spilt milk.* Sighing, she logged out of her email and closed the laptop. She'd reply to Cara when she was in a better frame of mind and actually had something of interest to report.

CHAPTER TWENTY-THREE

Mattie barely tasted the food in front of her. Not that there was anything wrong with it. No, she loved a steak as much as the next girl, and the tender fillet was a fine example. It was the person she was sitting opposite, in a back booth at Porter House in New Bridgeton, who was the cause of her lack of appetite.

Charlie had arrived, right on time, earlier that evening to pick her up. She'd spent far too long fiddling with her hair, which had grown as shaggy and wild as it had been when she was a girl, before finally giving up. She was self-conscious about the scar on her cheek, but had to admit it was fading with every passing week. Who knew, Bianca's cream might just have worked.

He wouldn't tell her where exactly they were going. 'Don't you like surprises?' he'd said as they got in the car. Mattie, shifting a raft of tasting notes and labels out of the front seat, grumbled, 'I usually prefer to know exactly what's going on, I'm afraid.'

Charlie laughed. 'Well, hopefully you won't be disappointed.'

She wasn't. The restaurant was dimly lit, with dark timber walls and a long bar, behind which a bearded barman whirled and shook and stirred fancy-looking cocktails. She barely registered the amazing smells coming from the kitchen, but she noticed the tang of Charlie's aftershave as he leaned across to usher her into the booth.

'This is all a bit sophisticated for the valley, isn't it?' she asked as they sipped on a thirst-quenching and utterly delicious blend of gin, paperbark-smoked grenadine and plum nectar spiked with orange bitters. 'Not that it isn't delicious,' she added quickly.

'Times have changed, Matilda Cameron. The valley's not the backwater you think it is,' he teased. 'Anyway, I thought we'd go somewhere where we won't be interrupted.'

'Mmmm,' she said, savouring the cocktail and agreeing with him. 'Can't fault that reasoning.'

'So, Mattie ...'

She looked up from her drink and found his gaze on her. Looking into his twinkling blue eyes, her throat went dry. She licked her lips, tasting the sweetness from the cocktail as desire swirled through her like smoke, sparking a heat in her belly. He reached for her hand, his thumb lazily stroking her palm, turning it over as if to read her future. Moments passed. The noise of the restaurant went on around them, but they might as well have been in a world of their own. She cleared her throat, trying to get a grip on herself. 'Yes?'

'The lamb or the beef?' Charlie said, relinquishing her hand.

She burst out laughing, the tension of the moment dissolved.

When their orders had been dispatched, he started to tell her of his plans for Windsong and what it was like to work with his father and brother, the challenges of getting his father to agree to new methods. What it had been like to return to the family business after spending so much time in France. 'Probably fairly similar to your own experience,' he said.

Mattie struggled to concentrate on his words, noticing instead the way he used his hands as he spoke, how his eyebrows wiggled when he wanted to emphasise a point. The warmth and humour and intelligence that sparkled in his eyes.

She managed only about half of her steak before admitting defeat, but Charlie, who'd not left a scrap, ordered dessert – something gooey and chocolatey, from the looks of the plate that was delivered to their table several minutes later. 'Here, you have to try this,' he said, offering her a bite. The intimacy of the gesture only served to make her think of other things she'd like to taste … Mattie was finding it harder and harder to focus on their conversation, her imagination running wild.

It was getting late by the time they'd finished. After the initial heart-stopping silence, they'd not ceased chatting, finding much in common in the time they'd both spent away from the valley, and living in Europe. She glanced at her watch, surprised by how quickly the evening had flown.

Charlie noticed and signalled for the bill. 'Come on then, hopalong. Let's get you home.'

The drive back to Kalkari went all too quickly, and Mattie found herself wishing the evening wasn't over. She couldn't remember the last time she'd enjoyed herself so much, even if she'd been off her food. As they crunched to a halt outside the main house, Charlie killed the engine and turned to look at her. She wondered whether or not to ask him in to the barn, which would mean only one thing ... which suddenly didn't seem like such a bad idea ...

'I had a great evening, would you —'

'Thanks, Mattie —'

They both spoke at once, stopped and then laughed. He leaned towards her and their lips met. Time stood still. As the kiss deepened she felt as if she'd been waiting her whole life for it. Lost in the embrace, Mattie curled her fingers through his hair, delighting in the feel of him, the rasp of his chin and the softness of his lips... She'd never been kissed like that by anyone and she immediately wanted more, feeling a hunger for him that she couldn't sate.

As they broke away to catch their breath, the part of her that would be forever fifteen years old couldn't believe the fact that *she was kissing Charlie Drummond* ... She had to suppress a giggle that threatened to bubble up from deep inside her. She reached for him again, wanting the feel of his lips on hers. As if moving to a tune of their own, her hands ran along his broad back, feeling the planes of muscle beneath his shirt. She reached to the front of him and undid the buttons, pinging one onto the car floor in her haste. She wanted – no, she *needed* – to feel his skin, silky and warm, against hers. Charlie began to trail kisses down her throat, lingering at the hollow there. She groaned, caught up in the heat, the desire that had so quickly flared between them.

'Tilly …' He cleared his throat, pulled back. His eyes locked onto hers.

She realised in that moment that she could really fall for him – properly this time. Not a silly schoolgirl crush, but the real thing. It was utterly terrifying. She barely had time to register the thought before he reached for her again and she willingly surrendered to his searching lips until she could no longer think straight.

A while later, as her eyelids fluttered open, she saw that a light had gone on on the verandah. The front door opened and Mark's voice rang out. 'Is that you, Mattie?'

They broke away like guilty teenagers.

Charlie grinned at her. 'Busted!'

CHAPTER TWENTY-FOUR

Despite the mining threat hanging over the valley – reports of engineers assessing the land at Tarrawenna hummed along on the grapevine – the sun still rose and set and life went on. A week after Mattie's date with Charlie, the long, golden autumn abruptly gave way to winter, and a freezing wind howled over the Shingle Hills, shaking the remaining leaves from the trees and delivering chilblains to those unfortunate enough to be out pruning.

Mattie rested her feet – cosy in a pair of thick socks knitted by Mrs B – on the belly of the kitchen range. Astrid was sitting with Max and Rose was there too, planning for the annual Longest Table Shortest Day lunch, an event that brought most of the wineries in the valley together for a mid-winter celebration. Mattie remembered it from when she was a girl: the Narrow Track, a tiny side lane that snaked its way off the main Eumeralla Road, was closed to farm machinery, and one long table was set up along the middle of it. A temporary camp kitchen was established at the far end, and participating restaurants and wineries collaborated on a menu and shared the cooking. This year, Rose had volunteered to chair the organising. She had already enlisted Mattie's help in designing a poster that now adorned most of the shop windows in Eumeralla, and which had gone out to the mailing lists of all the wineries involved.

Now Rose was deciding on a menu. 'Do you think we should serve polenta or rice with the lamb?' she asked Mattie.

Mattie shrugged. 'I dunno, depends on how you are thinking of cooking it, I guess.'

'I was thinking we'd marinate and then spit-roast it on site, Italian-style. In which case ...' Rose tapped her pencil against her thigh. 'Polenta is probably a better option. It might be a nightmare to cook on site though. If last year is anything to go by, we're looking at about 200 plus.'

'What about grilled polenta instead? That way you can make it in advance and warm it through before serving it?'

'Of course!' cried Rose. 'Genius. Thanks, Mattie!' She beamed at her and began scribbling away.

Astrid disengaged Max's fist from her hair. 'Last year they were all still there drinking in the dark, according to Thommo. He went from the lunch straight to the pub and didn't get home until nearly midnight – I remember, I was up with Max and he made a hell of a noise when he came in,' she grimaced.

Mattie chewed on a fingernail. 'Do you need any help with the theme? With dressing the tables, setting the scene?'

'Are you kidding? That would be fantastic. I'm good with the food side of things, but the aesthetics, well, it's not exactly my strong point.'

'But Trevelyn's Pantry? It's hardly devoid of style, Rose. You'd have to have rocks in your head not to notice how beautiful it is.'

'Actually Astrid did most of that.'

Astrid looked up and smiled. 'I spent hours at jumble sales and op shops,' she said. 'Loved every minute of it.'

'Do you think you'd like to help me out with this?' Mattie asked her. 'I reckon it'll be too big a job for one person, in any case.'

Astrid's eyes lit up. 'How about making a kind of Italian alfresco scene, lots of terracotta, reds and oranges?'

Rose and Mattie nodded enthusiastically.

'We'll have braziers to keep everyone warm, and there's a stash of blankets somewhere from previous years that we can use too,' said Rose.

'I can also do the calligraphy for the place names, if you'd like,' said Astrid.

'We'd better get cracking then,' said Mattie. 'It'll be here before we know it.'

The morning of the lunch dawned bright and clear. Ticket sales had been strong, and the last few places had been snapped up the week before. 'Helped in no small part by your beautifully illustrated poster,' Rose told Mattie.

The two women had risen before the sun and were sitting in the kitchen at Kalkari, having a coffee in the early morning quiet. Astrid was going to meet them at the Narrow Track, where they were expecting delivery of the plates, cutlery, glasses, tables and chairs loaned from each of the restaurants.

'All set?' Mark appeared in the kitchen, running his fingers through dishevelled hair.

Rose nodded. 'Yep. Looking forward to it. Are you bringing Leo and Luisa at noon?'

'Uh-huh. Thommo's coming later too, with Max. We'll be at the kiddies' end of the table, God help us.' Max was at that age where he took great delight in seeing how far he could throw his food, and would only sit still for a few minutes before wanting to be off, exploring. 'Toddlers,' he said, grimacing.

Mattie noticed a pained look on Rose's normally sunny face.

'Dan's bringing the Kalkari chardonnay and shiraz in his ute, and we've been able to borrow a refrigerated trailer to keep it all cool,' Rose said. 'Not that there's much chance of it getting too warm.'

'It feels like it's about five degrees out there,' said Mattie. She had dressed carefully for once, wearing a moss-coloured cashmere sweater that brought out the colour of her eyes, and cream jeans with her favourite boots. She'd also applied a touch of gloss to her lips and her cheeks were pink from the cold. She couldn't wait to see Charlie again; he'd promised to be there. He had been on her mind ever

189

since their interrupted date nearly a month ago. They'd swapped several messages, but Charlie had been travelling in South Australia and they hadn't managed to catch up since. It had been a long few weeks for Mattie.

'Once that sun comes out it'll warm everything up, you'll see. Looks like it's going to be a beaut of a day,' replied Mark.

Rose drained her cup. 'Right then, let's get cracking.'

As they pulled up at the entrance to the Narrow Track, Mattie could see that there was plenty of activity already underway. Portaloos had been delivered the previous day, trestle tables were in the process of being assembled along the centre of the lane and an assortment of chairs had been stacked at the far end. Mattie retrieved the linen table-cloths from the boot of the van and went over to where Astrid was helping to set up, while Rose headed over to the camp kitchen, where whole lambs were already turning slowly over a spit. Waving to Dave and Wayne, two chefs from The Tin Shed, a new restaurant on the other side of Eumeralla, Rose unwrapped her knives from their protective roll and began to prep the mountain of vegetables she'd brought with her in the van, topping and tailing beans with effortless efficiency. 'How's it going, guys? Everything under control?'

'So far so good. Bloody freezing though.' Wayne rubbed his hands together. They were all rugged up in thick parkas, but the same couldn't be said for their hands, which had to be bare.

'I'll go and see if I can pinch one of those braziers.'

Rose gestured to the huddle of metal gas heaters at one end of the track.

'Good idea. I'll help you shift it,' said Wayne.

The rest of the morning flew by, and the weather grew warm enough for the chefs to cast off their heavy coats. Mattie and Astrid put the finishing touches to the tables.

'It looks amazing, Mattie,' Rose called out, looking up from her work.

Mattie turned and gave her a grin. 'I know, hasn't Astrid done a great job?'

'You both have,' she replied. 'It's spectacular.'

The long line of tables was clothed in starched white linen, and glasses and silverware gleamed in the sunlight. Crimson berries interspersed with winter-crisped vine leaves added colour and warmth to the setting. It was simple, but breathtaking.

'What a day!' exclaimed Astrid, who was joining Thommo and his parents for lunch. Mattie was going to be sitting with Mark and the kids, and Dan and his wife were coming as well. 'We've got the last of the place names to set out and then we're done. Phew!'

'You've earned your lunch, that's for sure,' said Rose. 'Thanks so much for all your help.'

'Don't even think about it,' replied Mattie, her eyes shining with pleasure at the scene.

'Looking forward to seeing Charlie?' Rose teased.

Mattie grinned at her. 'Maybe ...'

*

When almost all of the guests had sat down and the first course was served, Mattie took her place next to Mark, Rose, Leo, Luisa and Dan and his wife, all the while keeping a lookout for Charlie. She checked her phone again. No messages.

The main course was just being served when she noticed him arrive. Her heart stopped. He looked as heart-stoppingly sexy as she'd remembered and it was all she could do to prevent herself from racing over to him. In fact, she was about to do just that when she noticed a chic-looking woman, swathed in a thick scarf and wearing impossibly skinny jeans, accompanying him. They were holding hands.

Her joy at seeing him turned to an icy dread.

She saw the rapt expression on the woman's face as she laughed at something Charlie said to her, his blond head angling towards her dark one. What the bloody hell was going on? Was this Marie-Claire? Somehow she knew it must be. Wasn't she supposed to be back in France? And wasn't their relationship supposed to be completely over?

The mystery of his companion was soon solved. Charlie brought her over to where Mark and Mattie were standing and, though he didn't quite meet Mattie's eye, introduced her. Her instinct had been right. Marie-Claire. The French fiancée. Mattie forced herself to exchange a few words, and found her completely charming, with delightfully accented English. *Bugger*, Mattie thought. She couldn't even find a reason to dislike her. Charlie, on the other hand, had a serious amount of explaining to do …

The rest of the afternoon was a blur of food and wine as Rose and the rest of the team worked to make sure everyone was fed and watered and Mattie silently fumed, doing her best not to stare at Charlie and Marie-Claire, who were sitting further down the table.

Mattie saw Rose on her way to the camp kitchen and jumped up. 'Need some help?' she asked.

'Thanks, that'd be great.'

Amanda, who'd come to the lunch with her banker husband – Jonathan or George or something, Mattie couldn't quite remember – joined them. 'So,' Amanda said, 'that's the mysterious Marie-Claire then?'

Mattie glanced at her but said nothing.

Amanda continued, undaunted. 'I have to say she's not as pretty as I thought she would be. But,' she added quickly, 'she's certainly *très chic*. There's something about French women, isn't there? They seem to have style oozing out of every pore. Let's hope she can tame Charlie, hey? He always was a wild one. Mattie, do you remember that time at primary school when he let the phasmids out of their enclosure at recess?'

Mattie smiled faintly.

'And when he collected tadpoles and put them in the teacher's coffee mug? Hilarious!' Amanda gave a trill of laughter. 'Well, anyway, she seems lovely and I'm sure he doesn't get up to those kind of tricks any more,' she said, picking up another bottle of wine and returning to the table.

'Are you okay?' said Rose when Amanda was out of ear-shot. 'It's all a bit of a surprise, isn't it? Did you know Marie-Claire was coming?'

'Nope. He didn't mention her at all when we went out for dinner, nor in his messages while he's been away. Funny that.'

'Oh, Mattie,' said Rose, giving her a squeeze.

Mattie shook her head. 'Damn it if she isn't nice as well. Ugh. I can't even … Men! They're all the same. Feckless bastards.'

Soon afterwards, Mattie excused herself from lunch with a headache. As she left, she inadvertently caught Charlie's eye and he flashed her a brief look of apology. She flicked her gaze away angrily. She told herself she didn't care, that Charlie was welcome to do as he pleased. They'd only shared a kiss … it meant nothing.

As she drove home, she wondered if it might be a good idea to leave the valley sooner rather than later.

CHAPTER TWENTY-FIVE

'A nyone up?'

At first Mattie thought she must be imagining things. That voice belonged half a world away, its owner most likely propping up a bar in deepest Kensington, knocking back a neon-coloured cocktail, not at here at Kalkari when the sun had barely risen over the Shingle Hills.

'Hey! Anybody home?'

Mattie had heard a car pull up, but thought nothing of it. However, she'd know that husky tone anywhere. A voice that would carry across three suburbs. She wrapped herself in a dressing gown and hobbled to the door.

'Bloody hell!'

'Well, that's a nice welcome if ever I heard one, mate.' Cara stood next to an unfamiliar car, arms folded in mock annoyance.

Ignoring the sting of the gravel as it cut into her bare

feet, Mattie stumbled forward and hugged her friend tight. 'How? Why? What the hell?' She was almost lost for words, laughing and crying at the same time.

'Come on, mate, it's bollocks bloody freezing out here. Can we go inside?'

'Oh, of course.' Mattie suddenly noticed that her feet had turned to blocks of ice. 'Come over to the barn. I'll just nip in and get my uggs. Oh, Cara I can't believe you're here!'

Cara followed her. 'Nice. Really nice,' she said, looking around and taking in the old stone house and the winery as they walked. 'You didn't tell me you lived in such a gorgeous set-up. It was a stunning drive up here from the city – well, once it got light, that is; I was up at sparrow's fart. That's jet lag for you. The vineyards are gorgeous. Roos, sheep, everything. Honestly, the whole place looks like something out of a freakin' tourism brochure.'

'It is pretty, isn't it?' Mattie agreed. 'But I'm still in shock at the sight of you. The last thing I expected was you turning up on the doorstep like this. I thought you were never going to come back to Australia. What are you doing here, in the Shingle Valley, of all places?'

'Have you seen the weather in England recently? It's been a shithouse summer. One more rainy day and I thought I might slit my wrists.' Cara grinned at her. 'Nah, I got busted for swearing at our biggest advertiser. Arrogant fuck-wit. He *so* deserved it. Bit of a career-limiting move though. Bianca made sure that the entire industry heard about it, so no one will hire me now. Witch.'

Mattie gasped.

'So I sublet my flat, got out my credit card and booked a seat on the first flight home,' Cara continued. I figured it was about time I played the prodigal daughter card. I'm staying with the olds in Vaucluse, and Mum lent me her car for a while. So,' Cara paused, flinging her arms wide. 'Ta da! Here I am. I thought you might be starved for some decent company.'

'Knock me down with a feather, Car. I really can't believe it. How long can you stay for? You are staying, aren't you? There's plenty of space; you can easily bunk with me in the barn. I'm sure Mark won't mind at all. There's a spare bedroom, so you won't have to put up with my snoring. It's even tidy in there – no more using the floor as a wardrobe,' Mattie said as she ushered her friend into the barn, her words tumbling over each other in her excitement.

'No way!' Cara's eyes widened as she looked around the immaculate room. 'Things *have* changed, Matilda Cameron.'

'Maybe just a little,' she said, grinning. 'So, can you stay?'

'Of course! I didn't drive all this way just for a cuppa. Though, come to think of it, something to warm me up would be good.' She was wearing a quilted down jacket with skin-tight white pants and knee-high leather riding boots, but Cara shivered exaggeratedly in the morning chill.

Mattie smiled again at the sight of her perfectly-accessorised-for-the-country friend. 'Of course, let's go over to the house. The kids should be up by now and it'll be heaps warmer over there.'

They clattered into the cosy kitchen. 'Rose, this is my friend Cara, from London,' said Mattie. Rose was standing at the range, stirring a vast pot of porridge while Leo and

Luisa sat by the window, teasing Gin and Tonic with a ball of string.

'Hello, Cara,' said Rose, waving a spoon at them. 'Welcome to Kalkari. Fancy some breakfast? There's plenty, more than enough in fact. I do tend to forget that I'm not feeding 500.' She laughed.

'Isn't she a dead ringer for Nigella Lawson's younger sister?' said Mattie. 'Cooks even better than Nigella too.'

'I reckon,' said Cara. 'And if you're sure, that'd be great. I had such an early start, and I've only had servo coffee to keep me going.' She shuddered at the memory.

'Nigella, eat your heart out,' said Rose. 'This will be the best porridge you've ever tasted – especially with my maple-pecan topping.'

'Porridge is my favourite,' said Luisa gazing in wonder at the glamorous new arrival.

Cara certainly cut a striking figure. A beanie covered her head and a cream scarf peeked out over the collar of her puffy jacket. With her fair skin and white-blonde hair she looked more *Game of Thrones* ice queen than flesh and blood human.

'Oh, mine too,' she agreed, pulling off her hat and shaking out her hair. 'Brown sugar or honey?'

'Brown sugar,' Luisa replied seriously.

'Snap!' cried Cara. 'That must mean we are soul sisters.' Cara held out her pinky finger to Luisa and the little girl smiled and grasped it in her own.

'Well, I see you've found a fan,' said Mattie, handing her a mug of tea.

'I love little girls. Especially ones as adorable as this munchkin.' She winked at Luisa.

A loud rapping on the back door drew everyone's attention.

'Come in,' called Rose.

'Sorry to disturb you so early.' Jake appeared in the doorway. There was a pause as he glanced around the room, his eyes coming to rest on Cara, who was, like the rest of them, looking up at him with curiosity.

Mattie could almost see the sparks fly, an electricity that seemed all at once to illuminate both of them, setting them apart from everyone else in the room.

Uh-oh, she thought. *This could be interesting.*

There was silence for a brief moment as Jake shook his head and seemed to be trying to refocus. 'Sorry to barge in, Rose,' he said, 'but some idiot seems to have blocked the track to the winery. Got any ideas? It's a flash Beemer.'

'Oh, that'd be me,' said Cara, smiling unapologetically at him and holding out her hand for him to shake. 'The idiot in the flash Beemer.'

'Right, okay then,' said Jake, taking her hand. 'If you wouldn't mind ...'

'It'd be my pleasure,' She gave him a wide-eyed smile and sauntered past him out of the kitchen door.

Less than half an hour later another car pulled up outside the house and then there was a knock at the door.

Jeez, it's like Clapham bloody Junction around here today,

199

thought Mattie. Rose was packing lunches for Leo and Luisa, so Mattie went to answer the door, wondering who on earth it could be this time.

She was shocked to see a uniformed policeman standing on the doorstep. He introduced himself as Officer Brock Doyd.

'I'm afraid Mark's away at the moment, if it's him you're after?' Mattie said.

'Perhaps I might come in?'

Had something happened to Mark? 'Of course,' Mattie said, 'excuse my manners. I'm just not used to police officers showing up on the doorstep. It's nothing bad, is it?'

'Why don't we talk inside?' suggested Officer Doyd.

Her stomach filled with a leaden dread. 'Is it Mark?' she said quietly, not wanting anyone else to hear.

'I'd like to speak with you, and anyone else in the residence, if I may,' he said, ignoring her question.

Mattie led him into the hallway and through the kitchen. 'Rose, Mark's partner, is here, and my friend Cara, though she only arrived this morning.'

Officer Doyd visibly choked when he entered the kitchen. Cara, who was leaning against one of the cupboards, long legs stretched out in front of her, had shucked off her down jacket and scarf, revealing the sheer white singlet underneath. Cara wasn't wearing a bra and her nipples stood out like peanuts, thanks to the cold draught he'd brought in. Keeping his eyes firmly on her face, he reached for his notebook. 'Miss, er, um, Rose?'

Cara smirked. 'Not me, Officer.'

'That's me,' said Rose, drying her hands on a tea towel. 'What's going on?'

The tips of Officer Doyd's ears had turned pink. 'We've had an incident of vandalism. At the property on the Wybree-Eumeralla turnoff' – he consulted his notebook – 'Tarrawenna. There are reports of three males and one female, all Caucasian, between twenty and fifty years of age, being seen in the area last night. I will need to take a formal statement from each of you as to your whereabouts in the past twenty-four hours. It's no secret that Tarrawenna is now owned by Tin Pei Resources, and that there's been considerable local opposition to that purchase,' he continued. 'As Mark is the head of the Shingle Valley Preservation Association, I will also need to speak with him in regard to the incident.'

CHAPTER TWENTY-SIX

Later that week, Cara and Mattie drove into Eumeralla. 'The Southern Cross is about all there is in
terms of nightlife in the valley,' Mattie apologised as
they got out of the car. 'But it's not bad, as pubs go.
Be thankful that it's too cold for the weekly cockroach races.'

Cara looked horrified. She was a city girl through and
through. She quickly recovered herself and waved an airy
hand. 'As long as there's cold beer and hot men, I'm in.'

Mattie spluttered. 'Very funny, Car. You know you've
only been here five minutes and already you've got half the
town talking.'

'What do you mean?'

'Astrid said that she'd heard it from Thommo Drummond, who heard it from God knows who, that Officer
Doyd was more than a little dumbstruck by your appearance
the other day, not to mention that Jake's been hanging
around a lot more than usual.'

Cara laughed and twirled in front of her. 'What can I say? If you've got it ... C'mon, let's go in. I'm dry as a drover's dog, not to mention bloody freezing.'

'Freezing? In that?' Mattie indicated Cara's fluffy rabbit-fur vest and the gold sequinned balloon-sleeved shirt underneath it. 'Babe, the Southern Cross isn't going to know what's hit it.'

'They're statement sleeves,' she said, lifting her arms in and wafting the gauzy fabric in the air. 'They're a thing.'

'A thing?'

'Too much?' Cara looked at her doubtfully.

'On you? Never!'

Giggling, they entered the pub to a roar of conversation, and Mattie soon spotted Jake in the far corner. He gave them both a high-wattage smile, and Mattie nudged her friend. 'See?'

'He's looking at you too, you know,' Cara replied.

Mattie made a scoffing sound and they went to the bar. 'My shout, what'll you have? And before you ask, I don't think they run to a Slippery Nipple. Now, on the other hand, if you were after a Bundy and Coke ...'

'Better make it a beer, hey?' Cara replied.

After they'd been served, they went over to where Jake was sitting and he moved over to make space for them.

'How do you like the valley so far, Cara?' he said.

'I like it pretty fine, thank you. Mattie never mentioned how stunning this place is, did you, Mats?'

Mattie raised her glass at her friend. 'Some things are best kept on the down-low. Cheers.'

'Wait till you see it in spring and summer, though I reckon autumn's my favourite season,' said Jake. 'Pruning's started and it's a bit bleak out there at the moment, I'm afraid.'

'Well, I'm certainly glad I packed my thermal underwear,' replied Cara.

Jake shifted in his seat and his eyes glinted. 'Did you now?'

She looked at him boldly. 'Lace-edged La Perla.'

Jake clapped one hand to his chest. 'You're killing me,' he mouthed.

Mattie, observing the sparks once again flying between them, suddenly felt flatter than an old bicycle tyre. She didn't think she could ever be as carefree and flirtatious as her friend, and she was, she realised suddenly, jealous of that. She looked over to the bar and spotted Charlie across the other side of the pub. Then she saw Marie-Claire standing next to him and her mood flattened even further. *Fickle bastard.* What gave him the right to have taken her out, to have kissed her like he meant it, when he had Marie-Claire waiting in the wings? He'd been conspicuously uncommunicative since the Shortest Day lunch. Nothing. Not a call, not a voicemail, or even a text. She'd had too much pride to message him. The last thing she wanted was for him to think she cared, as clearly it hadn't meant anything to him. She should have known better – he was still the knockabout larrikin he'd always been. Would she ever learn to be a better judge of men? Or were they all as bad as each other?

'Hey!' Mattie was startled out of her self-pity. 'Dude, did you hear any of that?' Cara asked. 'We were talking about photography. Jake says he dabbles a bit. You took some brilliant shots when we were in London. Why don't you give it a go here? There's so much scope.' Cara waved her arms around, nearly upending Mattie's drink.

Cara looked so excited, Mattie felt churlish not to summon up some enthusiasm. 'Yeah, I suppose. I did study photography as part of my course at art school. I loved it, actually. Toyed with the idea of taking it up seriously, but then with work ... I never seemed to have much time for it. I was shortlisted in a competition for one of my shots last year – do you remember, Cara?'

'I do.' Her friend nodded enthusiastically. 'Come on. Why not then?' They both looked at her hopefully. Were they in cahoots, trying to get her interested in something? Whatever their plan, it worked. Mattie and Jake were soon swapping camera stories, getting technical about apertures and f-stops, until Cara nudged her. Officer Doyd was walking towards them. She almost didn't recognise him in his civvies. The short-back-and-sides haircut was a dead giveaway though. He was wearing a tight pair of Levis and an even tighter black t-shirt that showed off the planes of what must surely be washboard abs. Mattie noticed her friend sitting up a bit straighter. 'The Shingle Valley is crawling with gorgeous men, Mats. They're all fit as Mallee bulls,' Cara whispered to her. 'Why didn't you tell me? I'd have been here sooner.'

'Stop it!' begged Mattie, only half serious.

'G'day, Officer,' Cara drawled.

'Brock, please. I'm off duty now.' He blushed, probably remembering the sight of Cara in the white singlet in the kitchen at Kalkari. 'Couldn't miss you even from over there.' He indicated the far side of the bar. 'I didn't realise pets were allowed – does this have a name?' he said, touching the edge of her furry vest.

'Careful, it might bite.'

He chuckled but removed his hand. 'Mind if I join you?'

Cara nodded and inched along the bench seat, giving him just enough room to sit down. Jake looked less than impressed.

'So, Brock, how's your week been?' Cara asked. 'Catch any bad guys?'

He shook his head.

'Any more news on the Tarrawenna vandalism?' asked Mattie. When he had called at Kalkari earlier that week, he'd told them that the fences along the property had been plastered with signs saying 'Frack Off Our Valley' – which the girls had smirked at – but, more seriously, that the entrance had been blocked by what must have been several truckloads of rubble.

He shook his head. 'Dead end at the moment. Everyone I've spoken to can account for their whereabouts on the night in question. But it looks like Tin Pei haven't had time to put up any security cameras yet, so there's very little evidence as to who the perpetrators might be.'

'Can't say I'm exactly sorry,' said Mattie.

'I'll pretend I didn't hear that,' said Brock, his tone serious. 'Vandalism is still vandalism, no matter what.'

'Oh, I couldn't agree more,' said Cara, batting her eyelashes. 'Don't you think so, Jake?'

*

'Excuse me?' The accent was French.

Mattie had grown bored of Cara's flirtation with Officer Doyd and Jake and had excused herself to the bathroom. She emerged from the stall to see Marie-Claire washing her hands.

'You are Matilda, yes? We met at the lunch the other week?'

Mattie nodded.

'Charlie has told me so much about you.'

She raised an eyebrow. 'Oh really?'

'About your terrible accident, but also that you have recently returned from London, where you had a *très* important job.'

'Well, I'm not sure that it was that important. Advertising …' She shrugged. 'Not exactly brain surgery, is it?'

'We may have something in common.' *You're not kidding*, thought Mattie. Marie-Claire continued, undaunted by Mattie's lack of response. 'I work in marketing, in Bordeaux. I love my job very much, but now … well, I am wondering what I can do if I move to *Australie*.'

'Oh, I'm sure there are opportunities here if you look for them,' said Mattie.

'Yes, but I would be leaving so much behind …'

'And you can't persuade Charlie to move over there,' Mattie finished for her.

'*Exactement.*'

'Well, only you can make that decision.'

'I know, but it would help if I knew I could make friends here too. Other women who have a career, yes?'

As Marie-Claire washed her hands, Mattie suddenly noticed that there was no diamond sparkling on the left one. Marie-Claire caught her stare and spread her fingers out in front of her. Mattie saw the perfectly manicured shell-pink nails, a complete contrast to her own blunt ones. 'Charlie wanted me to wear his grandmother's ring, but it was, how do you say ... not exactly so *chic*.'

Mattie was unsurprised. A jaw-dropping rock like those by DeVere & Soames would probably be more Marie-Claire's style.

'Anyway, I hope we can perhaps get to know each other better, Matilda?'

Mattie knew that Marie-Claire was asking her to extend the hand of friendship, but she wasn't feeling generous. 'Actually, I'm not sure how long I'll be in the valley; I'm really here just to recuperate before I return to London. But I'm sure you'll find it a friendly place.'

Marie-Claire looked at her in surprise. 'Oh, but Charlie said you were living here now.'

Mattie dried her hands fiercely on a paper towel. 'Well, he's got that wrong, I'm afraid,' she said, flinging open the bathroom door.

As she was walking along the corridor she looked up to see the cause of her current troubles coming towards her. He opened his mouth to speak, but she threw him a withering look and pushed past him, returning to Cara and her admirers.

*

Emerging from the shower the next morning, Mattie saw her phone light up. Grabbing it with one hand, the other clutching her towel, she saw a message.

It was from Charlie.

Sorry I missed you last night. Really need to talk. Come to Windsong first thing this morning?

What was that all about? She had no desire to see him. It was bad enough knowing she'd bump into him in town or at the pub, but to put herself deliberately in front of him and Marie-Claire? The two of them together?

Another day perhaps, she wrote.

The message pinged back. *Come as soon as you can — promise it'll be worth it.*

She was a tiny bit intrigued.

Another message pinged. *You won't want to miss this.*

She pondered as she got dressed. What on earth could be so important? On the other hand, he did owe her an explanation … perhaps it would help to clear the air between them. *Okay*, she eventually texted back, her curiosity getting the upper hand. *Be there in a couple of hours.* She wasn't going to rush.

Arriving at Windsong later that morning, she walked over to the enormous shed that housed the winery and spotted Charlie coming out of the door. He walked towards her.

She braced herself.

'Mattie,' he said, 'I haven't had the chance to speak to you —'

'No Marie-Claire?' she interrupted.

He looked uncomfortable. 'About that ... Look, I had no idea she was coming, you must believe me. She turned up out of the blue. I wanted to tell you before I saw you but I —'

'It's alright, Charlie.' The fight went out of her. 'You don't owe me any explanations. We're just mates, right?' Mattie decided right then that the best way to deal with her hurt and humiliation was to brush it under the carpet, pretend that she was just fine, that the kiss they'd shared hadn't meant anything.

'I don't know what's going to happen.'

'Well, that's between you and her. Certainly none of my business. I wish you the best. She seems like a lovely girl.'

'That's just the thing ...' He shrugged.

'Was that all you wanted? Because if that's it, I've really got a busy day ahead of me.' She turned to go.

'No!' He put a hand on her wrist and Mattie shivered involuntarily at his touch, her body betraying her. 'There's something else. Something really exciting. Come and see for yourself. She's in the back paddock,' he said, pulling Mattie around the side of the winery shed.

As they rounded the building, Mattie heard a whinny. Not that that was unusual — she knew the boys still kept a few horses on the property. But then ... she couldn't believe her eyes. She looked at Charlie in wonder. 'You're kidding me?'

He grinned. 'Nup.'

'What? How?' Mattie didn't stay to listen to the answer

but broke into a limping run, her bad leg almost forgotten as she raced to the fence. A chestnut mare with a white blaze tossed her head and began to neigh. Reaching the split-rail fence, Mattie ducked under it just as the horse, which had cantered over, came to an abrupt stop right in front of her. Mattie threw her arms around the old mare's neck. 'Shakira! Look at you, Shakira darling,' she crooned. 'All whiskery and grey now.' The horse nuzzled Mattie's face, whickering in recognition. 'You've missed me, huh? Oh, I've missed you too, baby.'

Charlie stood back, arms folded, as she fussed over the horse. After a long while, Mattie turned around and looked at him, an ear-to-ear grin splitting her face. 'I can't believe it. Where did you find her?'

'Been keeping my ear to the ground. I knew that you'd sold her to someone in the area —'

'Yes, the Willoughbys. They wanted her for their daughter, and I was off to the UK. I needed the money for my trip and I didn't want her sitting around in a paddock, never being ridden, so it seemed like the best thing to do,' she said. 'I tried contacting them when I got back, thought I could go and see the old girl, but they'd moved away.'

'Yep. I knew that too, but I happened to find out who they'd passed her on to. It took some negotiating, but, well, here she is. Now it's just up to you to get back on the horse, so to speak.'

She couldn't believe it. Her Shakira – here? 'Oh, Charlie, that's the most amazing thing anyone has ever, *ever* done for me.' Mattie's heart swelled.

'No thanks necessary. When I told them that the original owner had been in an avalanche and lost almost everything, they agreed to sell, to let her come back to you.'

'I can't believe it,' said Mattie. 'I can't believe you found her for me.'

'So are we mates again?' he asked.

Caught up in her happiness, she left the horse to give Charlie the fiercest hug she could, his betrayal overshadowed by her joy at being reunited with her beloved horse. She nearly knocked him off his feet.

'Steady on there, Mats,' he said, but his arms wound around hers and held her tightly, not letting her go.

CHAPTER TWENTY-SEVEN

Wet weather over the following few weeks kept everyone inside – that is, except for the poor pruning team, who had to brave the sodden conditions to cut back the vines. The mud in the vineyards was almost up to their ankles, and they trudged great clods of it along the paths. Rose made vats of vegetable soup to warm them up when they came into the winery at lunchtime, and Leo helped them hose off their boots when they'd finished at the end of the day. After staying with Mattie in the barn for a couple of weeks and having most of the single males – and, truth be told, even some of the taken ones – panting in her wake, Cara had disappeared back to Sydney. 'But I'll be back as soon as I've spent some time with the olds and caught up with a few school friends, never fear,' she promised Mattie. 'I love it here – I can see why you'd want to stay. So much talent.' She winked. 'Keep an eye on Jake for me, and Officer Doyd.'

Mattie was confused by her comment. She'd never mentioned to Cara that she was thinking of staying, not for the long term in any case. London and her old life did seem so far away, but she couldn't stay in the valley forever. For a start, she needed to earn a living, and the odd bit of design work probably wasn't going to be enough to support her. She also wasn't sure if she could take the constant reminder of Charlie and Marie-Claire practically on her doorstep. On the plus side, her leg was almost completely healed now, and apart from the odd twinge, her shoulder was in pretty good shape too. The scar on her face was still there, but she hadn't decided if it was bad enough to warrant seeing a plastic surgeon – apart from anything else she didn't know if she'd be able to afford it. She visited Shakira when the rain allowed, spending hours stroking the old mare's mane and whispering to her, but still hadn't worked up the courage to put a saddle on her and go for a ride.

'I'm not used to lounging around all day,' she moaned to Rose as they chopped veggies for dinner. 'I love helping you and Astrid out with the kids, but I really need to find something more to do with myself or I'll go batshit crazy.'

'Go easy on yourself, hey? You're still recovering from a major injury,' Rose reassured her. 'Don't stress too much about it. You know you're welcome here for as long as you like. What's meant for you will find you.'

'Humph.' Mattie wasn't impressed with trite philosophising. She'd seen enough of it on her Facebook feed when she was in London recovering from her accident. She knew her friends had meant well, but seeing phrases like 'Time heals' and 'You're never sent more than you can handle' had made her want to throw her laptop across the room. A card from one friend, with the words, 'Hey, little fighter, soon it will be brighter,' was particularly offensive. She glared out of the window, as if the rain were somehow responsible for keeping her there. She felt irritable and out of sorts with the world. It didn't help that Marie-Claire seemed to have charmed everyone the length and breadth of the valley. Even Mrs B, who had dropped by earlier that day, was singing her praises.

Finally, when Mattie thought she would die of cabin fever, the clouds cleared and she woke one morning to clear skies. Filled with a new sense of purpose, and determined to do something positive rather than sit around whingeing, she wrapped herself up in her warmest clothes, picked up the camera she'd brought with her from London and headed out into the vineyards. The early morning light was perfect and she wanted to get some moody shots of the vines with the Shingle Hills in the background before the mist cleared. She breathed in the cool, fresh air and noticed the heady scent of star jasmine from the vine that clung to the barn walls. Looking down, she saw the delicate blooms of wild snow-drops, their bell-like flowers nodding in the breeze. Spring was finally on its way to the valley.

Mattie clicked away, adjusting the camera settings, trying a range of exposures. Her fingers were completely numb, but she didn't want to stop and go back for gloves. The view from the top of Trevelyn's Hill was stunning, the dark streaks of the vines stretching across the valley, mist still lingering in the furrows. Switching to a macro lens, she trudged down the narrow footpath until she reached the valley floor again. She wanted to get some close-up shots of the bare vines, of their gnarled old trunks – something a bit more abstract. Dew glistened on the canes as she narrowed her focus on a vine at the end of the row. Bending down to get the right angle, Mattie suddenly lost her balance and fell backwards, landing in the thick, slippery mud. She swore loudly as she sat, feet in the air, camera held high so it didn't suffer the same muddied fate as her arse had.

'Need a hand?' Mattie heard an amused voice behind her. What the hell was Charlie doing there? Perfect bloody timing. She hadn't seen him since he'd found Shakira for her, and although she'd always be grateful for his thoughtfulness, it didn't mean she'd completely forgiven him for not telling her about Marie-Claire. However, after some hard thinking, she'd decided to see if they could salvage a friendship. The valley was too small a place for resentment to fester.

'Yeah, thanks,' she said, with as much dignity as she could muster, holding out a hand.

'Suffering for your art, hey?' he said, pulling her up.

'Something like that.'

'Mind if I take a look?'

The two of them bent their heads over the camera screen as Mattie flicked back through the shots she'd taken that morning. She couldn't help but be aware of his nearness, the toothpaste freshness of his breath, his white teeth and parted lips, his tawny skin ... She felt almost dizzy with desire, but then scolded herself. For better or worse, he was with someone else. End of story.

'They're fantastic, Mattie. You've really got a feel for this. These are amazing. Really they are,' he said, enthusiasm brightening his face.

Mattie blinked. 'You think? Sure you're not simply being kind?'

'No, really. These are brilliant. Look at the way you've captured the light on the leaves there.'

She grinned. 'Thanks.' An idea quickly formed in her mind as she looked Charlie up and down. 'You know, what I really need is a human element. Would you mind?' She smiled sweetly at him.

'You mean like this?' he said, giving her his best Blue Steel impression.

'No, you idiot! Can you stand over there, and turn sideways a bit and look over in that direction?'

Charlie muttered that he really needed to find Mark, but nevertheless did as he was asked.

'Fab. Now twist a little to your right.' The sun rose higher, touching the scene with gold, and Charlie became an outline on the horizon as Mattie crouched down and clicked the shutter rapidly.

After a while, he became restless. 'I'm not used to such scrutiny,' he complained. 'Anyway, have you got enough now? I really do have to find Mark before he disappears for the day.'

'Okay. I reckon I've got the shot I was after,' said Mattie, swiping through the frames she'd taken. For the first time in ages, excitement fizzed through her veins. This was how she had felt when she was working, creating. Her mind felt sharp again, the fog of the previous months lifting like the clearing mist. She couldn't wait to get back to the barn and download the images to her laptop and sort through them, check the quality was up to scratch and that she'd got the focus and depth of field just right.

'You know, you should show these to your brother. He might want to use them for Kalkari. Well, the ones without me, that is.' Charlie grinned.

'What do you mean?'

'On the website, the tasting notes, maybe even at the cellar door.'

'Nah. I'm just messing around for now.'

'I mean it, Mattie,' he said emphatically. 'They're really good. Amazing, in fact.'

'Whoa, who covered you in mud?' Rose asked later as Mattie ran into her outside Kalkari House.

Mattie glanced over her shoulder at her filthy backside and grimaced. 'Long story. Is Mark around?'

'He'll be back later today; went over to New Bridgeton for a meeting with Jeremy Bell about the mining thingo.'

'Okay, I'll try to catch him this evening. Better go and clean up. Beautiful day, isn't it?' she called as she strode over to the barn, her limp barely slowing her down.

Mattie didn't see Mark until just before dinner. She'd spent most of the day editing the photos and doing a bit of digital retouching, before selecting a dozen of the best shots. Carrying her laptop over to the house, she placed it on the kitchen table in front of him. 'Would you mind taking a look at these? I'd love to know what you think.'

Together they slowly scrolled through the shots. Bare vines were silhouetted against the morning sky, mist blanketing the ground; in one, a necklace of raindrops hung from a cane, and finally, there was a shot of Charlie, his profile turned to face the sun and the light catching his hair, making it a golden halo. She couldn't help lingering on it. Damn, he was attractive. Even just looking at his photo made her heart flip-flop.

'Wow. Where did these come from?'

Mattie gave him a mischievous look that carried more than a hint of pride.

'No!'

'Uh-huh.'

'You're kidding! When did you take these?'

'This morning. There was finally some decent light.'

'Incredible, Mattie. They're outstanding.' He waited a beat, thinking. 'Can we use them?'

'Only if you think they're good enough.'

'Good enough? Of course they're good enough!'

'Well, I was going to mention it at some point – the Kalkari website could do with an overhaul. I'd be happy to take a look at it if you'd like, do a bit of a redesign and include some of these.'

Mark thought some more. 'I've been wondering for a while whether or not the whole brand could do with a spruce-up. What do you say to that? Logo, stationery, website, labels … It's a big ask, but you'd do a brilliant job.'

'Are you sure?'

'Never more certain. It's what you do best, isn't it?'

Mattie's eyes shone. 'You're on!'

'Okay, well, why don't we have a proper chat about it tomorrow? I can give you a rough brief and you can tell me how long you reckon it might take, and what the fee would be.'

'Fee?' Mattie was incredulous. 'Don't be bloody ridiculous, Mark. I'm living here rent-free and eating dinner with you every night. I reckon that more than covers any fee, don't you?'

'Okay, it's a deal. Consider it in lieu of rent if you like.'

'Any luck with Jeremy Bell?'

'Well, he saw us, at least, thanks to Dad putting in a good word. Says he'll do some investigating and get back to me. It's not clear yet whether Tin Pei have bought the land as a strategic foothold in the valley, or whether they intend to start drilling in the near future.' He ran his hands through his hair. 'Apparently they can also drill horizontally, under neighbouring land, which doesn't look good for Windsong. Charlie and Thommo are even more worried than the rest of us.'

'So it's not as if they have to buy up the whole valley before they can start drilling,' Mattie concluded. 'Hooley dooley …' She whistled.

'Exactly. Tarrawenna is just shy of sixty hectares, which is more than enough for what they need,' he said, sounding harassed. 'Tell you what, I could do with a drink tonight, that's for sure. What shall we open? I've been meaning to see what you think of this one.' He held up a bottle of Italian red that was sitting on the dresser and went to fetch a corkscrew.

Leo appeared in the doorway. 'Dad?'

'Yes, mate?'

'Don't suppose you've got time for chess?' He held up a small box.

'Think you can thrash me again, hey?'

'I'll try.' Leo grinned.

'Alright, son, bring it over here.'

As Mattie sipped her wine and watched Mark losing good-naturedly to Leo, she realised with surprise that it had been months since she'd had a gut-wrenching stomachache of the kind that she'd experienced on almost a daily basis in London. She no longer had emergency packets of Rennies stashed in her handbag and in the medicine cabinet. Nor could she remember the last time she had a thumping head-ache. Two things at least to be grateful for.

CHAPTER TWENTY-EIGHT

'Isabella's back,' said Mark. He and Rose were out for a run, braving the early morning chill. Though it was spring, they both wore gloves and beanies as a defence against the cold air. All around them budding vines etched their shapes across the hills. The sun had barely risen, but was already tinting the faint wisps of clouds brilliantly crimson. Rose gasped, sucking in breaths. It had been ages since they'd been out running and she felt like her legs were made of lead. 'She sent me a text from the airport; she'll be in the valley later today,' he added as they reached the top of the hill behind Kalkari.

'Oh. That's sooner than she planned, isn't it?' Rose huffed, breathless from the effort of keeping pace with him. 'But I'm sure the kids will be pleased. Should I see if Astrid can drop them off to her after school?'

'No, don't worry about it. We can go and pick them up and take them over this afternoon, have lunch in Eumeralla first if you can spare the time. Isabella said she wanted to talk to me about something. Said it was to do with the kids. Might as well see what she wants sooner rather than later.'

Rose enjoyed the routine of her life when Isabella was out of the country. Now it was going to be disrupted again and God only knew what fresh drama would result. Still, she couldn't begrudge Leo and Luisa being able to see their mother more often. It would give her a break too. Perhaps she and Mark might be able to get away for a few days, she thought idly. Somewhere warm would be nice. She would mention it at lunch. A holiday on their own could be just what they needed, something to take Mark's mind off the catastrophe that might be caused by the mining company.

'Lunch would be great,' she said. Some time together might also give her the opportunity to have a serious chat about the baby thing. Lately it seemed as if it were all she could think about. Spurred on by this promising idea, she sped up, overtaking Mark as they ran down the hill towards the Trevelyn's vineyards.

'Hey!' he cried. 'Where do you think you're going?'

'Catch me if you can,' she laughed.

'Ah, my babies, there you are!' Isabella knelt down to hug Luisa as she raced across the front garden of the cottage in Eumeralla. Leo hung back, staying close to Mark and Rose, reserved. 'I have missed you so, so much.'

'Did you bring us a present?' asked Luisa, excitement in her dark eyes.

'I haven't had a chance to unpack yet, but I think something might have slipped into my luggage. How have you been, my little ones? How is Buttons? Are you riding him every day?'

Luisa looked serious. 'Well, not every day. Daddy and Rose are at work a lot and Astrid has to look after Max as well. But I bring him carrots.'

'That is good. And you, Leo? How is school? Come here, let me give you a hug.'

Leo allowed himself to be embraced. 'Good, yeah, okay …' he mumbled.

'Listen, why don't you both go and play for five minutes while I talk to your father?'

Luisa reluctantly let go of her mother and Leo took her hand, leading her to the back garden. 'Do you remember the frogs we found last time, Lulu?' he said. 'Let's go and see if they're still there.' Luisa nodded happily and skipped along beside him.

As the gate shut behind them, Isabella turned to her ex-husband, completely ignoring Rose. 'Mark. I want to talk to you. About taking the children back to Spain.'

'Well, it'd have to be in the holidays,' he replied. 'I don't think Leo especially should miss too much school.'

'Actually, I wasn't suggesting a vacation. I thought they might like to come and live there with me.'

'What? But they're Australian! They live here. Kalkari is their home.'

'They are also half Spanish, you know.'

'But they've been brought up here. Anyway, they barely speak a word of Spanish.'

'I am not suggesting that they come to live with me in Spain forever, merely for a year or so. I'd like them to have some experience of the culture. My family there needs me now. *Padre* is getting more frail and I must help out.' Isabella came from a celebrated winemaking family in the north of Spain – the family's winery was one of the Navarra's oldest.

'A *year*? Are you out of your mind? What about school, their friends here? What about Luisa's pony?'

Rose opened her mouth to speak, but closed it again, thinking better of it. This was between Mark and Isabella.

'She will have a horse in Spain if she wants, and they will make new friends there,' Isabella said, dismissing his concerns with a wave of her scarlet-tipped fingers.

'Can they not just go for a visit? In the long summer holidays, perhaps?'

'I would like them to both become fluent in Spanish. It is important. Languages are so good for children, for their brains, for their future. There is a school nearby that their cousins go to; they will have total immersion in the culture. They hardly know their Spanish *familia* and I'd like to give them the opportunity to do so.' She took a breath. 'Please, I would like you to think about it, Mark. If they don't come now then Leo will soon be too old to move schools easily. It will be a great adventure for them. And you cannot deny them their family there.'

'But what about their family here?'

Isabella stared him down. 'They have lived with you for a long time now. It is my turn to show them Spain. A year is all I ask. Then they can return and live here.'

'Do I have a choice?' he asked, exasperated. 'When exactly were you thinking of taking them?'

'Next month. Before *vendimia* begins.'

'I don't like it, not one bloody bit,' Mark fumed to Rose as they drove away. 'I don't know why she's suddenly got this ridiculous idea in her head. She's never suggested taking Leo and Luisa away with her for this long before. How do I even know if she'll bring them back when she says she will?'

'Oh God, Mark, I know how much you adore them, and they you.' Much as she'd been looking forward to some time alone with Mark now Isabella was back, she'd never wished for a moment that they would go and live with their mother, and certainly not in Spain. She was almost as devastated as Mark, but quelled the rising feeling of loss, took a deep breath and tried to see Isabella's side of things. 'Although I suppose she does have as much right as you do to spend time with them. Not that it makes it any less heartbreaking,' she said. 'But has she considered what the kids will say about having to leave here? I'm not sure Leo will be too thrilled.'

'God knows. Leo especially – he's been so much happier since we built him the treehouse, and he seems to be doing well at school again. This will completely throw him off-balance.'

CHAPTER TWENTY-NINE

'Ungggh...'

Mattie could hear a mumbling on the other end of the line. 'Is that you, Car? You sound like you've got a mouth full of marbles.'

'Nup, a lamington,' Cara replied.

'Where are you?'

'At the parentals. Though it's driving me crazy. Mum's treating me like a teenager, wants to know what I'm up to all the time. Keeps trailing me around the house. Honestly, Mats, I don't think I can stand it for much longer.'

'Good,' said Mattie.

'Good?'

'Yeah. Listen, I've been thinking ...'

'Un-uh ...' Cara's mouth was still full of cake.

'Well, the thing is, I was wondering if you fancied coming back down here for a while and helping us out? The cellar door manager quit and they're about to open up again for the season and, well, we're desperate. I can do some of it, but I can't be on my feet for too long and I'm also working on the website and a few other things. It really needs someone full-time. I remembered that you said you used to waitress way back when, and thought you might be interested. Of course, it's not quite the same as styling celebs and photoshoots in the big smoke …' There was silence on the other end of the line. 'Oh, forget it, it was just a thought.'

Mattie heard Cara swallow her mouthful. 'Is a frog's arse watertight?'

'Really? Is that a yes?' said Mattie, thrilled by her friend's response.

'Yep, you heard me. It'll be fun. I love working with you, and I'm a bit over Sydney, to be honest. And I adore the Shingle Valley, it's so gorgeous.'

'Not to mention some of the people who live here, huh?'

'Well, there is that added attraction,' Cara said drily. 'What's not to like? Hey, I won't have to wear a ghastly uniform, will I?'

Mattie laughed. 'No, of course not. An apron maybe, but not a uniform. And Dan can train you up in all the wine lingo – he'll give us both a session on the Kalkari varietals. Even I don't know as much as I should.'

'Right then. When do you need me to start?'

'How about yesterday?'

Cara arrived at Kalkari as the babydoll sheep, which had been introduced to keep the weeds down in between the vines, were lambing. She and Mattie watched, captivated, as the newborns gambolled in the orchard behind the winery, jumping on all four legs like springs.

'Oh, they're so cute and fluffy, look at their little noses!' Cara said, leaning against the fence.

'I know,' Mattie agreed as she snapped some shots. Being out and about with a camera had ignited a long-forgotten passion and she rarely went anywhere without taking photos these days. She'd also been spending her evenings reading books about technique, borrowed from the New Bridgeton library. 'Though sheep muck still stinks,' she added.

Cara wrinkled her nose. 'Don't they ever get any bigger?' she asked, pointing to one of the ewes.

'Nup. They're an ancient English breed, I think – you should ask Jake, he brought them here. They're brilliant for keeping the grass down, apparently.'

'Speaking of Jake, where is he? I'm looking forward to seeing a certain spunky viticulturist again.' She smiled lasciviously.

Mattie gave her friend a knowing look. 'Settle down. Mark said he's taken some personal leave. Gone back to Adelaide. I think his dad is a bit crook.'

Cara's face fell.

'But he's due back at the end of the week, so cheer up, sunshine. Now, enough of admiring the pretty sheep, we've got work to do.'

And work they did. The Kalkari cellar door closed over winter; there weren't enough visitors to their part of the valley to make staying open worthwhile. Anyone who did arrive unexpectedly was ushered into the winery and, often as not, treated to a private tasting. Spring, summer and autumn, however, were a different story, and the northern end of the valley especially was jammed with visitors all keen to taste a wine or three, kick back on the lawn with a bottle and a platter of cheese and salami, or barbecue at one of the fire pits Mark had dug on a rise above the winery. The views from there were spectacular, with a panorama over almost the entire valley and across to the Shingle Hills.

That day the girls went over to the winery, where Dan had agreed to give them a tour of the place, and then a tasting of the wines that were going to be on offer at the cellar door. 'Over there you've got the tanks,' he said, pointing to the hulking stainless-steel cylinders that towered over everything else in the winery. That's where we keep the younger whites – your pinot gris and your riesling.'

Mattie and Cara nodded.

'And then here' – he indicated the rows of oak barrels, stacked sideways on racks on top of each other, each with chalk scrawls on the base – 'these are the reds. Your cab sav, shiraz and pinot, as well as some chardonnay. We use a mix of old and new oak, and then Mark and I make up the final blends before bottling. This is where you might have heard the term "the angels' share".'

'The angels' share?' asked Cara.

'It's what we fondly call the small amount of wine from each barrel that gets lost to evaporation – it means that what's left is all the sweeter so we gladly give up a fraction to the heavens.'

'Cute,' said Cara.

'When I was a kid, I thought that angels really did fly down and siphon off some of the wine,' laughed Mattie. 'I kept asking my dad when they were going to come so I could stay up and try to see them.'

'Now, come along to the office and I'll run you through the wines. There are some tasting notes for you to study, but you'll find that most people want only a little bit of info about the wine as they taste. You'll soon learn to spot those who want to know more, but the key is not to overwhelm them to begin with – it's a social thing, mostly, and usually people are with their friends, or their partners. Of course you do get the odd show-off, the ones who think they know it all and try to catch you out. Mostly blokes, by the way.' He took a closer look at Cara. 'But I'm sure you can more than handle them.'

They reached the office, where two rows of small tasting glasses were lined up, with a spittoon at one end. Dan poured the first bottle. 'Right, ladies, let's begin.'

'Could there be any more dust?' Cara complained later as they steamed and polished every single one of the cellar door's hundred-odd tasting glasses, most of which were cloudy from lack of use.

'I reckon the spiders were worse,' Mattie shuddered. She'd discovered a nest of hundreds of the tiny wriggling black things behind the tasting bench. It was enough to give her the heebie-jeebies for a week. She and Cara had called for backup, and Dan had been persuaded to come in with the Mortein. It was several hours before they ventured back to the cellar door, and only after his assurances that all traces of the offending eight-legged creatures had been removed.

'Do you think Mark might spring for some new furniture?' said Cara as they looked at the dated wrought-iron chairs and dark wood tables, some of which had most definitely seen better days. 'Perhaps something a bit more contemporary? Bring the place into the twenty-first century?'

'I'll see if I can pin him down tonight. What do you reckon we ought to change?'

Cara needed no further encouragement. With her stylist's eye she quickly assessed the place, taking in the fusty curtains at the large windows that looked out over the valley, and the ochre-coloured walls. 'At the very least give the place a coat of paint – soft grey with white trim, I reckon. And get rid of those curtains. It wouldn't hurt to add some bench seating out on the front verandah either.'

That evening Cara showed Mark some images she'd put together of how she thought the cellar door could look. Mark was surprisingly quick to agree to their suggestions. 'I'd been meaning to do something about it for a while, but hadn't had the time to get around to it – or the imagination. And I've got bigger things to worry about now.' He sighed. 'Okay, it's all yours, girls – stick to the budget and you've got free rein.'

Cara looked at her friend with excitement. 'Nothing thrills me more than making things over, people or places.'

'Don't I know it,' said Mattie with an easy grin.

By the end of the week, the girls were covered in paint and completely exhausted, but the cellar door was sparkling. Light streamed in from the windows, bounced off the newly painted dove-grey walls, and Rob the chippy had been commissioned to construct two long tables and benches to go either side of the front door. Cara had sourced a bolt of charcoal linen and arranged for it to be made up into cushions for the benches, and found new lighting for inside the cellar door.

'Golly, it looks so much larger and lighter in here,' said Rose, admiring their work, 'and I love these fittings. You've done a brilliant job. Wait until Mark sees it, he'll be thrilled.'

'It might help put him in a better mood too,' added Mattie hopefully, thinking of Leo and Luisa's impending departure and the mining worry hanging over all of them.

CHAPTER THIRTY

Rose had planned a dinner for the family, together with Cara, Astrid, Thommo and Max and Jake, who was due back from Adelaide that afternoon. It was the last night that Leo and Luisa were to be at Kalkari before leaving for Spain with Isabella. She was doing her best to create a festive mood, despite Leo's obvious sadness. He'd been withdrawn all week, and had refused to pack a bag. Rose could see that he wasn't coping and ended up sorting through his clothes and shoving a pile of shorts and tees into a suitcase that now sat outside the door to his bedroom. She'd found herself nearly in tears as she folded Luisa's tiny dresses and cardigans, and had to sit down on the little girl's bed and take several deep breaths to steady herself. She was sadder than even she had imagined she would be, now the day was nearly upon them.

'Anything I can do to help?' Mattie came into the kitchen to see Rose standing at the range, stirring a big cast-iron pot. 'God, that smells delicious. What's for dinner?'

'*Potage Saint-Germain*,' replied Rose. 'Pea and lettuce soup. It's based on something Philippe, my Bondi friend, used to cook at Rustica. I want to trial it at the restaurant, so I thought I'd give it a go here first. Mark brought me some yabbies that I thought I'd pop on top at the last minute.'

'Smells freaking amazing, whatever it is,' said Mattie.

Rose laughed. 'That's probably the garlic. It'll be followed by osso bucco and risotto. At least the kids will eat the risotto, if nothing else.' She indicated the pan where grains of rice glistened with saffron and stock, which she was stirring with the other hand.

'Want me to take over?'

'Sure, that would be great. I'll duck upstairs and change. Just add a bit more stock as the rice absorbs it.'

Rose bumped into Mark in the hallway. 'Hey. How are you doing?'

Mark shrugged, his eyebrows drawn together in a frown. He'd looked this way for the past few weeks.

'Oh, babe, I wish there was something I could say.' She moved towards him, wrapping her arms around him and drawing him close. She loved the way they fitted together, as if they were two halves of a whole.

'I know. It helps just having you here,' he said, murmuring into her hair. After a moment, he reluctantly pulled away. 'What can I do? I can't stop her. She's their mother, and I've got to give them the chance to see their other family. They need to get to know that side of their heritage.'

'It still doesn't make it any easier to see them go, especially for so long. I think you're being very civilised about it though, and that'll make it easier for the kids in the long run.'

'They'll be back for a holiday at Christmas. She's promised me that.'

'The time will fly by,' Rose tried to reassure him.

'Thought I'd bring along this hungry reprobate,' said Thommo as he arrived. Charlie smiled apologetically at Rose. 'Hope I haven't put you out.'

'Not when you turn up with wine, you don't,' said Mark, coming across to shake his hand.

'Of course you're welcome, Charlie,' said Rose. 'There's always room for one more at Kalkari.'

'I've been meaning to quiz you all about Bordeaux, in any case,' said Mark. 'Is Marie-Claire with you?'

Charlie shook his head. 'She, er… she wanted an early night.'

Dinner, at the long mahogany dining table, was a noisy affair. Max was installed at a high chair at one end, with Astrid and Thommo, Luisa sat between Mattie and Cara, and Leo placed himself next to his dad at the head of the table. Jake and Charlie sat opposite the girls. The soup was a hit with everyone, even Max, who banged his spoon for seconds. Rose's heart contracted. He was such a sweet little boy, the spitting image of his dad.

Charlie looked across at Mattie. 'So have you been spending much time with Shakira?' he asked.

'Uh-huh,' she mumbled through a mouthful of soup. 'Thanks again for letting me keep her at your place.'

'Not a problem. She likes the company there, I reckon. When do you think you'll be ready to ride her?'

Rose saw Mattie freeze.

'Come on, Mats,' Charlie cajoled. 'I'll come with you, if you like. You know you've got to get back on her sooner or later.'

'I'll think about it,' she said.

'Dig in,' said Rose, after the soup had been cleared away, as she hefted giant dishes of veal and risotto onto the table.

Jake poured the wine he'd brought back with him from Adelaide. 'Tell me what you think of this, boss. It's a new mob up in the hills. Pretty smart stuff, I reckon.'

'How's your dad, Jake?' asked Rose.

'He's not too crash hot. It's his ticker. The old man needs to take it easy, but he won't be told. My mum's got her hands full trying to keep him in the house.'

'Sorry to hear, but it must have been good to see him.'

'Yeah, I don't get back there very often. Makes me real-ise how much time is passing. They both look a little more fragile each time I see them.'

'I know what you mean,' said Mattie, thinking of her own parents.

Cara, sitting opposite Jake, seemed to be completely tongue-tied.

Rose caught Mattie's eye. She wasn't the only one who had noticed the unspoken attraction between the pair. Of course Rose knew of Jake's reputation – and she remembered the wedding at Trevelyn's with amusement – but figured that if anyone was up to the challenge, it would be Cara. In fact, the more she thought about it, the more obvious it was how well matched they were. That is, if they ever got over this sudden, completely out-of-character shyness around each other.

'Can we take Barnsie out?' asked Leo when dinner was nearly finished. Astrid had gone to put Max to bed upstairs, and Jake, Thommo, Charlie and Mark were deep in conversation. They seemed to be discussing a plan to get the valley specially zoned. Rose wasn't sure what exactly; she'd only been listening with half an ear.

'Sure,' she said, knowing how much Leo was going to miss his almost constant companion. 'Watch out for your sister and don't be too long. It's dark out there and it's nearly bedtime.'

Mark wasn't the only one who was going to be heartbroken when the two kids left the house. Rose had been a stand-in mother to them on and off for nearly three years, and loved them both as if they were her own. Their imminent departure had crystallised the longing inside her for a child to a point where it was almost constantly on her mind now: when she was driving along the Eumeralla Road to Trevelyn's, when she was kneading dough, stirring a sauce or weeding the veggie patch. She could imagine herself, a baby wrapped to her chest as she hung out the washing, or with a green-eyed toddler banging a wooden spoon on the floor as she cooked. But she knew that now wasn't the time to raise the subject with Mark, even if they did manage to get away for some time alone together. Having a baby wasn't an answer to his other children leaving, and she didn't want him thinking she would ever imagine that would be the case. You couldn't simply replace one child with another.

She got up to start clearing the table. The wine, though delicious, had given her a headache and she thought longingly of her comfortable bed. She took one look at the men gathered at the head of the table, Thommo opening another bottle, and knew it was going to be a late night.

'Tea, anyone?' she said hopefully.

'Sure,' said Mattie. 'But let me clear up. You look absolutely beat. You've really been doing too much, you know, running the restaurant as well as looking after all of us.'

Rose smiled. 'I guess I am a bit tired. I love it though. And I'm really going to miss those two little tackers.'

'You're not the only one. I feel like I've only just got to know them and now they're going to be so far away.'

After Rose had finished her tea, she called the kids in. They stopped to say goodnight to the guests before Mark took them upstairs.

An hour or so and another bottle of wine later, Astrid and Thommo gathered up a sleeping Max and headed home with Charlie.

'I'd better call it a day as well,' said Jake, yawning. 'It's been a long one.'

'Me too,' said Cara. 'I can hardly move after all the painting and cleaning this week.'

'Sounds interesting,' Jake said.

'Go and take a look,' said Mark. 'They've transformed the place. Almost didn't recognise it when I saw it this arvo.'

'Care to give me tour?' Jake asked Cara.

She nodded.

'Night, boss. See you Monday. Thanks again for dinner, Rose,' he said as they left, heading over to the cellar door.

Despite feeling that she would be asleep as soon as her head hit the pillow, Rose followed Mattie over to the barn to collect a book she'd left there. She was dying to discuss Charlie turning up to dinner alone, and she seized the opportunity for a private chat. 'Sooo,' she said as they walked outside.

'What?' asked Mattie.

'Marie-Claire ...' Rose was round-eyed with unspoken questions.

'I know, but I'm sure it doesn't mean anything. Everyone's entitled to a night on their own every now and then, right?'

'I suppose, but I reckon something's happened.'

'Nah,' Mattie scoffed. 'Not likely. They seemed pretty into each other the last time I saw them together.'

'Don't be too sure.'

'Well, it's got nothing to do with me, in any case,' said Mattie.

Rose raised an eyebrow. She didn't believe it for a minute. She'd seen how Mattie looked at Charlie when she thought no one was looking. And how Charlie looked at her.

'Can you credit it?' Cara exclaimed, bursting in a few minutes later.

Rose and Mattie looked up, astonished.

'Nothing. Not a thing happened. Did I read the signals wrong? I thought he was definitely interested. I must be losing my touch.' She sounded surprised and a little wounded. 'He just blathered on about plants growing faster during a full moon because there is more moisture in the soil. Some biodynamic shit. I mean, really! The guy needs to work on his approach, don't you think?'

'Perhaps he's simply taking his time?' suggested Rose gently.

'Taking his time? That doesn't sound anything like the Jake I've heard about.'

'Well, maybe he sees you a bit more seriously?'

'You're kidding, right?'

'What's wrong with that?' said Rose. 'You know you shouldn't be so afraid to take him seriously either. It is possible to have more than a no-strings fling. Maybe that's why he's backing off.'

'Oh, come on. I'm not buying that,' said Mattie before Cara had a chance to reply. 'Jake – and, for that matter, Johnny – are both the same. They charm their way into a girl's heart and then you don't see them for dust the minute things get a bit tricky. I'd include Charlie in that group too.'

'Oh, Mattie,' said Rose sadly. 'They're not all that bad.'

'Johnny certainly was.'

'Okay, perhaps he was a total arse – and believe me, I've known a few of those in my time. I can't even begin to tell you about the complete fuckwit who was my boyfriend before I met Mark. But don't think that every bloke's like that.'

'Well, I'm not holding my breath for Mr Right to come along. I'm better off on my own, I know that.'

'Yeah, but you've gotta have some fun, right?' said Cara. 'Life's too short to be bitter, babe. Just go along for the ride.'

'Humph,' snorted Mattie. 'That's easy for you to say.'

CHAPTER THIRTY-ONE

The morning brought a flurry of activity to Kalkari. Rose, still tired despite a heavy sleep, was simultaneously clearing up the remains of dinner while making pancakes for the kids. She felt like a zombie; the last time she'd been this exhausted was when she was working double shifts in a London cafe and surviving on pies and doughnuts, lurching from one sugar crash to another. She couldn't find a reason for it. It wasn't as if she'd even had that much to drink last night – she hadn't felt like a second glass, even though there were some gorgeous wines on the table. 'Come down now, guys!' she called up the stairs for the third time. 'Leo! Luisa! Pancakes! It's your favourite.'

There was silence. *Odd*, she thought. Normally that would have brought them, Luisa at least, running to the kitchen. She looked at her watch. Eight o'clock. They definitely should have been up by now. With a sinking feeling, she turned the stove off, wiped her hands on a tea towel and made her way upstairs.

She looked into Leo's room and found it empty. Walking faster now, she went down the hallway to Luisa's room. Also empty. Their pillows were missing, and a blanket from Luisa's room. Her heart in her mouth, Rose flew down the stairs and went in search of Mark, who had just come in from a run. 'I can't find Leo or Luisa,' she gasped. 'They've gone!'

'What?' he said, running a hand through his hair. 'Gone where?' Realisation quickly dawned on him. 'You're kidding?'

'I wondered why they hadn't come down to breakfast, and when I went to look, both of their rooms were empty. They were there, asleep, when we went to bed last night. I checked on them.'

Mark was silent for a minute and Rose looked at him, wondering wildly what they should do. 'Do you think they could have run away? Oh Christ. I knew Leo wasn't happy about leaving. Do you think he's taken Luisa with him?' Her heart was racing nineteen to the dozen.

'Let's try to think calmly for a minute,' said Mark, though he looked as worried as she felt.

'They can't have gotten far, not in the middle of the night. Do you think they went over to the winery?'

'It's not possible,' he said. 'It would have been locked up last night.'

'What about the cellar door?'

'Same.'

Rose's heart was caught in her mouth as she thought of the two children walking down the long Kalkari drive and onto the Eumeralla Road in near-pitch darkness. Anything could have happened to them. 'They've even taken their pillows. And Leo's overnight bag is missing too.'

'I'd better get on to the police,' said Mark, reaching for his phone. 'God only knows where they could have gone.'

Twenty minutes later Rose heard the scrunch of gravel as a squad car came to an abrupt halt at the top of the drive. 'I've put out a bulletin to the Eumeralla Shire force,' said Officer Doyd as he emerged from the car. 'If they're anywhere in the area, and they most probably are, we'll find them.'

'Thank you,' she said, feeling a tiny bit reassured.

'Have you contacted their school friends, anyone who might have seen them, or overheard them talking about what they were going to do?'

'I've tried all the ones I can think of. No one's seen or heard from them, or heard Leo talking about anything unusual — other than moving to Spain, that is.'

'Hmmm,' said Officer Doyd. 'Alright, I'll see about setting up a search party. We'll put out an appeal for members of the public to come and help.' Rose noticed his eyes flick over to the dam, which was glistening in the early morning sun, and felt a fresh worry grip her. 'Have you looked everywhere on the property? Kids often hide in the most unlikely places.'

Just then, another car came up the drive. Rose recognised it immediately. Isabella. Early for once. Christ, that was all they needed.

'Are they ready?' Isabella said to Mark as she got out of the car. 'I want to make good time to Sydney.' She looked curiously at the policeman.

'I'm afraid that we, er, can't seem to locate them just at the moment,' Mark admitted.

'What? I do not believe it,' she fumed. 'The lack of discipline here is really showing. Those kids run wild, like savages. I knew it was time to have them with me.'

'That's enough, Isabella.' Mark's tone was calm, but cold. 'There is no sense in throwing unnecessary accusations about. I could just as easily say that they are so unhappy about leaving Kalkari that they've run away, rather than go to Spain with you.'

Probably the more likely scenario, thought Rose, noticing that Isabella was taken aback by that suggestion.

'So what are you doing to find them? We cannot miss our flights.'

'That's what Officer Doyd' – Mark indicated the policeman – 'is here for. He was just telling us the next steps to take.'

'I'm so sorry, Isabella,' Rose said. 'I swear we had no idea Leo was thinking of anything like this. And they were there when I checked on them last night, fast asleep. I can't imagine what must be going through your mind. We're completely beside ourselves.' It was the most she'd ever said to Mark's ex-wife.

'Well, no, I suppose you can't imagine it; you are not a mother,' Isabella said.

Rose held her tongue despite the sting of her words, and turned away. 'I'll be in the house if you need me,' she muttered to Mark.

CHAPTER THIRTY-TWO

'And you say you checked on them at midnight, and then only realised that they had disappeared by' – Officer Doyd consulted his notebook – '8am? Are you sure you've looked everywhere?'

Mattie, who had come over from the barn, looked at Mark, who appeared to be wracking his brains. 'We've checked the house,' he said. 'Even under the beds and in the cupboards. Nothing. I'm sure they've run away. It's the only explanation.'

'Try not to worry too much,' said Officer Doyd. 'They can't have gotten far.'

'That's what I'm concerned about,' said Mark grimly.

'Perhaps we should each search a different part of the valley?' Isabella suggested.

Mark nodded in agreement. 'Let's go inside and figure out a strategy.' He turned towards the front door, ushering everyone in.

Mattie was about to follow them when a thought suddenly occurred to her and she changed direction, hobbling down the drive as fast as she could manage. Reaching the junction with the Eumeralla Road, she halted and looked up at the big liquidambar tree where Leo's treehouse was perched.

'Leo, mate. Are you up there?' she called out.

The lonely caw of a blackbird was the only answer.

'Come on, mate. I reckon you're in there. I'm coming up, ready or not.' Mattie grabbed each side of the timber planks that had been nailed to the trunk and hauled herself up the tree, not caring about her recently healed leg and shoulder. It was harder than it looked. Puffing, she reached the entrance to the treehouse and peered in. It was hard to see clearly, but she could just make out a huddle of blankets in the far corner.

'What's going on here then, kids?' she said gently.

There was an indistinct murmur and the blankets shifted. Her instincts had been spot on.

'Oh, Leo, sweetheart. I realise it isn't exactly your choice, but you never know, Spain might be alright. And it's not forever.'

Silence. Mattie bit her lip, feeling awful for what the poor boy was going through.

'You know we all have to do things we don't want to sometimes,' she said. 'And when that happens you have to suck it up and get on with it. Drink a cup of wet cement, as your granddad used to say.'

Mattie heard a faint gurgle, something between a laugh and a groan, and then Leo's head emerged from the blankets, his dark hair, so like his father's, sticking up at all angles. Luisa, too, popped her head up.

'Hello, sweetie. Did you have a bit of an adventure?' The little girl shook her head and stuck her thumb in her mouth. Mattie turned her attention back to Leo. 'You know, sometimes we all feel like running away – I know I have from time to time. But sooner or later you have to be brave and face things.'

'But what about my soccer team?' said Leo, an agitated expression on his face. 'I can't let them down. There's three more matches left of the season and then we might be in the grand final. And if I leave now, they might not let me back in next year.'

Mattie softened. 'Oh mate, of course they will. They're gonna miss you, that's for sure, but I know they'll have you back next season.'

'How? How do you know? They might not. Someone else might come and take my place.' Leo's voice was strained with the effort of holding back emotion.

'I'll tell you what, why don't we call your coach and have a chat to him?'

Leo looked a little more hopeful. 'Can we?'

'Promise. Now come on down, will you? I can't balance up here much longer and Rose has made pancakes – I know they're your favourite. Your mum's here too.'

'Okay,' he said resignedly. He gathered up the blanket and pillows and handed them to Mattie, who tossed them to the ground below. She wondered if her leg, which was now aching, would hold up on the ladder, but she took a deep breath and waited as Luisa came towards her.

'That's it, sweetie,' she said. 'Now just turn around and I'll come down with you.'

'Too high,' said the little girl anxiously, still with her thumb in her mouth.

'It's okay, I'm here. I'll help you climb down. Come to Auntie Mattie, sweetie.'

This time Luisa did as she was asked and kneeled down at the entrance. Holding onto the ladder with one arm and guiding Luisa with the other, they slowly descended.

Leo followed, then picked up the blanket and pillows from where they lay on the grass, and the three of them walked back up the drive, Mattie holding Luisa's hand.

They clattered into the kitchen and Mattie saw the relief on everyone's faces. Rose looked like she was blinking back tears, and Mark sprang forward to hug both kids.

'Where were they?' Isabella said accusingly to Mattie while gathering Luisa to her. 'Did you know you gave us all a fright?' she said, looking at Leo.

'It's alright, Isabella, he and Luisa were just having an overnight adventure in the treehouse. Weren't you, mate?' Mattie said. 'Silly me had forgotten all about it; he told me that's what they wanted to do last night,' she lied, exchanging a look with Mark.

'Yes, Mum, Auntie Mattie's right. It was just a sleepover in the treehouse,' said Leo. 'We were perfectly fine.'

'Sorry to have bothered you, mate,' Mark said to the policeman.

'Better safe than sorry, hey?' said Officer Doyd. 'I'll be off then.' He began speaking rapidly into the radio on his chest, calling off the search, as he exited the kitchen.

'Okay then,' said Rose, with a show of false cheerfulness. 'You two must be starving. Who wants pancakes?'

After an awkward breakfast, Isabella hovering in the background as Rose cooked, it was time for them to leave.

Blinking rapidly, Rose went to hug Leo. 'Bye, darling,' she said. 'Have a wonderful time in Spain. Christmas will be here before you know it.' Leo looked at her with desperate eyes but Rose gave him her best encouraging smile.

Luisa wrapped herself around Mark's knees like a vine. He picked her up and hugged her. 'Bye bye, sweetie,' he said, his voice cracking with emotion. He released her and handed her over to Rose. The little girl clung to her.

'It's okay, darling. You're going to have such a lovely time with your mummy,' said Rose, squeezing her tightly.

After planting a splashy kiss on her, Luisa let go of Rose and ran into her mother's arms.

'Don't forget to feed Buttons,' Luisa called out from her car seat. 'And give him lots of apples.' She was too young to realise what going away with her mother was really going to mean; she had only a young child's concept of time.

Rose and Mattie came around the side of the car to say a final goodbye. Isabella glanced at them without saying anything, then asked Mark to load the suitcases into the boot.

Mattie hugged Leo, reassuring him that she would personally call his soccer coach, and then poked her head inside the car to say goodbye to Luisa. 'See you soon, baby girl,' she said, showering her with kisses as Luisa giggled.

Mark hugged his son fiercely, then ruffled his hair as he released him. 'It's not forever, mate, okay? You'll be back before you know it. And we'll Skype you. Every day, if you want.'

In a flash they were gone, Isabella's car kicking up a cloud of brown dust as they rumbled along the drive.

The house was going to be very quiet now, thought Mattie sadly.

Mark put an arm around Rose as they watched the car disappear into the distance. 'I'm heading to the winery,' he said eventually, and walked off in that direction.

'Coffee?' said Mattie.

Rose smiled faintly at her. 'Perhaps now's a good time to teach you how to use the beast.'

'The beast?'

'The La Marzocco. Where's Cara? You're both going to need to learn.'

CHAPTER THIRTY-THREE

'Mark, it's *Vineyard Life* on the phone. Something about next Wednesday's photo shoot?' Rose held the receiver out to him with a quizzical look on her face. She handed it over and busied herself clearing away the lunch dishes, keeping one ear open to eavesdrop. It had been nearly a week since the kids had left with Isabella, and the yawning silence about the place hadn't gotten any easier to bear for either of them. She kept forgetting that she didn't need to get their breakfasts, cook their dinners, or make school lunches. For once, the house was immaculately tidy, but rather than enjoying the peace and tranquillity, she found she hated it. She could scarcely believe it, but she actually missed the mess and almost constant chaos and couldn't settle to anything; she couldn't bear to go into their bedrooms. She also missed having Astrid, who had found work with a family in New Bridgeton, and Max about the place. She'd loved the sweet little-boy plumpness of him, his skin like a fresh-baked soft roll, and had always stolen cuddles whenever she could. She was as fond of him as she would have been of her own nephew. No doubt about it: it was far too quiet with everyone gone.

Mark spent longer hours at the winery, only coming into the house when hunger struck, and so she divided her time between Trevelyn's Pantry and the cellar door, where Mattie and Cara were learning the ropes. She smiled to herself as she overheard Cara chatting away to a group on a buck's weekend, mesmerising them with the swing of her hips as she expertly poured the wine and gave them the spiel Dan had drilled into both her and Mattie. Business was increasing as the weather warmed up. That at least was something to be thankful for, Rose mused, thinking of the wedding bookings for Trevelyn's that had been coming in steadily since the first one earlier that year. Mattie had revamped the restaurant's website and included a section on functions with photos she'd taken of the dining room all set up for service. And Cara had 'Instagrammed the shit out of it', whatever that meant. It all seemed to be making a difference, and her reputation was spreading beyond the valley, with enquiries coming from as far away as Sydney.

'Look, I don't remember agreeing to this, but if you say I did then I guess we'll have to go ahead with it,' Mark was saying into the phone. 'Yes, yes, of course. We'll all be ready for you next week.'

'Well?' asked Rose when he'd hung up.

'Apparently I agreed to let the magazine come and

photograph us. Bugger me if I can remember it. I tried to put them off, but they were insistent. God help us.'

'It won't be that bad, surely?'

'Well, they want to show the family side of the winery so they weren't too thrilled when I explained that the kids weren't here right now,' he said. 'But they're still coming. Wednesday. Do you think you can rustle up some food? They want to show us, all dolled up, having a meal on the verandah – you know, the sort of thing we do every day of the week.' Mark raised his chipped mug of tea to her, revealing the holes in the elbows of his favourite ratty jumper.

'Hah!' She laughed. 'The girls will be pleased though. Give them a chance to get involved. And the magazine will go nuts for them – two lovely young things at the cellar door.'

Mark grunted. 'Hey, you're not exactly a dried-up old bag yourself, you know.'

'Oh, so you noticed?' Rose circled her arms around him and gave him a kiss. It was the first light-hearted comment she'd heard from him since the kids had left.

As Rose had predicted, Cara was excited at the prospect of the photo shoot. 'It'll be like old times,' she said, grinning at Mattie.

'Er, actually, this time you'll be in front of the camera, not behind it,' Rose warned.

The two girls looked at each other and then at her.

'What?' said Cara.

'No kidding. They want the whole team. You two included.'

'Well, I hope they're bringing hair and makeup with them,' said Mattie, grimacing and running her fingers through the tangled mop on top of her head. 'We're gonna need it. Not to mention wardrobe.' Since she'd been back in the valley, Mattie had worn either jeans and boots or shorts and thongs, and her face was almost always makeup free.

'One thing's for sure, I'm certainly not putting another rinse on mine,' said Rose, remembering the results of her effort on Luisa's birthday.

'That's probably for the best,' laughed Mattie. 'Katy Perry purple probably wouldn't go over too well in the pages of *Vineyard Life*.'

Cara's eyes lit up. 'Can I style everyone? Rose, would you let me go through your wardrobe?'

'Sure,' said Rose, 'though I doubt you'll find anything suitable. There's not much call for haute couture in the Shingle Valley. Haute cuisine maybe, but not haute couture.'

'I reckon between us we can rustle up something. I brought quite a few things with me,' said Cara with confidence.

'Why am I not surprised by that?' asked Mattie.

Rose was up early on the Wednesday morning, wanting to squeeze in a quick run and get on with some food prep before the shoot crew arrived. With Mattie and Cara's help, she had scrubbed the house from top to bottom and tidied away the worst of the clutter out on the verandah. Her heart twisted as she stowed Luisa's tiny mud-encrusted boots in the shed.

They set up a long table outside and covered it with a freshly starched linen cloth. Cara had ironed the clothes she'd picked out for all of them and had been true to her word – they were all going to look the epitome of country chic, from the crown of their akubras to the tips of their newly polished boots. Even Jake and Dan were to be in on the act, and had been given strict instructions to spruce up and change out of their usual grimy jeans and moth-eaten sweaters. Of course they had grumbled about this, but Mattie was adamant and cajoled them both into moleskins and polo shirts. 'Never met a pair of RMs I didn't like,' Cara said approvingly, checking Dan over.

'Where would you like us to set up?' The photographer's assistant, a fresh-faced boy who looked all of about fifteen, enquired.

Mattie, who had greeted the team at the door, led them through to the back of the house and onto the verandah. 'Rose and Mark thought you might like to get some shots out here, the whole crew having smoko, the house and the hills in the background, that sort of thing.'

'Terrific!' The assistant was enthusiastic. 'We also wanted to get some in situ shots – Mark in the vineyards, in the winery, among the barrels.'

'Of course,' said Mattie. 'You tell us where and when. We're at your disposal.' She flashed him a quick smile. 'Why don't I give you a guided tour and then you can decide where you'd like to start?'

The previous day, Rose had made lamb and rosemary pies and baked a fruitcake for the shoot and the visitors. She was pulling a tray of scones out of the oven when Mattie led the photographer, his assistant and the writer through.

'Oooh, lovely,' said Wendy, the writer, as she caught sight of the scones' golden tops. 'Smells delicious. You must be Mark's partner – Rose, isn't it?' She checked her notes. Rose nodded. 'Oh good. I'd love to have a quick chat with you as well, once we're done with Mark. You look like quite a cook.'

'Well, I run Trevelyn's Pantry, a restaurant a bit further down the valley,' said Rose.

'Sounds fascinating,' Wendy said eagerly, 'we can certainly mention that as well.'

'Mark, Jake and Dan are all waiting for us over at the winery,' said Cara, coming into the kitchen. The assistant's jaw dropped when he saw her. She was channelling full-on prairie-girl chic, with knee-high cocoa-brown leather riding boots, a full skirt in some sort of fine wool and a cream silk blouse topped by a broad-brimmed hat tipped insouciantly over one eye.

The day was hectic, with Mattie and Cara posing at the cellar door, Mattie making endless coffees and Cara pretending to be polishing tasting glasses. Rose sighed with relief that they'd finished the revamp. The final bits and pieces of furniture that Cara had ordered had arrived the week before and the place was utterly transformed.

'I'm itching to take up the camera myself,' Mattie confessed to Rose as they looked at the shots that had come through on the photographer's laptop. 'It looks gorgeous, really photogenic. Thank God we painted the place, hey?'

Rose nodded. 'And Cara looks amazing,' she said. The girl's fair skin and white-blonde hair shone in the shots. 'She should have been a model.'

'You're not too shabby yourself, Rose!' insisted Mattie. Mattie had been reluctant to be in the photos herself. 'The scar ...' she'd said to Rose. 'Nonsense. You can hardly see it any more,' Rose had reassured her. 'Don't sweat it, babe,' said Cara, coming to her rescue. 'A dab of concealer will fix that right up.' Mattie felt uncomfortable with a face full of makeup, but unless you looked closely, the scar was hard to see. Cara had done an amazing job.

Mark and Jake had spent what seemed like hours patiently strolling up and down the vines, and then Mark was made to stand in front of a backdrop of old barrels in the winery. 'Reckon you've got enough of me now,' he protested.

'And me,' echoed Jake.

'He's gorgeous, isn't he?' breathed Cara, sidling up to Rose, who was watching from a distance. Cara's eyes were fixed on Jake.

'Mmmm ...' said Rose, who was looking at Mark. She'd seen him spruced up on plenty of occasions in the past, but now, through the eyes of the photographer and with Cara's styling, it was as if she was seeing him anew. With a delicious shiver, she remembered the time he'd taken her to a dinner in Sydney, how he had kissed her afterwards – their first kiss ... She looked around at the gorgeous landscape, her handsome partner ... She'd got everything she wanted, so why was there this emptiness threatening to overwhelm

her? The hunger to have a child of her own, a baby to nur-
ture, was growing stronger by the day. She knew a baby
would only complicate things – she had enough on her plate
with the restaurant and it was taking more and more of her
time. She knew Mark wasn't keen on the idea of more kids,
so why couldn't she let it go? It was totally irrational, but she
couldn't help herself.

Finally, they began to set up on the verandah. The sun
was low in the sky and cast a golden light across the honeyed
stone of the house. Rose brought out a platter of pies and
chutney and one of scones, together with heaped bowls of
blackberry jam and whipped cream, which she laid on the
table. They'd skipped lunch and everyone was starving. The
six of them pretended to pass each other the food and laugh
while doing so. 'Forget I'm here,' the photographer instructed.
Rose couldn't help being self-conscious; she wasn't used to
it, but Mattie and Cara were acting like naturals, managing
to effortlessly pour tea and ham it up for the camera at the
same time. Jake was sitting opposite Cara, and Rose couldn't
help notice the tension between them – they kept locking
eyes and then looking away. They seemed as wary around
each other as a pair of stray cats. Jake did look good, Rose
had to admit, freshly shaved and in a clean shirt that perfectly matched his eyes. Earlier, she had seen Cara ruffling
his dark hair, teasing out the curls, which gave him even
more of a gypsy appeal.

'Top tucker, Rose,' said Jake, sensing her gaze.

'Amazing,' said Cara as both she and Jake reached for
the last scone at the same time.

'Ladies first,' he said, winking at her. 'Gotta love a woman with a good appetite.'

'How about we go halves?' said Cara, slathering part of the scone with jam and cream and presenting him with it.

'Generous too,' he said.

Rose could feel the temperature rise just looking at them.

'That's it, guys. It's a wrap. We've got everything we need,' said the photographer after Rose had raised her tea-cup to her lips for what seemed like the hundredth time.

'Thanks for everything,' said Wendy, who had been hovering in the background all day, making copious notes in her spiral-bound notebook. 'Jake, you've been particularly helpful. I can't thank you enough.' She pressed a hand on his arm and looked up at him with a radiant smile.

Rose was astonished at Jake's lack of reaction; normally flirting came as naturally to him as breathing. Come to think of it, he hadn't been the same since he'd come back from visiting his parents in Adelaide. Could his father's illness have something to do with his new, more sober, approach?

'No worries,' he said. 'I hope you got everything you came for.'

'Well, perhaps not everything,' Rose heard the writer say to him under her breath.

CHAPTER THIRTY-FOUR

A typical Friday night in the Shingle Valley revolved around the Southern Cross and its legendary chicken parma, and, while she admitted the dish was mighty good, Mattie was looking forward to a bit of a change this coming Friday.

A group of the local vignerons were hosting a dinner in New Bridgeton to showcase their new-release reds, and Mark had invited Mattie and Cara along as a thank you for their work in running the cellar door.

Mattie dressed with care, applying just enough makeup to conceal the scar and enhance her skin and naturally rosy lips. Cara had persuaded her to wear a simple sheath dress, its emerald colour making her eyes seem even greener, and a pair of low-heeled ankle boots that offset the prettiness of the dress and were stable enough for her to walk in without fear of tripping and wrecking her leg again. She slicked her hair back and tucked it behind her ears. She wanted to at least hold her own against the other guests at the dinner, one chic Frenchwoman in particular.

'Can you do me up?' asked Cara, coming into Mattie's bedroom with a rustle of fabric. Mattie let out a low whistle. Her friend had gone all out in a silver jumpsuit, the front of which was slashed almost to her navel. With scarlet lips, smoky eyeshadow and her blonde hair pulled back in a smooth chignon, she looked the epitome of glamour.

'Dressing up again, Car? Anything to do with a certain viticulturist?' she teased.

'Oh, come on, you know I always make an effort.'

'Yeah, but this ...' Mattie paused. 'You look gorgeous, babe. Jake won't be able to resist you.'

'Well, if he does then I don't know what the problem is.'

'Come on then, we'd better go and find the others. If we don't leave soon, we'll be late. Mark said something about wanting to check the wines before they're poured.'

'Coming.' Cara slicked on a final coat of scarlet gloss and the girls headed out.

The spring night was cool, but the restaurant was cosy, with a crackling fire at one end of the long room. The tables were laid with white cloths and each setting had four glasses of varying sizes in front of it. The restaurant had arranged extra glasses to accommodate the wines that were to be served – Rose had lent fifty of her own from Trevelyn's Pantry. The place had yet to fill up, but almost immediately Mattie spied Thommo, Deano and Mick, and Charlie, who was deep in conversation with Jake but looked up and smiled as he saw her. She cast around for Marie-Claire, but couldn't spot her.

'Hey, girls,' said Jake, seeing them arrive. Mattie noticed that he was unable to tear his eyes away from Cara.

'Wow, Mattie, you look amazing,' said Thommo.

Mattie felt rather unremarkable compared with Cara, but it was nice to get the compliment. 'Thanks. It's not quite my usual style,' she said, indicating the dress.

'You don't say,' he laughed. 'But it really suits you.'

'How about me?' said Cara. 'Am I the dog's breakfast?'

Thommo laughed, a loud boom that echoed across the restaurant. 'Cara, sweetheart, you could never be that.'

A waiter approached with a tray of sparkling wine and Cara and Mattie accepted a delicate flute each, tilting their heads back to take a sip.

The room quickly filled up with couples and groups as waiters moved through the crowd, ushering guests to their seats. It was time for the food to be served and the first of the wines to be poured.

Mattie found herself seated to Charlie's left, and further along their table she could see Cara sitting directly opposite Jake. Still no sign of Marie-Claire. She leaned back to allow the waiter to place the first course in front of her while another poured the wine. Sangiovese, by the look of it. She picked up the glass, swirled it and sniffed. The familiar aroma of sour cherries and dusty earth pricked her nostrils and her mouth immediately began to water. One of her favourite wines.

'What do you think?' Charlie was watching her.

'Mmm. Pretty good,' she said after taking a swallow.

'It's ours. We replanted a block at the top of the property a few years back. This is the first decent vintage. Have to say I'm damn pleased with how well it's turned out.'

'How have things been at Windsong?'

'Well, we're none too pleased about the mine, that's for sure.'

'You and Mark are leading the opposition to it, aren't you? Do you think you can stop it?'

Charlie's normally sunny face was serious. 'I've no idea. But if it goes ahead it'll change everything about the valley, I know that much. We're going to do everything we can. I'll chain myself to a bulldozer if I have to.'

Mattie barked with laughter. 'Sorry, I know it's not funny, but somehow I can't imagine you in chains.'

'Yeah, well. You never know what a man will do when he's backed into a corner. This is our land, our heritage, our bloody livelihood and none of us want to see it destroyed.'

Mattie nodded. She knew what this valley meant to so many of those who lived in it, those who had grown up here, whose families had farmed the land for generations. 'You didn't have anything to do with that truckload of waste that was dumped at Tarrawenna, did you?' she asked, something in her brain clicking into place.

He gave her the barest hint of a wink.

'I knew it! Charlie Drummond, you'll get yourself into all kinds of trouble. Will you ever grow up?' she scolded in a whisper.

He shrugged, looking like a schoolboy caught doing something he shouldn't, but knowing that his charm would probably mean he would get away with it. 'Not if I can help it.'

'What would Marie-Claire say if she knew that her fiancé was completely irresponsible?'

'I dunno. She's in France, isn't she?'

'Oh, I wasn't aware of that. But she's coming back, right?'

Charlie was about to reply when there was a chink of cutlery on glassware and Mark got to his feet.

Frustrated, Mattie threw back another slug of wine and wondered what Charlie had been about to reveal. She noticed Cara sitting further along the table, seemingly engrossed in a conversation with the couple alongside her, and completely ignoring Jake. She wanted to bash their heads together and tell them what idiots they were being, but she knew she had to let them sort it out themselves.

As the chairman of the Shingle Valley Vignerons Association, Mark welcomed the guests and began to talk about the previous year's vintage, how the conditions had affected the fruit, and the style of the wines they had in the glasses before them.

'He's incredible, isn't he?' Mattie whispered to Charlie, who nodded in agreement. Mattie had always been a little in awe of her big brother, but seeing him taking centre stage, his passion for his work shining through his words, gave her a sudden rush of pride.

Mark called on each host in turn, inviting them to say a few words about their wines. As first Thommo Drummond, then Deano and then Bob Drayfield and several more wine-makers got up to speak, the guests finished off their entrées and the main course was served. Mattie didn't get the chance to return to her conversation with Charlie about Marie-Claire's expected return.

Later, after the food had been cleared away, and people were lingering over coffee and dessert wine, Mattie saw Cara push back her chair and head out of the room. Excusing herself, she followed, wanting to talk to her friend about what was going on, but Jake was too quick for her and reached Cara before Mattie could. She hung back, anxious not to interrupt.

'Cara, are you feeling okay?' he said.

Mattie couldn't hear her friend's reply.

'Here, take this.' He handed her his jacket, letting his hands linger on her shoulders. 'It's still cold in the evenings.'

'Thanks.'

'Are you sure you're okay?'

'Yep. A bit light-headed, that's all. It was warm in there.'

Mattie knew she should probably get back to the restaurant; she felt like a voyeur. But she couldn't help but stay to hear what would happen.

'You know I can't stop thinking about you,' Jake blurted out.

Mattie saw her friend's eyes widen in surprise.

'I'll probably regret this,' he said, taking a step towards her and placing a hand on her chin. He tilted her lips to his. Mattie wasn't able to suppress a cough and blushed furiously at the thought of being discovered eavesdropping, but the two of them were oblivious.

She dragged herself away, feeling a mixture of happiness and despondence. She truly was pleased for her friend, but everyone around her seemed to be pairing up. It was like a bloody couples' Noah's Ark.

As she returned to the table, Charlie called out, 'Did you find her?' He stopped when he saw her expression. 'Hey? Everything okay?'

Mattie tried to put on a brave face. She knew she wasn't being rational, but she'd had it up to there with rationality. She grabbed her glass of wine, taking a reckless gulp. 'Fancy going dancing?' she said to Charlie. She'd completely forgotten that a recently healed broken leg might limit her capabilities on the dance floor. The alcohol appeared to have numbed any lingering pain in her limbs.

'In New Bridgeton? Really?' He stood up. 'C'mon Mattie,' he said, putting a steadying arm around her. 'Perhaps it's time to call it a night, hey?'

Mattie wriggled out of his embrace, wobbling slightly. 'If you won't take me, then I'll find someone who will.' She enunciated her words, careful not to slur them.

He paused for a moment and then grinned. 'Alright, I'm up for it if you are. There was that dodgy nightclub in Waverly Street, but I think it closed down last year.'

'Anyone else?' she asked the table. There was a murmur of dissent from those who remained. 'Looks like it's just you and me, Charlie Drummond. Come on then, what are you waiting for?'

They said their goodbyes and hopped in a cab that was

waiting outside the restaurant. 'Know anywhere that's open late around here, mate?' Charlie asked the driver.

A few minutes later they found themselves in a part of town that Mattie had never been to, on the other side of the railway line that bisected the town. 'Wrong side of the tracks,' she laughed as they stepped out of the cab and towards an unlit doorway. 'Where the hell are we?' she asked, leaning on Charlie's arm.

'I've heard of this place, but I can't say I know it. Well, Fearless ...' They approached the bouncer, who waved them inside and down a set of stairs. 'Here goes.'

Mattie could feel the pulse of a thrumming bass, and a fug of heat rose from the dimly lit basement. A tangle of bodies, writhing to an insistent beat, filled the room.

'Drink?' Charlie shouted.

Mattie shook her head, pulling him into the middle of the throng of dancers. She didn't need any more alcohol; she craved a different drug. In the far reaches of her responsible mind she knew that she was well out of order to crack onto someone else's fiancé, but she deliberately ignored the tiny voice of reason and reached out to Charlie. Pulling him close, she began to move sensuously against him, inhibitions cast to the wind, desire surging through her. She didn't care if this was only for one night; she wanted to have some fun for once. Everything could change in an instant, she knew that now; what was so wrong about living for the moment?

Charlie didn't miss a beat, matching her move for move as their bodies locked in a rhythm. *He is good at this*, she thought with surprise before closing her eyes and losing herself in the music and the feel of his hard-muscled body against hers.

As the beat changed she gazed up at him, squinting slightly to focus. *He really does have the most incredible eyes,* she thought hazily. Then, as the music slowed, she became aware of his hands stroking her back, his fingers slowly making their way down her spine, making her shudder with desire and giving her chills despite the heat of the nightclub. Charlie loosened his embrace and reached for the tip of her chin with his finger. The question in her eyes was answered as he lowered his mouth to hers.

CHAPTER THIRTY-FIVE

Mattie was up early the following day, determinedly ignoring the stinking hangover that clouded her brain and thumped behind her eyes. She couldn't remember exactly how she'd gotten home the night before. She'd woken up, fully clothed, her boots abandoned in the middle of the room as if she'd just kicked them off and collapsed like a felled tree onto the bed. To make things worse, she was completely out of painkillers. Her stomach roiled anxiously.

She peered into Cara's room and saw her friend, face down and spark out. Mattie remembered the sight of her and Jake kissing outside the restaurant the previous evening. As she thought about seeing them entwined, the full force of what *she'd* done the night before came back to her. Oh Christ, how could she have been such an idiot? Was she ever going to be able to face Charlie again?

Throwing down a glass of water, she grabbed her camera and climbed into her car. She was due to take some shots at Trevelyn's Pantry when it was set up for a wedding, and wanted to get there in plenty of time to capture details of the tables and flowers as well as the plated-up food before it was eaten.

She glanced at her watch. If she was quick she'd have time to take some early morning landscape shots before meeting Rose at the restaurant. There was a lookout at the far end of the valley that she'd been meaning to hike up to – she thought her leg could just about handle it, despite the previous night's shenanigans – and the conditions were perfect. As she trundled along the Shingle Road, she was forced to slow down to let a stray cow cross the road, then, as she sped up again, her eye was caught by a flash of silver in the vineyards on the Tarrawenna property. On little more than a hunch, she yanked the car to the right and pulled into the lane that led up to the old winery buildings.

Killing the engine, she got out of the car, camera in hand. It was eerily quiet; even the birds seemed to have been silenced. Mattie felt a shiver of apprehension run through her, but told herself not to be silly and strode, undeterred, towards the vineyard. Coming around the side of the winery, she noticed the graffiti that Officer Doyd had been investigating but there was no sign of the dumped rubbish; she supposed it must have been cleared away. She was almost upon the vineyard, where she could still see the scrap of silver that had caught her attention. It was, incongruously, a shiny babydoll nightie, sewn with sparkly, tinselled thread, that had been draped over a vine trellis. Something to scare the birds perhaps? Cursing herself for having been taken in – in her befuddled state she'd thought it was Cara's jumpsuit, though how it would have got there God only knew – she retreated a few metres and snapped a few shots. If nothing else it would make a good story to tell the others back at Kalkari. She was so absorbed in her task that she didn't hear the footsteps behind her.

'Just what do you think you're doing here? This is private property, didn't you see the sign?'

Mattie whirled around and saw a man towering over her. He was built like a brick shithouse and looked none too happy about her presence in the vineyard. Not the kind of person to argue with. She noticed the tag on his jacket. Security. *Of course.*

'I'm sorry,' she said. 'Honestly. I'm not causing any trouble. I just —' She didn't get the chance to finish her sentence. A meaty hand came down on her camera with shocking swiftness. One minute she was holding it and the next it was torn from her grasp and in the dust. She cried out as his huge boot crushed it.

'I'd get out of here pretty quick if I were you,' he said, reaching for her. 'Or there will really be trouble.'

Mattie was too fast for him, even with her bad leg. Ducking under his outstretched arm, she ran as fast as she could towards her car, throwing herself behind the wheel and gunning it down the drive.

She was approaching Trevelyn's by the time her heart had begun to stop hammering. She was furious, and incredulous. Had that really just happened? In the Shingle Valley? Her poor camera ...

'Rose!' she cried as she raced into the restaurant. 'Rose, you won't believe what just happened!'

'You're kidding?' Rose was as incredulous as Mattie when she'd told her the story. 'Oh, darling girl, you're shaking.'

It was true; Mattie was quivering like a leaf. 'Oh God. I can't work without it,' she said. 'What am I going to do?'

'Right,' said Rose, a note of determination in her voice as she got out her phone. 'I'm reporting this to the police.'

'But I was technically trespassing,' said Mattie.

'Doesn't matter. Didn't give that goon the right to damage valuable property.'

Rose made the call and handed the phone over to Mattie, who relayed the rest of the story. Eventually she hung up, having been reassured that they would dispatch a car to Tarrawenna to investigate.

Rose looked sympathetically at her. 'Coffee?'

'Do I look that bad?'

Rose smiled. 'I've seen worse, if that makes you feel any better. Come on, have a seat and I'll make you a cup. I can spare a minute.'

'I don't suppose you've got any painkillers too?' The effect of the adrenaline that had surged through her had worn off and Mattie's hangover had come back with full force.

Rose brought two espressos, a glass of water and a blister pack of Panadol over to a table at the verandah at the back of the restaurant. Mattie swallowed two tablets and took a grateful sip of her coffee. She looked out over the small kitchen garden Rose had planted.

'I know, they grow like weeds as soon as the weather warms up,' Rose said, following Mattie's gaze. 'Not that the soil is that great around here. It works well for the vines but not so well for my greens and pumpkins. A lot of sweat, not to mention chicken manure, has gone into that patch, but it's been worth it.' Rose took a sip of her coffee and made a face. 'Does this taste okay to you? God, I must be losing my touch, this is awful.'

'It tastes fine to me,' replied Mattie. 'Why, what's wrong with it?'

'Not sure. Too bitter perhaps? Maybe it's the new beans that Bevan sent over from Sacred Grounds? I'll have to ask him next time I see him.' Rose put her coffee cup down, distracted. 'Anyway, I'd better get on, there's still loads to prep.'

'It looks gorgeous,' said Mattie, noticing the snowy-clothed tables and massed bowls of roses adorning the room. Each bloom had been nurtured to the peak of perfection. 'I'm so sorry I can't get the shots I promised.'

'Don't be silly. There'll be other weddings – we've got four more booked in already this spring. Anyway, we've only got about fifteen minutes before everyone's due to start arriving.'

Mattie took the hint. 'I'll head off then. Good luck with it all today.'

'No worries.' Rose grinned at her. 'You look after yourself – you've had a nasty shock. Take it easy, okay?'

*

Mattie returned to Kalkari and spent the afternoon holed up in the barn, retouching the shots she'd had the foresight to upload to her laptop the day before. She was trying to take her mind off that morning's bizarre events, not to mention her actions of the previous night. She felt utterly shame-faced that she'd gone after Charlie so brazenly, especially as he was engaged to someone else. Cutting someone else's lunch wasn't her style. One thing was certain: she'd well and truly blown any chance they'd had of platonic friendship.

Several hours passed as she worked, absorbed in her task. Finally, as the sun was beginning to set, she closed the computer and went in search of her friend. The cellar door was probably her best bet. It had been a sunny Saturday, so she was sure Cara would have been kept busy.

Cara was wiping down the long slab of the oak counter, getting ready to close up, as Mattie walked through the door. 'Dude, how's it going?' Cara asked, giving Mattie a tired smile. 'What happened to you last night? Out dancing, so I heard?'

'Um, er, yeah,' said Mattie ruefully. 'Probably not the best move after so much wine. Anyway, more importantly – what about you and Jake, hey? Cara Claythorne, are you actually blushing?'

'Pah!' Cara looked embarrassed despite her denial.

'Come on.' Mattie fixed her with a firm gaze. 'Spill.'

'It was only a kiss …' Cara said. 'And then we got a lift home with Mark and Rose, so that kind of put the brakes on anything else. Just as well though.'

Mattie was confused. 'Why? I thought you liked him?'

'That's the problem. I do. Perhaps a bit too much.' Cara held up her mobile phone. 'And has the guy called today? Texted? Has he fuck!' she exploded.

'Calm your farm, Cars. Give him a day or so before you jump to conclusions.' Cara's phone began to peal. 'See!' cried Mattie. 'It's probably him!'

Cara, however, didn't look quite as delighted as Mattie thought she should.

'Movies?' she was saying into the phone. 'Sure, why not? Yep, I'm sure Mattie would love to come too. See you then.'

'Was that Jake? You could have sounded more enthusiastic. And surely you don't want to drag me along as well?' Mattie was puzzled.

'Nah, it wasn't Jake. Seems Officer Doyd is keen to go on a double date.'

'And you agreed?' Mattie said, horrified.

'Why not? It's not as if I'm knocking back any other offers. Besides, there's nothing like a bit of healthy competition.'

'Yeah, well, in this valley the word'll get out and back to Jake, that's for sure. But do you really want me along too?'

'He says he's got a colleague who's moved here recently and doesn't know a soul. So we've got a night out with the boys in blue.'

'Do we have to?'

'Yes! It's only the movies. Anyway, you really need to get out more. Though you were having a good time last night, by the looks of things. Where exactly did you get to with the delicious Charlie Drummond?'

Mattie shrugged. 'A club.'

'In Eumeralla?'

'I know, right?'

They grinned at each other.

Mattie deliberately didn't mention kissing Charlie in the nightclub; she was too embarrassed to admit to cracking onto a guy who was involved with someone else.

'Now, about this date —'

'Alright, if I have to,' Mattie sighed. 'When?'

'Tomorrow,' said Cara, her good humour restored. 'Hey, there's something I almost forgot to tell you. Earlier this afternoon a lady came in, said she's from the new spa that's opening up on the other side of Eumeralla – you know the one, where they're going to get people to bathe in grape skins.'

'Oh yeah, the one at Lilybells?'

'That's the one. Well, she'd heard about the makeover we'd given the cellar door and she came over to take a look for herself. Seems she wants some help with the interiors of the spa. Get this, it's going to be called "Spa-kling"!' Cara roared with laughter. 'Can you believe it? Anyway, she loved what we did here so I reckon I might have a commission.'

'Perhaps even a new career?' Mattie pointed out.

'I hadn't thought of that – how cool would that be?'

'Brilliant, mate. Brilliant. I reckon that calls for a drink.'

'Of spa-kling?'

The two girls dissolved into fits of laughter, and woes, hangovers and heartache were temporarily erased.

*

Despite Mattie's low expectations, or quite possibly because of them, the movie night turned out to be okay. Officer Doyd's – Brock's – colleague, who had the improbable name of Billy Bluestone, was easygoing company, and good-naturedly brushed off Cara's suggestive teasing about truncheons and the back seat of paddy wagons. 'You can't help yourself, can you?' Billy winked at her. 'You'd better be careful or you could find yourself handcuffed to Brock. And I'll have the keys.'

'Did you have any luck with the security guard at Tarrawenna?' Mattie asked Brock while they were waiting in the cinema queue.

'What security guard?' Cara asked.

'The one who destroyed my camera yesterday morning,' said Mattie.

'Wait, what?'

'Oh God, I forgot to tell you. I was just standing in the vineyards at Tarrawenna, minding my own business – well, I stopped because I thought I saw your jumpsuit, but that's another story. Anyway, this oaf of a security guard came along and threatened me. The next thing I knew he'd knocked my camera out of my hand.'

'What?'

Mattie could see the shock in Cara's eyes. 'Ground it under his boot for good measure too,' she added.

'I hope you'll be pressing charges,' said Cara, glancing at the officers they were with.

'My colleague is managing the case,' said Brock. 'But I do know they went over and spoke to the guard and retrieved the camera.' Mattie looked suddenly hopeful. Perhaps it was salvageable? 'Though they'll be holding onto that as evidence,' he added.

'Oh okay. I'll follow it up on Monday,' said Mattie.

'I can't believe you didn't tell me,' said Cara. 'Are you sure you're alright, mate?'

Mattie smiled wryly. 'I'm fine – it's the camera that's probably not. It'd take more than a steroid-pumped rent-a-cop to scare me for long.'

The movie itself was forgettable, but they headed to the local Thai afterwards and ordered vast quantities of pad see ew and penang chicken, washed down with a couple of bottles of riesling that Mattie had brought along. As the door clanged shut and they stood on the street saying their good-byes, Mattie noticed a familiar figure on the opposite side of the street, and nudged Cara. It was Jake. She couldn't tell if he'd seen them or not. She went to raise her arm. 'Don't,' urged Cara in a whisper. 'I've got more pride than that. If he was going to call, he should have done it by now. He's had all bloody weekend, for God's sake!'

'Okay, if you insist.'

Mattie, on the other hand, found herself fending off callers over the next few days. First, Billy, the policeman from the movie night, and then Charlie, had been in touch. Billy rang to say how much he had enjoyed meeting her and that perhaps they could do it again sometime soon. She managed a non-committal response. Then, on Monday night, Charlie rang.

'Fearless!' he said when she picked up.

As she heard his voice, the memory of dancing with him surfaced again and she blushed beet-red. 'Charlie,' she said. 'Listen, I'm really sorry. I don't know what happened. All that wine ...' She wanted to get in before he could say anything. Anything at all about what had happened between them in the nightclub. She shook her head, but far from dispelling the memory, it became clearer – the heat of the club, people dancing wildly, surrounding them, pushing them closer, her fingers entangled in Charlie's blond curls, pressing her body up against his then breaking away to dance in front of him, putting on a show, teasing him ... the full force of what they'd done came rushing back to her. She remembered pulling him closer, her body moulded to his, hip to hip, chest to chest, their eyes locked, lips meeting, then drowning in the softness, the addictive sweetness of his kiss ...

'Don't worry about it,' Charlie said after a pause. 'I reckon everyone's entitled to tie one on every now and then. Do you remember our plans for next Sunday?'

Phew. He wasn't going to make her sweat over it. Perhaps he was as shame-faced as she was. But then why did he want to see her again? 'Plans?' she asked, puzzled.

Charlie laughed at her on the other end of the line. 'Never mind. I'll be there to pick you up at eleven, mate.'

CHAPTER THIRTY-SIX

'**B**loody hell, you cleaned the ute!' Mattie exclaimed as Charlie showed up at Kalkari on Sunday morning. Sure enough, the car was free of its usual muddy spatter. 'I hope that wasn't on my account.'

'Nah,' said Charlie, looking sheepish. 'It was long overdue. I don't think the paintwork's been that shiny since I bought it though. It was about time the old girl got a spruce up.'

'So, where are we going?' she said, hopping in the passenger seat.

'I thought we'd take the valley road, drive up to the lookout on the other side of the hills, if you think you can manage the walk.'

Okay, a walk. Interesting.

'I'll be right. My leg aches sometimes, but even that will eventually disappear, according to the physio. She said the best thing for it is exercise.'

'Good. By the way, I'm sorry about what happened. To your camera.'

'News travels fast in the valley, huh? Yeah, it's a total suck-fest,' she said despondently.

'You've had more than your fair share of bad luck, Mattie Cameron.'

'I'm kind of partly to blame for this one though. I shouldn't have been there.'

'But the goon was completely out of order, by all accounts.'

'Even so …'

The sun was high in the sky by the time they reached their destination, and Mattie was surprised by the heat as she stepped from the air-conditioned cool of the ute's cab.

'It's not too far from here,' said Charlie, reaching into the back and retrieving a small rucksack.

'Okay,' said Mattie, looking around. 'God, I haven't been up here for years.'

They were both out of breath by the time they reached the top of the escarpment, and Mattie had grass stains on the knees of her jeans where she'd stumbled on the way up. 'It's steeper than I remember,' she gasped.

'No, I reckon we're not as fit as we were when we were kids,' said Charlie.

They turned around. The valley spread out before them like a child's drawing: rows of vines forming neat grids across the plain, trees dotted between the vineyards, silvery triangles of dams catching the sunlight. 'Wow, it's still amazing, isn't it?' said Mattie once she'd gotten her breath back. 'I'd forgotten how beautiful it is.'

'Yup. Can't imagine how different it'll look if the mines get in,' said Charlie. He shucked off the backpack and pulled out a couple of water bottles.

'Thanks,' said Mattie as he handed one to her. 'Completely forgot we might need water. Shows how much of a city girl I've become.' She gulped it down thirstily, wiping her mouth with the back of her hand when she was done.

'Good job I'm here then, hey?' said Charlie. 'Come on, let's sit over there.' He pointed to a couple of tussocks of grass.

Sitting cross-legged, he pulled out a brown paper bag and offered her a bun dripping with icing.

She groaned with appreciation. 'Eumeralla Bakery still makes the best cinnamon scrolls I've ever tasted.'

'Nowhere better.'

'This is a bit classier than our old smoko fare, isn't it?' she said, recalling the white-bread sandwiches with Vegemite or pink slices of Devon that had been their sustenance as kids.

'Some things change, Mattie Cameron.'

'I guess they do,' she said. 'Charlie?'

'Mmm?'

'Can I ask you something?'

'Anything.'

'Remember that cross-country competition?'

'How could I forget it?' He laughed. 'The one where you trounced me and most of the valley?'

'That'd be the one.' She couldn't help grinning at the memory.

'What about it?'

'Why did you leave so suddenly? Did you really hate losing to me so much?'

'Do you really want to know?'

Mattie nodded.

'I was all set to congratulate you,' he said, looking suddenly embarrassed. 'But as you came down from the podium some other lucky bugger swept you off your feet. Figured you didn't need me there, playing third wheel.'

Mattie blushed. 'Oh. I had no idea.'

Both of them fell silent, looking out at the view.

'Now it's only fair that I get to ask you something,' said Charlie.

'Okay. I suppose.' Here it comes. She felt herself grow hot with shame.

'Do you really not remember the other night in New Bridgeton, after the dinner?'

'Well …' she said carefully, 'I remember going into the nightclub. And a bit of the dancing – those were quite some moves you pulled,' she said, trying to make light of it. 'But I've no idea how I got home, I'm afraid.' She couldn't look at him. She *was* telling the truth – well, partially.

He waited a beat. 'Don't worry,' he said eventually. 'We had a dance, but then you were practically falling over with tiredness. I made sure you got home okay.'

'Ever the gentleman,' she said, relieved that he was going to let it lie there. 'I don't normally cut loose like that,' she said, an apologetic look on her face. 'I think I've spent too long convalescing.'

He nodded. 'I reckon it's safe to say that your recuperation is nearly complete.'

'Nearly?'

'I've yet to see you back on Shakira.' He looked at her pointedly.

'Yeah, well …' Mattie shrugged. She still hadn't got up the nerve to ride again. After the pounding her body had taken in the avalanche, she was too scared to do anything that might set her recovery back or do even more damage.

'Hey, Charlie?'

'Yeah?'

She wanted to ask about Marie-Claire. If he was planning on going to France, or if she was coming back to the valley. But she wasn't sure if she wanted to hear the answer. She hesitated and the moment was lost. 'Nah, it's nothing. Doesn't matter.'

CHAPTER THIRTY-SEVEN

T he meeting in the main bar at the Southern Cross
Hotel was getting increasingly rowdy. Everyone
was there, as far as Rose could see: Thommo,
Charlie, Ben, Deano and Angie, Jake, Dan,
Bevan, Bob and Sadie … all of the vignerons in the valley,
plus the bed and breakfast owners, the restaurateurs, the cafe
proprietors, the hoteliers, the boutique owners. Everyone
whose livelihood and future was under threat if a mine at the
southern end of the valley went ahead. The pub was packed,
and doing a roaring trade as people ordered schooner after
schooner, thirsty from their shouted conversations. Rose
could sense an ominous tone to the conversations. People
were frustrated. And angry at the lack of progress. It wouldn't
take much for the meeting to get out of hand. She hoped
Mark would be able to keep them under control.

Mark signalled to the publican to ring a ship's bell at
the end of the bar that was used to call time. At the sound,

the hubbub died down and there was a shuffling of feet, a few coughs, then relative quiet as people ceased their conversations and turned to listen.

'Alright, everyone,' Mark called out. 'Let's get this meeting underway. It's great to see so many of you out tonight, and thank you for coming. Now, I've spoken with the State Planning Commission and as yet they've not had any applications for licences to mine in the area. But I reckon it's only a matter of time. We need to be ready with all guns blazing the minute we hear anything. Amanda, what are your thoughts on a PR campaign?'

'Well, I think they can frack off!' she yelled. The crowd laughed, as much at the thought of this diminutive blonde going up against the behemoth company as at her joke. As the laughter subsided, Amanda continued. 'For a start we're going to need some funds.'

There was a collective groan from those assembled. Amanda held up her hand. 'Hear me out. I think there's a way we can raise some money and get a bit of publicity for our cause at the same time.'

'C'mon then, spill,' said Bob. 'Tell us what you're thinking of.'

'I'm proposing we hold an auction. A wine auction. If all the local vignerons donate a case or two from their museum stocks, and we hold it in the city, I reckon we'll score some great coverage and raise money to fund our campaign. Two birds with one stone.'

'I like it,' said Mark. 'Great idea. I'll take care of assembling and cataloguing the wine, if everyone can email me with the details of what they can donate. Amanda, can you work on a venue and an invite list? Perhaps some of our other businesses can donate prizes for a raffle too? A few nights' accommodation, a couple of meals, that sort of thing?'

Amanda nodded, her blonde hair flipping about her face. 'There's no reason that it can't be online, too – that way anyone can bid.'

'But then what's in it for those who come?'

'How about we open a few bottles, some older vintages – give people a chance to taste wines they'd never normally get to? Meet the winemakers …'

'Terrific idea. Well done.'

She nodded, accepting his praise with a satisfied smile.

'In addition, Thommo and I have also been working on a proposal to have the entire valley zoned for tourism. At the moment, it's only the northern end that has the zoning. If we can get it extended, it'll really put the kybosh on anyone digging up the area. It's going to take a lot of work to put together a comprehensive submission, and we'll need to make it our number one priority.'

There was a murmur from the crowd, then Bob Drayfield spoke up. 'Now what's this I've been hearing about an assault?' he asked. 'On young Tilly.'

There was more chatter, which soon escalated loudly and Mark had to hold up his hand to speak. 'An over-eager security guard, that's all. The matter is being handled by the police. I don't think it will change anything, though it's not great publicity for Tin Pei. But' – he looked around the room – 'it's best that everyone stays well clear of the property. We don't want any accusations of foul play, especially not after the graffiti incident. Everything we do has to be done the right way. This is no schoolyard fight we've got on our hands here.'

Rose's eye was caught by a movement at the end of the bar. She was surprised to see an unfamiliar face there, waiting to be served. In the three years she'd lived in the valley, she reckoned she knew just about everyone, though even on a Wednesday night in spring she supposed there might be the odd stranger passing through. Then she noticed a logo on his fleece pullover, a blocky *TPR* picked out in red and white embroidery. *Uh-oh.* She recognised it immediately from Mark's computer searches. Tin Pei Resources. Christ, if anyone else saw it and knew what it stood for, all hell would break loose. She tried frantically to catch Mark's eye, but he was now deep in conversation with Bob and Thommo. Threading her way through the throng of people she squeezed next to the man just as he was about to be served. 'I'm not sure that's a terribly good idea,' she said quietly.

The man turned to look at her. 'Is there a problem? Perhaps the lady would like a drink too?' he said to the publican with a leer.

'Er, actually,' Rose said, 'your shirt. Probably not the best thing to wear around here.'

He looked bemused for a minute. 'Oh, right,' he said, understanding at last. 'Look, lady, I'm just doing my job —' he started.

'I get it,' she said, 'but in case you hadn't realised it, you've just walked right into a hornet's nest.' She inclined her head towards the crowd. 'That's a meeting of locals who oppose everything that Tin Pei stands for. Don't stir up any more trouble than you already have. Most of them don't know what that logo means, but there are a couple who do ... I'd be leaving before things get ugly, if I were you.'

He looked over at the crowd, hesitated, then signalled the publican. 'I'll get a six-pack to go instead, mate.'

Rose breathed a sigh of relief as he exited the door. Crisis averted. For now.

CHAPTER THIRTY-EIGHT

'Honestly, Mats, I don't know what to do. I've never had a guy come on so strong and then disappear off the radar. It's bloody frustrating.' Cara and Mattie were sitting on a couple of old chairs outside the barn. 'I'm not used to being ignored. He's hardly been at the winery for the past week, doesn't answer my texts —'

'Wait,' said Mattie. 'You've been texting him? Isn't that the number one mistake in the dating rulebook?'

'I couldn't give a shit about that right now. I'm more pissed off than anything else. How dare he say what he said to me and then act as if I don't even exist!' Cara threw the magazine she'd been reading onto the floor. 'Anyway, it was only one text. Just to see how he was. Keeping it casual.'

'What exactly did he say to you at the wine dinner?'

'Oh, you know, can't stop thinking about me, he's completely smitten, blah blah blah …'

'Wow. That is full on. I'm stumped,' said Mattie. 'I mean, I'd heard all the rumours about him, but I found them hard to believe. Do you want me to speak to him, find out what's really going on?'

'No way! I'm almost over the whole thing actually. Arsehole.'

'Are you sure?'

'Nah. I'm trying to make myself feel better about it. I might have even agreed to meet Broccoli at the pub on Friday.'

'Broccoli?'

'Officer Doyd. Brock.'

Mattie was silent. Cara had always needed admirers, but she sensed that her friend cared about Jake more than she was letting on.

'Okay, so let's see what you've done so far,' Mark said to Mattie in the kitchen at Kalkari later that day. Cara had gone over to the cellar door for the afternoon shift, and Rose was busy at Trevelyn's, prepping for another Saturday wedding. Mattie powered up her laptop and clicked on the mocked-up Kalkari website. She turned the screen around so that Mark could navigate through the site. He was silent for several minutes. She really wanted to please her big brother. He'd done so much for her, especially in the last few months, letting her – and her best friend – stay rent-free.

She could hold back no longer. 'Well?'

Mark looked at her, respect showing in his eyes. 'Sis, I think it's bloody brilliant. So much better than what we've had in the past. Love it. Love all of it. But ...' Mattie's spirits deflated.

'I think the real talent here is in the photography,' Mark went on. 'Who knew you could make old Dan look that good?' He pointed to the screen. 'And these, of Luisa.' His eyes glistened as he looked at it. 'They're incredible. You've completely captured her cheekiness.'

Mattie smiled back at him. 'Thanks, Mark, that means a lot. It really does.'

'Actually, you've given me an idea. I need to speak to Rose, but I reckon we could hold an exhibition of these photos.'

Mattie was taken aback. 'Really? Do you really think so?'

'I'm certain.'

'Oh wow. But I've just been mucking around, really. And now my camera's been destroyed I'm not sure if I even have enough for something as ambitious as that.'

'Why don't you have a look? 'Cause I reckon you do. These are better than someone just mucking around, sweetheart.' Mark put his arm around her shoulders. 'What a bloody clever sister I turned out to have.'

'Hey!' Mattie protested. 'I've always been clever.'

'Is that so?' he teased.

'Why do you need to speak to Rose?'

'Well, I think Trevelyn's Pantry might be the best venue for it.'

'Oh, I see. Um ...' She paused, not knowing how to frame her doubts. 'I'm not sure if I can afford the framing costs.'

'Don't worry about that – we'll sort something out. Now, I've had another flash of inspiration.'

'Watch out, Einstein, the world may not be ready for two of your great ideas on the one day.'

'Do you think you might be up for designing a wine label too?' He pointed to a close-up she'd taken of rose bushes that bloomed at the end of a row of vines. 'I want to do a special bottling of our rosé this vintage. I thought Rose might get a kick out of me naming a wine after her. That photo, or something similar, might look really good as part of a label.'

'Aww, Mark, who knew there was a romantic bone in there somewhere?' Mattie grinned and elbowed him in the ribs. 'She'll love it. How about if we do this one as a black and white shot?'

'That sounds great. I'm happy to leave the design up to you, but keep it a secret for now. I want to surprise her. I thought I might show her on her birthday. "Rose's rosé" – what do you think?'

'Isn't that a bit ordinary?'

'Oh. Got any better suggestions?'

'What about "a rosé by any other name"?'

'Isn't that a bit long-winded?'

'Nah, I don't think so,' she said confidently. 'I reckon I can make it work. Let me mock it up and you'll see what I mean.'

'Okay, you're the expert. But keep it under your hat for now.'

'Yes, big bro, got the message, loud and clear. And I'm glad you like the website. I'm really pleased, in fact.'

'So am I, Mattie. So am I. In fact, I've got another request.'

'Oh yes?'

'Do you think you could help me with the rezoning proposal? I've got all the evidence together, and Charlie's helped me out with the report, but we need someone to design it, make it look official …'

Mattie couldn't refuse him. 'Of course.'

The exhibition was all organised with lightning speed. Mark spoke to Rose, who agreed that Trevelyn's Pantry was the perfect venue. A date was set, and Mattie was flat out selecting the best shots, finding someone who could handle the job of producing large-format prints, and figuring out the best way to hang them from Trevelyn's hundred-year-old walls without causing damage.

'I've found somewhere to print and frame them for a really good price, but I'm going to have to go to the city to pick them up,' she said to Cara as they sipped their coffee out on the verandah one morning. 'The framers reckon they'll be ready next week. I might see if I can borrow Rose's car; there's no way they'll all fit in mine.'

Cara raised her eyebrows at Mattie. 'Are you thinking what I'm thinking?'

'I dunno, what are you thinking?' she asked, mischief in her voice.

'Road trip!' they both chanted in unison.

Good, thought Mattie. It would help take Cara's mind off Jake, who'd been conspicuous by his absence, spending all his time out in the vineyards and not dropping in to the house or the barn as he'd done in previous weeks. She'd never seen her friend so affected by a bloke before, and worried that she might be about to get her heart badly dinged – which would be a first. She sighed. It had to happen to everyone once, she supposed.

'Do you think Rose would like to come too?' asked Cara.

'I reckon we can persuade her. If she doesn't have too much on at Trevelyn's. It'd do her good to have a break, she's been looking exhausted lately.'

'Cool. We can stay with the olds, and I'd like to go and check out some furniture warehouses. I haven't had a chance to tell you – the new manager at Spa-kling definitely wants me to sort out their interiors for them. And Lord knows my wardrobe could do with a refresh as well.'

'You're kidding, right? All you need is shorts and a t-shirt around here.'

'Maybe for you.' Cara wrinkled her nose. 'But some of us aren't going to let our standards slip, even if we are out beyond the black stump. Owww!'

Mattie had whacked her friend across the shoulder. 'You totally deserved that!'

Late that afternoon, Mattie found Rose on the sofa. In all the time she'd been at Kalkari she'd never seen Rose sit down, let alone lie down, in the middle of the day. She was usually a whirl of energy, in perpetual motion from sun-up to sunset. 'Are you feeling okay?' Mattie asked.

'Mmm?' Rose stirred. 'Sure. Just having a little lie-down.'

'Maybe you're working too hard?' Mattie suggested.

Rose sat up slowly. 'Things are busy at Trevelyn's, but I've coped with hard work before and never been this buggered. And with the kids away, there's a lot less for me to do here. I don't know. Maybe it's the weather. It's getting so hot again.'

'Well, I've got an idea that you might like. How do you fancy a few days chilling out in Sydney? A girls' road trip. We can go out to dinner, go shopping …'

Rose brightened. 'Sounds good to me. When were you thinking of going? I've got another wedding this weekend, but after that it's pretty quiet.'

'Next week is perfect. I've got to pick the prints up from the framers – oh, and do you think we can take your car? I'd never get them in the back of mine.'

Rose nodded. 'Of course.'

'Cara says we can stay at her parents' place – they've got heaps of space, and it's close to the city. Now, where do you fancy eating? Should I book?'

'Ooh, I've been meaning to go and check out a few new restaurants. I could do with some inspiration for our summer menu.'

'Okay, let me know where and then consider it done.'

The girls arrived in Sydney with enough time to leave their bags at Cara's parents and hop on a ferry to the city for lunch. It was a perfect day and the water glittered, its serene blue perfectly reflecting the colour of the sky. They all breathed in the salty air, tipping their faces to the sun like flowers. 'This is exactly what I needed,' Rose called to Mattie over the thrum of the ferry's engines. 'I feel better already.'

Moments later, they were seated at a waterfront table, starched white linen napkins unfurled and toasting the trip with a bottle of bubbles. Across the water, the Opera House shone, its white sails pristine against the blue of the sky.

'Here's cheers, ladies,' said Cara, raising her glass. 'Now, what's the plan of attack? After we've eaten I vote we hop in a cab and hit Bondi Junction. Then if we've got the energy, we can pop over to Double Bay.'

'I need to make it to the framers in Surry Hills before they close at five,' said Mattie. 'But I can always leave you to shop and go over on my own.'

'Sounds good to me,' said Rose, taking a sip from her glass. 'Ugh.' She made a face.

'What?' asked Mattie. 'Is there something wrong with it? We can send it back if there is.'

'I'm not sure. Just doesn't taste that great.'

Cara looked suspiciously at her. 'Is there perhaps some-thing you'd like to tell us, Rose?'

Rose looked confused. 'What?' Cara fixed her with an intense stare. 'What?' Rose repeated.

'Er, Rose,' said Cara, 'do you think ... well, do you think there's a chance you might be —'

'Pregnant?' Rose finished, her face colouring. She looked embarrassed, as if caught out. 'Actually, I've been try-ing to convince myself I'm not. Guess I'm not doing a very good job of it.'

CHAPTER THIRTY-NINE

'I reckon that's it,' said Mattie, standing back to check the last frame as it hung suspended on wire from the ceiling. Two weeks after they returned from Sydney they'd finally finished 'bumping in', as Cara called it, arranging the thirty images around the rough white walls of Trevelyn's. The damage to her camera meant that she hadn't had a lot to choose from, but as she looked over the images, she knew she'd made the right selection. A close-up of a curling vine tendril, a panoramic vineyard scene with the Shingle Hills in the distance, the weathered hands of a worker using pruning shears, a shed filled with barrels, a tender shot of Rose and Mark silhouetted against the sandstone of the house ... Together they formed a shorthand picture of life in the valley, of its joys and its heartbreaks, of the land and those who worked it to bring forth wines with soul and passion – a true reflection of this very special piece of earth. She let out a satisfied breath. It had come together even better than she'd pictured it in her mind's eye, the black and white images conveying the raw beauty she saw from the vantage point of the camera lens. She'd thought she'd been busy in London, but what with organising the exhibition and then designing the proposal for Mark, she'd been flat out. And never happier. She'd also included some of her photos in the proposal document, showing the valley in all its glory: the vines, the cellar doors, people tasting, barrels being checked, the sweep of the landscape. It made a pretty compelling argument for turning the entire valley over to wine production and tourism. She hoped it would be enough. Mark and Charlie had a meeting with Jeremy Bell to present it to him in two days' time.

'It looks amazing,' said Cara, who'd been helping her get everything ready.

'Incredible,' agreed Rose, who'd been in the kitchen, busy with the mise en place for the exhibition opening that night. Local media and members of the Kalkari Wines club had been invited, along with their friends from some of the surrounding wineries. Rose was putting together charcuterie plates, terrines and cheeses to feed the hungry masses and soak up some of the wine that was going to be there for tasting.

'Are you sure you're up to this?' Mattie looked pointedly at Rose's stomach, which had the barest hint of roundness.

'Don't be daft. I've never felt better – well, as long as I keep eating, that is.' Rose laughed and crunched on a carrot stick.

'Have you told Mark yet?'

Rose looked evasive. 'Er, not yet. I'm waiting for the right moment.'

'Really?'

'Yes,' said Rose firmly. 'It's got to be right.'

'Okay. You know him as well as I do.' Mattie shrugged. It was between Mark and Rose, though if it had been her she would have been shouting it from the rooftops. 'So how many are we expecting?' she asked, refocusing on the exhibition. She'd been caught up in preparing the photographs and not taken too much notice of the rest of the plans.

'Oh, about a hundred,' said Rose cheerfully.

Mattie gulped. 'A hundred? Shit. I was thinking it was going to be a handful of locals. Way to make me feel exposed.' This was her, up there on the walls: her vision, her perspective, her soul bared for all to see.

'Don't be ridiculous,' said Cara. 'You should be proud – these are truly amazing. I reckon I might not be the only one who's found herself a new career, babe.'

'Thanks,' said Mattie, feeling a thrill of pleasure at Cara's compliments. 'It's a shame Jake won't be here as well. That's a great shot of him there.' She indicated a black and white portrait that highlighted his gypsy charm, the whites of his eyes and his teeth gleaming in contrast to his tawny skin. He'd been at his family's home in Adelaide for the previous week.

'Mark told me yesterday that his father passed away in the early hours of the morning. Jake's staying on for the funeral and to help his mum and sisters out,' Rose said.

'Oh no, I hadn't heard that. How is he doing?' asked Cara.

'Okay, I think,' added Rose. 'It's gotta be tough though.

His father had been ill, but this was far more sudden than they'd thought.'

Just then the door opened and Mark strode into the room. He stopped and stared. 'Wow, sis. These look incredible.'

Mattie gave him a proud smile. 'Thanks, mate. And thanks again for the opportunity.'

'It works both ways – gives our new-release tasting some added class,' he said jokingly. 'We might do it again at the Shingle Valley museum auction in the city. That is, if you've any left after tonight.'

'Oh, I wasn't expecting to sell them,' she said to Mark.

'Why on earth not?'

'You really think people will want to buy them?'

'Hell, yes!' said Cara and Mark together.

'I'll buy one off you right now,' said Rose. 'I love the one of Mark and me in front of the house. Name your price. In fact, you'd better put together a price list for all of them.'

'Well, I'm certainly not going to sell my work to my brother and his partner, the very people who happen to be putting a roof over my head and helping me hold this exhibition!' Mattie protested.

'Consider it rent paid in full then,' said Mark.

'Up until the end of the year,' Rose added, laughing.

By eight o'clock that night the restaurant was heaving, a roar of conversation coming from the crowd, who were there to taste, gossip and socialise. Rose had opened up the doors leading to the garden, letting guests spill out onto the verandah. Brock Doyd had managed to score an invite and made a beeline for Cara, who was looking uncharacteristically demure, wearing a Peter Pan-collared black shirt and pencil skirt, her long blonde hair twisted into a severe bun. It was only when she turned around that Mattie noticed that the shirt was backless, showing off smooth, alabaster skin almost to the cleft in her buttocks. Brock nearly choked on his wine as he saw her rear view. 'How are you, Cara?' he said, regaining his composure as she turned to face him once more.

'Terrific, Broccoli – whoops! I mean Brock. How about you?'

Mattie was keeping a lookout for Charlie. It had been a week or so since she'd last seen him and she'd found herself, in idle moments, thinking fondly of their Sunday hike, the easy conversation and the way he made her laugh over the stupidest things. But he was off-limits, she reminded herself. They could only ever be friends. He hadn't mentioned Marie-Claire at all so she had to assume they were still working things out. She could see Thommo, so like his brother, over near the kitchen with Astrid, but there was no sign of the older twin.

'Hi, Thommo,' she said going over to him.

'Mattie! What amazing photographs. I had no idea you were so talented.' He bent down to give her a kiss on the cheek.

'Thanks,' she said. 'Truth be told I'm still coming to terms with seeing my work blown up so large; it's quite confronting.'

'I wonder what Charlie will think of them. Especially that one.' He pointed across the room. 'I guess we'll find out soon enough,' he said as he looked over to the door, where his brother had just walked in.

Mattie couldn't help it; her heart leapt at the sight of him, his untidy mop of curls, broad shoulders and cheeky grin. He leaned down to kiss her hello and she inhaled his warm, clean, masculine scent. 'Charlie. Thanks for coming,' she said, trying to gather her scattered wits. He gave her butterflies in her stomach like no one else ever had. 'I really appreciate the support,' she said to both brothers.

'I couldn't miss the chance to see the artist's work for myself,' said Charlie. 'Are you going to give me the guided tour?'

'If you like. Come this way.'

'Who's this bloke, then?' he said when they got to the shot she'd taken of him that winter in the vineyard. A glint in his eye and a larrikin smile on his face. 'Pretty good model, if I do say so myself.'

'Hmmm,' she said, pretending to consider it. 'He wasn't bad. I might even use him again.'

Charlie stayed by her side for the rest of the evening, only leaving it to bring her wine as her glass emptied. By the end of the night her photographs were a sea of red 'Sold' stickers and Mattie was on cloud nine. Perhaps, like Cara, she too had found a new career?

But before she could forge a new path, she had one more thing to do.

CHAPTER FORTY

'I'm coming with you,' Mattie said the following morning as she and Mark and Charlie were in his study going through the proposal one final time before the next day's meeting. Mattie had changed into one of her old London work suits, even donning heels and slicking back her hair. She knew that if she was to have any hope of convincing them to let her be a part of the presentation she had to look the part, even for the dress rehearsal she had planned for them. She placed her hands on her hips and lifted her chin defiantly as Mark looked up from the proposal document she had prepared. Including images and maps, it ran to more than fifty pages.

He raised his eyebrows when he saw her outfit. 'What?'

'Hear me out, Mark. One of the things I did best in my job in London was to present strategies. Advertising, marketing, rezoning – it's all essentially the same thing. We have to sell this to Jeremy Bell. It's a pitch. I'm the best person for this job.'

Mattie took the document from him, clicked onto a slide presentation she'd put together and began to speak. Ten minutes later, Mark gave Mattie a low whistle.

'Now I get the reason for the fancy duds,' he said. 'Well, I'm sold. How about you, Charlie?'

Charlie gave Mattie a nod. 'She's got the gig.'

Neither of them noticed her wipe her sweating hands on her trousers. She gathered up the presentation materials and was just about to close her laptop when she noticed an email. From Jamie Soames.

She left Charlie and Mark in the study and took her laptop to the back verandah. As she sat down, Gin came and curled up next to her. She gave the cat a distracted stroke before opening the message.

She gave an involuntary gasp as she read his email. Jamie had been so impressed with her work on the DeVere spring jewels campaign. He was looking for a creative director. He mentioned an eye-watering salary, her own office, a car, complete creative control for the future of the business. Would she be interested? He needed a quick decision.

It was the kind of job Mattie had dreamed of. It was all she could do to stop herself replying there and then.

Mattie was up early for the drive to Sydney for the presentation. They had to be in Macquarie Street for 11am sharp and

Mattie had insisted that they plan to get there at least an hour early. 'We can't risk being late.'

'Don't worry, Mats. We'll get there in plenty of time,' Charlie said. They were driving to the city together, Mark having left at lunchtime the day before for a meeting with his wine distributors.

'Who are we presenting to, apart from Jeremy?' she asked.

'The planning and environment minister, the tourism minister and the local government minister, according to Mark.'

'Quite a line-up.'

She noticed, as they sped along the highway, that Charlie was uncharacteristically quiet. Perhaps it was the early morning, or the gravity of the situation weighing on them both, but they spoke little, each lost in their own thoughts.

Once they'd parked and found the offices, there was plenty of time for a coffee. Mattie got out her phone to call Mark, and Charlie ordered for them. They'd arranged to meet him twenty minutes before the meeting, but she just wanted to check everything was okay. She saw a text from her brother.

'Oh Christ!'

'What's up?' said Charlie, who'd returned with their coffees.

'Mark. He can't make the meeting!'

'What?' His cup shook as he replaced it on the saucer.

'Apparently something's up with Rose. He's had to drive back to Kalkari.'

'Faark! That's all we need. No offence to Rose, of course, but this meeting's really important.'

'He knows that. It must be serious for him to miss it.' Mattie tried dialling his number but the call rang through to his voicemail.

She put her phone down and they looked at each other, both quietly horrified. 'It's just you and me, mate,' she said.

Agitated, Charlie ran his hands though his hair.

'Don't stress. It'll all be fine,' she reassured him, taking a deep breath. 'I've done hundreds of these things. I'll cover Mark's part of the preso – I know it inside out and backwards in any case, I've spent that much time on it, and you know your stuff, right?'

Charlie nodded and looked at her in admiration. 'You're a pretty cool customer, Tilly Cameron.'

'Come on then,' she said, all business. 'Let's go and sock it to 'em.'

More than an hour later, the two emerged from the building into bright sunlight. Mattie and Charlie looked at each other, a mix of exhaustion and exhilaration on their faces.

'How do you think it went?' he asked.

'They sure put us through the wringer. But at least they listened, and asked the right questions. Which, I might add, you were able to answer with ease.'

He grinned. 'You weren't too bad yourself, Mats. Especially when Jeremy asked about revenue projections.'

'Well, that was all Mark's work, but thank Christ his figures were sound.' The warm day had meant that her hair, which had been slicked back, was now falling around her face again and she impatiently brushed it away. 'I think I need a walk before we drive back,' she said. 'I'd forgotten about that kind of pressure.'

'It didn't show. When we were in there, I mean. You were amazing. You're a woman of many talents, Mattie Cameron – presenter, photographer, exotic dancer …'

She turned away so he couldn't see her blush. So he hadn't forgotten about that night in the club. 'How about we go down by the water?' she said.

'Exactly what I had in mind. It's not far away and it'll be cooler down there.'

'Let me just try to call Mark again.' Mattie dialled, but there was no answer. She left a brief message telling him that the presentation had gone as well as could be expected and that she hoped everything was okay with Rose. As she was about to hang up, she noticed a missed call from her dad. What could he want? She dialled his number as they walked towards the harbour.

CHAPTER FORTY-ONE

T he morning of the meeting, Rose had been woken
by a dull ache in her lower back. She'd seen the
doctor a few days after returning from Sydney
and he had confirmed her suspicions with a blood
test. 'Judging by your dates you're about ten weeks along,' he
said, 'though your hormone levels are rather high. But that
could just mean it's a good strong pregnancy.'

With the preparations for Mattie's exhibition and
Mark spending his evenings working on the proposal, Rose
felt like she'd hardly seen him for more than a snatched few
minutes in weeks – it was almost as bad as vintage. There
never seemed to be the right moment to broach the news
and she was becoming increasingly worried about what he
might say, given his throwaway comments about the horror
of the toddler years. They Skyped Leo and Luisa every few
days, and it seemed as though both kids had settled into life
in a new country. Luisa had a new pony and Leo had found

some of the local boys to play soccer with. He was struggling with the language, but proudly showed off a new phrase or words every time they spoke. She could tell Mark was finding it hard without them around, and was working longer and longer hours at the winery to compensate for the quiet around the house. Rose found that by the end of each day she was completely knackered, and was forced to take herself to bed early. 'We're two ships passing in the night,' she'd complained one morning as Mark grabbed a piece of toast on his way out the door.

'Sorry, babe. I'll make it up to you soon, I promise,' he said, stopping for a quick kiss before he left for the winery.

She had barely given a thought to the fact that it was her birthday the following week. With so much going on at the winery and at Trevelyn's, not to mention the secret she was carrying around, it hardly seemed important.

Rose felt another twinge of pain, and rolled over to one side to see if that would ease it. She had been surreptitiously reading up on pregnancy symptoms in quiet moments at Trevelyn's, but she didn't think back pain was supposed to start so early – everything she'd read said it was only really bad in the third trimester. As she moved, she felt wetness between her legs. She reached down and found that her pyjama bottoms were damp and sticky. As she brought her hand up over the covers, she saw that it was covered in bright red blood.

That was not good. Her heart started beating wildly as her brain scrambled to make sense of it. She suddenly didn't want to move, didn't want to do anything to make the bleeding worse. She looked across and saw her phone. She knew Mark was already in the city, so she tried Mattie's number instead. There was a chance she might not have left yet. No answer. Next she tried Cara, who – thank God – answered on the second ring.

'Cara, are you by any chance able to come over to the house?' Her voice shook.

'Yeah, sure. Is everything okay? You sound worried.'

Rose couldn't hold back. 'Oh Cara, I think I'm losing the baby!' she cried, admitting her worst fears.

'Don't move a muscle, I'll be there faster than a scalded cockroach.'

Two minutes later, panting and out of breath, Cara was in the room. She took one look at Rose's pale, frightened face and took charge. 'It's alright, Rose, don't panic. I don't think we should move you without getting help. I'm going to call an ambulance.'

Rose's eyes widened. 'Are you sure that's necessary?'

'Better to be safe than sorry,' Cara said. 'Don't stress, babe. They'll know what to do. It might only be a bleed. The same thing happened to my auntie, and now her son is fifteen and eating down the house. Never laid eyes on a healthier boy.'

Rose knew Cara was trying to reassure her, but she couldn't help thinking the worst. She hadn't even had time to tell Mark yet and it might all be too late.

It seemed an interminable wait until Rose heard the distinctive siren growing louder and closer, an age until Cara went downstairs to let them in.

313

Two paramedics entered the bedroom and began talking to her calmly and slowly, with Cara looking on anxiously. There was a loud knocking from downstairs.

'I'll get that,' said Cara, hurrying down the stairs.

'Oh, it's you,' Rose dimly heard Cara say. 'Are you back already? I'm so sorry about your father.'

'Drove through the night. Got back an hour ago. Was looking for you, actually. What's going on? I heard the sirens and saw the ambulance coming up the drive. Are you okay?' Jake's voice floated up the stairs.

'I'm fine, it's Rose who's in a bit of a bind.'

'Why? What's the matter?'

'Just a bit of bleeding, probably nothing to worry about.'

'Just a bit of bleeding?' Rose heard him say.

After that there was only whispering and Rose turned her attention back to the paramedic, who was taking her blood pressure.

Cara returned upstairs. 'That was Jake. He's going to get hold of Mark. Don't worry, he'll be here soon.'

'No,' Rose protested. 'He's got the meeting this morning. He can't miss it. Don't disturb him, I'm sure I'll be fine.' She grimaced and clutched her stomach.

'I think this is a little more important,' said Cara firmly.

'We're going to take her in,' said the paramedic. 'Do you want to follow us there?'

'Of course,' Cara replied. 'Which hospital?'

'New Bridgeton Base. There's only one in the area, love.'

'Oh, right. It'll all be okay, Rose. I'll be there as soon as I can. You're in the best possible hands now.'

The paramedics lifted Rose carefully onto a stretcher and carried her down the stairs and out to the waiting ambulance. She couldn't help but notice a single magpie perched on a power line that ran to the house. She closed her eyes. She was determined not to see it as a bad sign; it was a time for a mother-to-be's instinct, not random superstition. She tried not to worry as they sped towards New Bridgeton. Once at the hospital, she was admitted and wheeled to a ward on the first floor. Curtains were pulled around her bed and a nurse explained that as soon as they were able, they'd take her down to the ultrasound suite. She closed her eyes and prayed with every ounce of faith she had that the baby would be safe. She couldn't lose it, she just couldn't.

Cara, who'd arrived a few minutes after the ambulance, sat beside her and held her hand. 'Mark will get here as soon as he can. Jake spoke to him and he's on his way back from the city,' she reassured Rose.

She nodded. 'Alright. I wish I'd had a chance to tell him before all this. It's not exactly the way I planned on breaking the news.' She choked back a sob, trying but failing not to think of the worst. 'And he's going to miss the meeting.'

'I know, babe, I know.' Cara soothed. 'But Mattie and Charlie will have it all under control. I've seen her in a pitch – she's a pro. There's no one who can do a better job.'

Cara sat with Rose as nurses came and went, taking her blood pressure and temperature and reassuring them that a doctor would see them just as soon as one was free.

Nearly two hours passed and Cara looked as though she was just about to get up and demand for Rose to be seen, when there was a voice outside the curtain.

'Here, you say?' It was Mark.

He twitched the curtain to peek through, and, seeing her, rushed to her side. 'Oh, Rose, darling, what's happened? Jake told me to get back here as quickly as possible. I've driven like fury; luckily the highway was clear. What's going on? What's happened?' He took her hands in his.

Cara got to her feet. 'I'll go and grab a coffee. Call me if you need me.'

'Thanks, Cara,' said Mark, not taking his eyes off Rose. He stroked her face. 'What is it, darling girl?'

'Oh, Mark,' said Rose and burst into tears. She couldn't get the words out.

Just then the curtains were whipped aside by a nurse, who bustled into the space with an orderly. 'Right, then, let's get you down to ultrasound.'

Mark watched as they began to wheel the bed towards the door.

'Come on, then,' said Rose, getting her tears under control. 'You can come too.'

He looked momentarily stunned. 'Yes, of course.'

The gel on her stomach was cold and Rose shivered. She'd been here before, when Astrid was pregnant. If she wasn't mistaken, it was even the same technician.

'Okay now,' the woman said. 'Let's have a look. How many weeks did you say you were?'

Mark looked from the technician to Rose and back again, his eyes round with unspoken questions.

'Um, about ten or eleven, I think,' she replied. 'I'm not entirely sure. I've only just found out.' She looked pleadingly at Mark.

As the technician pressed the sensor down hard on her belly a whooshing noise like the sound of horses' hooves filled the air. Rose gasped. She remembered that sound from her previous visit.

'I'm not supposed to give it away, but that's definitely a heartbeat, love. Nice and strong, too.'

A huge smile spread over Rose's face. 'Oh, thank God,' she breathed. She turned to Mark. 'I'm so sorry. This is not exactly how I meant to tell you. I was waiting until there was a good time to break the news.'

Mark looked at her incredulously.

'Oh, wait a minute,' said the technician, running the probe over her stomach again. 'Yes. I thought so. There's more than one.'

Rose was confused. 'More than one?'

'Yep, there are definitely two heartbeats. Congratulations, love, it looks like you're carrying twins.'

'Bloody hell, are you sure?'

'Yes, love. Here, have a look.' The technician turned the screen around and, sure enough, there were two pulsating jellybean-like shadows on the screen.

They both gazed at the two blips on the swirling screen.

For a moment, neither spoke, then a grin spread across Mark's face. 'Double the trouble, hey?'

It took Rose a moment to register his comment. 'Oh, Mark! Are you sure you're okay with this? You said you didn't want to go through it all again. I'm perfectly prepared to do it all on my own if I have to – even twins.' She gulped at the thought.

'Did I really say that? If I did, I'm sure I didn't mean it. I'm absolutely delighted, Rose, how could I be otherwise? I love you, and I already love them.'

They were silent as their thoughts turned to the two children that were so far away.

'They'll be back before you know it,' Rose said, putting a reassuring hand on his, knowing what he was thinking. 'And hopefully they'll be thrilled to hear that they're getting two new brothers or sisters.'

He squeezed her hand. 'I know they will.'

CHAPTER FORTY-TWO

Mattie arrived back at Kalkari late that afternoon, having driven back from the city with Charlie. She felt like a wrung-out rag, all her energy used up in the presentation. She and Charlie had talked it over in the car on the way home, and although they both agreed that they'd done all they could, they had no way of knowing what the outcome might be. They'd worked so well as a team, better than she'd even expected. She'd made the main points, and he had been there to back her up and reiterate their message. As they'd walked along the harbourfront, it had been all she could do to keep from giving her real feelings away. Trust her bloody bad luck that he was in love with someone else. The offer from Jamie Soames couldn't have come at a better time – she could put herself far from temptation.

She went over to the cellar door, finding Cara cleaning up.

'Hey there. How's Rose? I tried to call her, and Mark, but couldn't get through to either of them. Mark said something had happened to her, and that was why he didn't make the meeting.'

'Oh, Mats. Rose had some bleeding, quite bad in fact, and she was rushed to hospital in New Bridgeton. I had to call an ambulance, I was so worried for her.'

'Oh God!' said Mattie. 'Is she okay? What happened?'

'She's fine now. Apparently it can happen sometimes in early pregnancy. A sub-chorionic haemorrhage, the doctor said it was called. They're keeping her in for a few days to rest. But that's not all.'

'What?'

'She's having twins.'

'Heavens! That's even more exciting. I'm going to be an auntie all over again! Twice!' Mattie was delighted. 'And what was Mark's reaction?'

'Yeah, what a way to find out, huh? Rose said he's thrilled.'

'I knew he would be. I told Rose she was worrying for nothing. Wow,' said Mattie as the news sank in. 'I should go and see her.'

'Visiting hours are most likely over for today, but I'm sure she'd love it if you popped over tomorrow. Jake came to the hospital too, he'd just got back from Adelaide, and we finally had a talk ...'

'And?' Mattie had wanted her friend to sort it out with Jake for ages; it was as obvious as tits on a bull that they were well suited.

'He's taking me out. Finally!'

'What's changed?'

'We talked about his dad, and he told me it had been a bit of a wake-up call. That he realised the importance of building something, creating and sharing a life with some-one you love. That he'd seen what his parents had and felt envious of them, probably for the first time in his life.'

'That's a bit heavy for Mr Slippery Salmon,' said Mattie.

'I know, right?'

'So?'

'So he said he's going to do things a bit differently from now on. Starting with asking me on a date – a proper date.'

Mattie raised her eyebrows. 'Well, thank Christ for that. I'm very glad to hear that you two are sorting your shit out,' she said.

'About bloody time, huh?' Cara replied. 'We'll see what happens. I do kinda like him though.'

'Can't say I noticed,' Mattie said, smiling at her friend. 'Hey, guess what? I had an email yesterday. From Jamie Soames. You know, DeVere & Soames? He's offered me a job – creative director. Complete control.'

Cara looked astonished. 'Holy crap, Mattie. That's an incredible offer. Are you going to accept it?'

Mattie hesitated. 'I'd be stupid not to.'

'Mattie!' Mark called out to his sister as she went into the house later that evening.

'How's Rose?'

'She's doing okay. Tired, but so relieved that it wasn't anything serious. They're keeping her in for a few days, to make sure she gets some rest as much as anything, I think.'

'Oh, good. I'll pop over to see her tomorrow.'

'So tell me how it all went – the presentation. I'm sorry for leaving you and Charlie in the lurch.'

'Don't be ridiculous. Rose's health is far more important. And anyway, we had it completely under control.'

'Go on, then – what was their reaction?'

'It's hard to say. They listened, asked lots of questions, and then said they'd let us know their preliminary findings in due course.'

'Whatever that means.'

'I know,' she sighed.

'Now, Rose is worrying about Trevelyn's,' Mark said. 'About the wedding that's booked for next weekend. But I've spoken to her sous chef and she's fine to take everything over, so do make sure you tell her we've got it all under control here and that she's not to worry.'

'Okay, will do. Oh, I forgot to congratulate you! How does it feel?'

He choked up. 'Oh, Mats, I'm thrilled. I couldn't be happier. She's an amazing woman.'

'I'm glad you realise that – sometimes I think you take her for granted.'

Mark looked surprised. 'Me? No.'

'Yes, you,' Mattie said firmly. 'She took on a lot, looking after Leo and Luisa like they were her own, you know, as well as everything else. I'm sure it hasn't always been easy, not that she'd ever complain – that's not her style.'

'God, we miss them both so much,' he said. 'Christmas seems so far away. It's been too bloody quiet around here without them.'

'I know, but it'll be December before you know it,' said Mattie. 'Actually, there's something else that'll be here even sooner – Rose's birthday. It's next week.'

'Yes – how have you got on with the label design? The one for the rosé?'

Mattie's hand flew to her mouth. 'Oh! I'd completely forgotten, what with the exhibition and the rezoning meeting. I'll get onto it straightaway, I promise. I've got an idea in mind, and I know somewhere that we can get a few samples printed up. I'll have something organised in time, don't worry.'

'Okay, good. Now what else should we do?'

'Well, Rose does love a good party.'

Mark smiled. 'I remember Rose's dancing at a party a few years ago, the one we had after Kalkari won the Jimmy Watson. It was probably the night I first realised that I was in love with her.'

'Aww,' said Mattie with saccharine sweetness. 'Ain't love grand?'

'Hey, that's enough cheek from you, Tilly Cameron! She won't be dancing the house down for a while, but I reckon a small party, just a few friends over, would be a great idea. The docs say that other than taking it easy for a few days, she'll be right as rain.'

'Well, if you think she'll be up to it, can you let Cara and me organise it? I know you've got a lot on. Please, Mark? I'd love to do something for her – she's made me so welcome here.'

'Done,' he agreed. 'Where should we have it?'

'I think in the garden at Trevelyn's. It's warm enough to hold it outside. We can set up on the verandah. Let me know who you'd like to invite.'

'That's easily done. And speak to the butcher in Eumeralla – he owes me a favour. We can spit-roast something, get people to bring a few desserts, keep it simple. I don't want Rose worrying about anything. Perhaps we should make it a surprise party. That way she won't be able to stress at all.'

'Leave it with me,' she assured him.

Mark headed off to the winery, and Mattie got out her laptop. Several hours later, she had a design for the label that she was pleased with. She just needed Mark's approval. A square photograph of a single pale rose. In flowing script underneath were the words 'by any other name'. It was simple, elegant and beautiful, much like Rose herself.

'I love it,' said Mark as she showed him that evening. 'Let's have forty or so labels printed for the party. We can do the full run later. How long do you think it will take?'

'I reckon my printer can turn this around in a couple of days. I've already given him the heads up.'

'Excellent.'

*

A few days later there was another meeting of the Shingle Valley Preservation Association in the upstairs room of the Southern Cross.

'There have been rumours flying about all over the place,' said Mark, trying to calm an increasingly agitated crowd. 'That doesn't make them true. They're just that. Rumours.'

'There's no smoke without fire,' shouted a voice, to a chorus of agreement.

'Charlie and Matilda met with Jeremy Bell earlier this week and made our submission for rezoning. Jeremy has also assured me that there are no current plans for a change of use at Tarrawenna,' said Mark.

'So why have we heard that Tin Pei has bought up another parcel of land in the valley?' demanded Bob.

'They have, but again, there are no current plans for any further mining licences to be issued, according to Jeremy,' said Mark.

'Unfortunately there's nothing we can do about who buys land in the valley,' said Amanda. 'We need to focus on what we can do, which is to create an awareness campaign.' She paused to hand out several pieces of paper. 'I've listed everything that's been done so far, with photocopies of the reports. If anyone's got anything to add, I'll be happy to consider it.'

'Thanks, Amanda, you've done a terrific job,' said Mark. 'We've been getting some great coverage in the press, and we need to keep the pressure on. We can't afford for people to forget about this. Our future and our children's future depends on it.'

'Hear, hear!' shouted a few in the crowd as the noise level rose.

Mark held up his hand for quiet. 'Now, next order of business. Plans are going ahead for the museum tasting in Sydney,' said Mark. 'Mattie here has very generously offered to include some of her photographs, and donate any money from their sale to the fund.'

Mattie grinned as a murmur of approval went around the room. It felt good to be able to help, but as she thought about Jamie Soames' email, she couldn't quell the queasy feeling in her stomach. Wouldn't they see it as a betrayal if she upped and left again?

CHAPTER FORTY-THREE

Mattie woke up very early – the sun hadn't even risen over the Shingle Hills – with one thing on her mind. It was time. Long past time, actually. She threw on a pair of long pants and a t-shirt, pulled a comb through her hair and splashed her face with water. Grabbing a hunk of bread from the kitchen at Kalkari House, she slathered it with butter and some of Mrs B's strawberry jam then headed out to her car, picking up an old akubra from the pile in the hall on her way. She slung a water bottle on the front seat and took off down the drive.

As soon as she drew up next to the paddock at Windsong, she heard the distinctive whinny. Her heart sped up and she hurried out of the car to see her horse. Shakira was standing with another mare under an old peppermint gum. A layer of mist blanketed the ground, droplets of morning dew trembled on spider's webs and the trees were still dark cutouts.

A sudden bark from one of the Windsong dogs startled the pair, and they kicked up their hooves and cantered across the paddock. As Mattie watched them in full flight, manes and tails streaming out behind them in the wind, she didn't hear the footsteps behind her.

She felt a tap on the shoulder and spun around. 'Oh! You scared me. I didn't think anyone was up and about yet.' Her heart skipped a beat.

'No worries. I saw someone over here and figured it was probably you. I thought you might like this.' Charlie held out a steaming mug of coffee. 'It's only instant, but it'll warm you up.'

'Thanks,' she said gratefully accepting it. 'It's cooler than I thought out here.'

'Well, it is barely light.'

'Yeah, I guess. What are you doing here at this hour?'

'Got a delivery of barrels coming, and had to make some space in the winery. Thommo will be here later to get everything unloaded so I was planning to take a break after I've moved them, maybe even go for a bit of a ride before it gets too warm. What do you say?' he asked casually. 'I promise we'll take it easy – not even so much as a trot.'

Mattie smiled. 'That's what I was here for, actually.'

'Yes! About time, Tilly Cameron,' he said. 'It won't take me long to finish up in the winery. Give me another half an hour or so.'

'Cool. Why don't I go and catch them and get them tacked up?'

'You know where everything is?'

'If I don't, I can figure it out.' Mattie handed him the now empty cup.

'See you in about thirty then.'

Catching Shakira was easy. The horse knew her, and came obediently at her whistle. The other mare was a different story, and Mattie was sweating by the time she eventually managed to throw a halter and lead rope over her. Leading them both to the tack room at the small stables behind the winery, she found bridles and saddles and set about her work. She was attaching stirrups to Shakira's saddle when Charlie reappeared. He was holding a tuckerbag. 'Looks like it's going to be a beaut of a day once this mist burns off. I thought we might go down by the river, perhaps make it to Carrolls Springs?'

'That's a fair way,' said Mattie. Carrolls Springs was named after one of the valley's early settlers, who, legend had it, lost his sweetheart there in a tragic drowning accident. His ghost was said to haunt the spot. It was at least a couple of hours' ride away.

'That's why I've got this,' he said, buckling the tuckerbag onto his saddle and grabbing a battered hat, not unlike Mattie's, from where it hung on a nail in the stable. 'Come on, Fearless, whaddya say?'

Mattie grinned at him. How could she refuse? 'Sounds good to me.'

With her heart in her throat, she gathered Shakira's reins in one hand and let Charlie boost her into the saddle.

She felt suddenly scarily high up, and thoughts of falling on her recently healed shoulder flitted through her mind, but Charlie stood alongside her, calming a skittish Shakira, who hadn't been ridden for some months.

'Okay?' he said, looking up at her.

She nodded and adjusted her seat, holding the reins loosely with hands that were slippery with sweat.

He scrambled up on the other mare, and kicked her off out of the stables. Shakira followed obediently, and Mattie's confidence grew. She leaned forward to give Shakira a pat to reassure herself and the horse.

It was hot by the time they approached the springs. Mattie's leg and hips had begun to ache, but she didn't let on to Charlie; she was revelling in the long-forgotten feeling of being on horseback. They rode easily together, side by side when the trail allowed it, and then in single file as it narrowed. Charlie kept up a steady chat, telling her about the last vintage at Windsong, his plans for it, Thommo's delight at being a father, the cuteness of Max, the latest blue at the pub ...

Honestly, thought Mattie fondly, *the guy could talk underwater*. The rhythmical sway of Shakira beneath her and the sultry heat as the sun rose overhead made her drowsy. Her eyes narrowed and she felt rather than saw the landscape, the sweeping valley floor, the towering gums and the familiar sounds of the bush, the sweet, familiar perfume of eucalypts and dry grasses that enveloped them. It felt like a gift: the perfect day to get back on the horse that she loved so much. There was a special quality to the air, as if it were touched with magic, and she knew that she would remember this day forever, even when she was back in London.

She swatted a fly away for about the millionth time and caught Charlie laughing at her. 'Bet you haven't missed those, hey?' he said.

'Can't say I have. But there's plenty else that I didn't realise I was missing.'

'Oh yeah?'

'Yup. This … Riding …' She shrugged.

He grinned at her. 'Told you so.'

They rode on in silence, Charlie's chatter having unaccountably dried up.

'Whoa there,' he said, pulling his horse to a standstill as they came upon the track that led down to the springs. It was too steep to take them any further on horseback. Charlie dismounted and looked for a suitable tree to tie them up. 'Here,' he said, reaching for Mattie to help her down.

'Thanks,' she said gratefully as she slid off Shakira, aware of his strong hands about her waist. She didn't want him to remove them; despite everything, she wanted him to keep holding her, but no sooner was she on the ground than he released her.

They left the horses grazing and ventured down the track, Mattie clinging onto tree roots to steady herself.

'Okay there, Fearless?' asked Charlie, who was a few steps in front of her.

'Piece of cake,' she replied. The sheen of sweat on her forehead cooled as they descended along the shadowy path.

After a while the track levelled off and opened out and,

rounding a corner, they came upon the springs. There was a flattish, sandy area in front of a dark pool of water almost completely surrounded by rocks. After Charlie's chatter during the ride, the sudden silence and filtered light gave the place an eerie feel. Mattie shivered in the cool, dank air.

'Don't know about you, but I'm famished,' said Charlie. 'How about that spot over there?' He pointed to a large, flat rock big enough for them both to sit on.

'Perfect,' said Mattie, shaking off the nagging feeling that she was being watched. She had heard the story of Phillip Carroll too many times as a child. How he had returned again and again, searching for the body of his true love, but never finding it.

'You know that's all a crock,' said Charlie, reading her mind.

'What?'

'It's all a big myth, that stuff about Carroll's wife drowning. It's made up to frighten little kids and stop them coming down here.'

'No!' Mattie was shocked. 'I believed every word! It was such a tragic story. Are you sure?'

Charlie nodded. 'Uh-huh. My dad told me it had been going around since before he was a boy.'

Mattie felt almost disappointed. They sat down on the rock, mere inches between them, and gazed out at the pool of water. She noticed a dragonfly hovering over the water, flitting this way and that over the glassy surface.

'Doesn't stop it being a very romantic place though,' said Charlie.

'How do you figure that?' There were sitting so close to each other that Mattie could feel his breath on her skin. She turned to look at him and saw that he was staring right at her, an unfamiliar look in his bright blue eyes.

Charlie shook his head. 'Mattie ...'

She decided to take control, to get in first. There was an ease to being with him, as if they spoke the same language, but there were still so many unanswered questions in her mind, not least of which was his relationship with Marie-Claire.

'What's going on here, Charlie?'

'What do you mean?'

'Well, do I have to spell it out?'

There was a pause. Seconds ticked by.

'No. No, Mattie, you don't. I've been trying to tell you.'

Her stomach clenched briefly. She didn't know what he was about to say, and it suddenly mattered a great deal.

'Tell me what?'

'That I'm crazy about you.'

She reeled. 'But what about Marie-Claire? Your, er, fiancée?'

'She went back to France. I told you.'

'But she's coming back, isn't she?'

A look of realisation dawned on him. 'I thought you knew. She came back to see if we could make it work again, but in the end she decided that she didn't want to leave France, and I couldn't leave the valley, this ...' He spread his arms wide. 'This is my home. My life. My world.'

'Oh.' Mattie was floored. That changed *everything*.

'I know what you mean,' she said as she tried to process the momentous news.

'You do?'

'I do. I didn't always understand it, but coming back here has made me see everything differently.'

'Still reckon you're a city girl then? You belong here too, you know.'

'There certainly couldn't be anywhere more beautiful, that's for sure,' she said, avoiding his question.

They sat together quietly, each absorbed in their thoughts.

'Do you remember the dance?' he said suddenly.

'The dance?'

'Yes, at the Eumeralla Hall. You must have been about fifteen or sixteen and I was a couple of years older. You walked into that room like you owned it. I was completely blindsided. The tomboy I'd grown up with had changed into a beautiful girl. I was so stunned I could barely think straight, let alone ask you to dance.'

'I do remember,' she said slowly. 'You weren't the only one to be blindsided.'

'Really?'

'Uh-huh.' She nodded emphatically at him. Mattie steeled herself to say the words she'd been rehearsing in her mind. 'I've got something to confess,' she said.

Charlie looked at her, curious.

'I remember everything about that night, in the club …' She blushed.

'I know,' Charlie replied.

'You what?'

'I know you do. It's one of the things I love most about you. You're utterly transparent, Matilda Cameron. Couldn't tell a lie to save yourself.'

'Oh,' she said, turning even redder. 'But you let me believe ...'

Charlie smiled, leaned forward and pulled her gently towards him, his lips meeting hers in a sweet, tender kiss that she felt all the way down to her toes. Time stilled. The sounds of the river and the birds faded, replaced by the insistent thrum of her heart. She was consumed by the feeling of his skin on hers, his hand cradling her head, the taste of him, the feeling of utter rightness at being there with him. She didn't want the moment to end.

Eventually, they broke apart, but she held his gaze. The look of joy on Charlie's beautiful, dear face was, she knew, reflected in her own. The thought of the job offer from Jamie Soames flew into her mind. Was she ready to break her own heart?

CHAPTER FORTY-FOUR

Rose stretched blissfully in the big bed in the master bedroom at Kalkari, enjoying the feel of the soft cotton sheets after the hospital's starched linen. It was so nice to be back home again. A slight breeze ruffled the curtains at the window and she lay listening to the warble of magpies and the occasional piercing note of a whipbird. The morning sounds of Kalkari were one of her favourite things about living there.

She placed a careful hand on the gentle swell of her stomach. No cramps. That was good. 'Come on, little fighters, you hang in there,' she whispered to the tiny jellybeans growing inside her. She eased herself out of bed and padded downstairs to the kitchen and put the kettle on. The doctors had reassured her that a sudden bleed was a common occurrence in early pregnancy, but she didn't want to take any chances. Making a mental note to look into organising some extra help at Trevelyn's, she walked over to the fridge for milk. She was just pouring the tea when there was a knock at the door.

Opening it, she got the surprise of her life.

There, on the doorstep was Isabella, resplendent in a black trenchcoat with the collar turned up, killer heels and a slash of red lipstick. Her normally perfectly styled hair was pulled back severely and her eyes were hooded and ringed with grey. She looked tired and wan. Rose was so shocked by Isabella's appearance that she completely forgot that she had yet to get dressed, and was clad in fabulous ice-blue pyjamas with polar bears gambolling across her chest.

'Ah, Rose. I am glad it is you. May I come in?' Rose was still absorbing the fact of Isabella's sudden appearance and took a while to answer. 'If that's not too much trouble?' Isabella said, a note of impatience in her voice.

Rose was surprised. Isabella had never spoken to her like this before. What was going on?

'Of course,' Rose said, standing back and opening the door wider for her to enter. 'I must say we weren't expecting you. I thought you were in Spain?'

'Well, obviously I am not. Not for now, anyway.'

'I'm afraid Mark's already left for the day. I think he said he was heading to the Trevelyn's vineyard.'

'Actually it is you I have come to see.'

'Okay. I've just made a pot of tea, actually. Would you like some?' Rose's natural politeness came to the fore.

'Coffee. If you have it.' Isabella's abruptness was something Rose could never quite get used to, though her rudeness no longer had the same effect on her as it once had.

As she led her through to the kitchen, she wondered where Leo and Luisa were. 'Have a seat and I'll bring some cups over,' she said, indicating the table.

'I expect you are wondering why I am here, no?'

Rose nodded and waited for her to say more.

'I am bringing the children back to Kalkari. They have had a wonderful time in Spain, but they miss their home and their father. Leo the most. He has been a very sad boy. He has tried not to show it, but I can see it anyway. He needs his father.'

'Oh, that's wonderful.' Rose could hardly believe her ears. 'Well, for Mark, anyway, I know he'll be thrilled. He has really missed them. We all have.'

'It's not easy, you know …' Isabella's voice trailed off and Rose felt suddenly sorry for her. Her hand went involuntarily to the curve of her belly. She couldn't imagine ever having to share her children in the way Isabella and Mark had to.

'I'm sure it isn't,' said Rose softly. 'Where are they, by the way? The kids, I mean.'

'Oh, they are over at Mrs B's. We flew in yesterday and stayed overnight in Sydney, but they were awake so early this morning that we drove straight to the valley. She's feeding them breakfast. They were desperate to come back to Kalkari, but I wanted to see you first, before bringing them back here.'

Rose's stomach rumbled at the mention of breakfast. She'd been fortunate not to suffer from morning sickness, but the flipside was that she was always starving. 'Er, I don't suppose you'd like some toast?'

Isabella gave her a look of disbelief. *Yes*, thought Rose, *you don't look like you eat carbs. Ever.*

'I know that you have taken care of my children in the past. Very good care. I am ashamed to admit that I have not always been the nicest person to you and I am sorry for that.'

Rose nearly fell off her chair. Wonders would never cease. 'Thank you,' Rose said graciously. 'You're right, it hasn't always been easy; for either of us. It's good of you to recognise that.'

Isabella took a sip of her coffee, winced, and put it down. Rose pretended not to notice. 'I have too much to do at my family's company. My father needs help, and my mother ... pah! She has no clue. I must be there to run the business, but I cannot do that and look after Leo and Luisa. It is a hard thing to say, but I think their place is here.'

'Golly, I can imagine that was a difficult decision to make.'

Isabella inclined her head. 'I must do what is right for my family. For all of my family.'

Rose got up and stuck two thick slices of bread in the toaster. Her hunger couldn't wait a moment longer. When the toast popped up, she slathered on butter and a dollop of strawberry jam and piled it onto a plate, putting it in the centre of the table. She could see Isabella looking hungrily at it, and got out a second plate. 'Go on, help yourself. It's Mrs B's prize-winning jam. The ladies of the CWA are never wrong.'

CHAPTER FORTY-FIVE

'A re you okay, dude?' said Cara as Mattie eased herself horizontally onto the sofa in the barn. She'd just arrived back from her day out with Charlie and was dusty and saddle-sore.

'I'm not sure I'll be able to walk for a week, but yes, I'm okay.' She beamed at Cara.

'Oooh, what have you been up to? Did it have anything to do with a certain blond-haired, blue-eyed, drop-dead-gorgeous winemaker?'

'It might have.' Mattie was coy.

'Go on then, spill ...'

'We took the horses for a ride, only it was quite a lot further than I planned. We stopped for a picnic at Carroll's Springs ...' She lost herself in the memory of Charlie's lips on hers, the way his arms wrapped around her, the feel of his lean body against hers ... Mattie wanted to hug the memory of that day to herself. She didn't know if there would be others.

'And the job?'

Mattie looked at her guiltily. 'I've asked for another week to make my decision. But what about you?' she said, changing the subject.

Cara gave her a Cheshire cat smile. 'You mean Jake?' she asked innocently.

'Yes, I mean Jake!'

'Pretty good,' she said. 'I reckon I can keep him on his toes.'

'Is that right?' asked Mattie, seeing through her friend's deliberate flippancy. 'You're not mucking around there, are you?'

'We'll see. Now, have you remembered that it's Rose's party tomorrow?'

Mattie groaned. 'I knew there was something I was supposed to do today – go to the post office in Eumeralla and pick up the labels. Christ, Mark's going to kill me!'

'Will you be able to get there first thing in the morning?'

'I guess I'll have to. What else do we need to do?'

'I've got the rest of it under control. The butcher's sending someone to help set up the suckling pig and spit-roast, everyone's bringing a salad or a dessert, we've got to pick up some bread tomorrow, and Mark's in charge of the wine – when you get the labels to him, that is.'

There was a loud knock at the door of the barn, a scuffle and some giggles.

'Expecting anyone?' said Cara.

Before Mattie had a chance to reply, the door flew open

and two dark-haired children burst into the living room.

'What the …?' said Mattie, completely taken aback.

'Auntie Mattie! We're back!' cried Leo. '*Hola. Como estas?*' he said triumphantly.

'*Hola*, Auntie Mattie!' said Luisa, throwing her arms around her.

'Oh my goodness, let me look at you two. I swear you've each grown at least half a metre! What have you been eating over there?' Mattie laughed with them. 'What are you doing back? I thought you were staying in Spain until Christmas?'

'Mama said it was better for us all to come back to Australia,' said Leo. 'Spain was good, but I really missed my friends. And you and Dad and Rose, of course,' he added quickly.

'Well, you've certainly given us the surprise of our lives. I bet your dad is pleased! And I'm so happy to see you both. Come here, both of you,' she said, reaching for them. 'We've got plenty of cuddles to make up for.'

Leo looked embarrassed, but succumbed to Mattie's embrace. Luisa had no such qualms and clung to her like a limpet.

'Auntie Mattie, did you know I'm going to have two little brothers or sisters?' Luisa's eyes were wide with excitement.

Rose and Mark must have told them the news.

'I know, isn't that wonderful?' She grinned at them. 'You're going to be such a good big sister.'

Luisa nodded solemnly.

'I hope they're boys,' said Leo with a shy grin.

'No, girls!' insisted Luisa.

'Well, we won't know for a while – perhaps it'll be one of each? Now, we'd better get you two scamps back to the house. Come on.'

Mark was opening a bottle of wine when they trooped into the kitchen, and Mattie noticed a look of joy and relief on his face that had been absent for months.

'Well, this is rather unexpected, isn't it?' she said.

'Out of the blue,' Mark replied. 'And cause for celebration, I'd say.' He handed Mattie and Cara each a glass of wine. 'Let's take these out onto the verandah.'

They went outside and Leo and Luisa began to chase Barnsie about the yard. Mattie felt Gin curl around her legs and then settle herself on her lap. Rose followed them out, carrying a plate of antipasti and a soda for herself. The sun was putting on a glorious show, colouring the sky with streaks of rose pink and orange. Mattie glanced over to the yard, where Leo and Luisa were trying to get Barnsie to play fetch. They'd reached a fever pitch of excitement at being home, but she could tell that they'd collapse with exhaustion before too long. She looked up and saw the flock of cockatoos coming in to roost, their shrieks shattering the evening peace. Once again, she was struck by how stunningly beautiful the valley was. How could she have taken it for granted for all those years?

Cara and Mattie sprang into action the next day. After an early morning trip to the post office to pick up the labels and then delivering them to Mark, the two girls snuck over to Trevelyn's to set up for Rose's surprise birthday party.

'Where do you want these, love?' The deliveryman pointed to the back of his van, which was open to reveal stacked boxes of Chinese paper lanterns, pink bunting and pompoms. Cara had ordered them online and Mattie heaved a sigh of relief that they had arrived in the nick of time.

'Cara, do you think you can give me a hand here?' Mattie called into the restaurant. 'These boxes need shifting into the dining room.'

'Yep, I'm on it,' Cara replied, putting down the stack of plates she'd been carrying and heading out to the van. As she was helping to unload the decorations, Mark drove up in his ute, the back of which contained several wine cartons.

'Got the labels on. Whaddya think?' he said, diving into one of the cartons and pulling out a bottle.

'Ohhh, they've come up brilliantly!' said Cara.

'She's going to love it,' agreed Mattie.

'Alright then, let's get these into the fridges and chilled down. What time is the spit-roast coming?'

'Later this arvo. We'll have this all decked out by then. And Mrs B is making one of her famous sponges – with rose-pink icing, of course.'

Mark raised an eyebrow. 'I'm sensing a theme here.'

The two girls grinned at him.

'Does she have any idea?' asked Mattie.

'Not a clue. I told her to take it easy today, and that we might head over to the pub for dinner with the kids later. Oh, Mattie,' he added, 'guess what?'

'Hmm?' Mattie was inspecting the wine labels.

'You had a parcel delivered by courier today. They came round to the winery.' He dug out a cardboard box.

'I didn't order anything else for Rose's party,' she said. 'I wonder what it is?'

'Been doing some internet shopping?' asked Cara with a wink.

'Hardly!'

'Come on then, open it,' said Cara.

Mattie peeled off the tape from the package and lifted a flap. 'Oh my goodness.' She pulled out a note and began to read. '*Dear Miss Cameron. Please accept our apologies for the unfortunate incident you suffered recently. We trust that this will prove a suitable replacement ...*' She pulled out a camera, lenses, and a bag from the box. 'It's from Tin Pei Resources. I'm not sure I can accept this.'

'What? Don't be an idiot!' exclaimed Cara. 'It was their fault. You weren't doing anything wrong.'

'Absolutely,' said Mark. 'I think it's the least they can do. Anyway, it's a drop in the ocean as far as they're concerned.'

'But it's worth so much more than mine,' protested Mattie even as she marvelled at its beauty. 'And it feels like blood money.'

Mark scoffed. 'Don't be ridiculous.'

The camera felt so right, balanced between the base of her thumb and her fingers. Solid, comforting. She held it up to one eye, closing the other, and gazed through the aperture. She hadn't realised how lost she'd felt without her own way to look at the world, to interpret it, to create beauty.

CHAPTER FORTY-SIX

'I thought we'd leave at about six. That okay with you?' Mark said to Rose that evening.

'How about we stay here instead?' she pleaded. 'I'm still a little tired, and the kids are both knackered too ...' She'd been feeling down all day, not least because no one apart from Mark – who'd given her a quick birthday kiss that morning – had mentioned her birthday. Were they so caught up in themselves that they'd all completely forgotten about it?

Mark gave her a concerned look. 'I'd really like for us all to go out. It is your birthday after all, darling.'

She sighed.

'And I promised Thommo and Astrid that we'd have a drink with them – Astrid's dying to see the kids again. We won't be late, I promise.'

'Okay,' said Rose. 'I'd better go and have a shower then.

I'm filthy after being down at the stables with Luisa and Buttons this afternoon.'

'Good. You'll feel better after that,' he reassured her. 'Why don't you wear your new dress too? The pink one?'

Rose looked at him, surprised. 'Isn't it a little dressy for the pub?'

'Not at all,' Mark replied swiftly. 'And besides, you look gorgeous in it.'

'Aw, thanks. I hope it still fits. My boobs have exploded.'

'Don't think I haven't noticed,' he said with a wicked grin. 'In fact, come here, my lovely girl. I haven't kissed you since at least this morning. How are my two little fishes doing in there?'

Rose showered and put on the dress – a pale pink silk wraparound frock with a deep vee that showed off her enhanced cleavage and skimmed the curve of her belly. She let her long dark hair hang loose down her back, and dusted her tawny skin with blush. A touch of mascara lengthened her eyelashes and a raspberry-pink stain on her lips completed the look.

'Yum, you look good enough to eat,' said Mark as she came downstairs.

'I'm famished myself,' replied Rose. 'God only knows what this pregnancy is going to do to me – I'll end up the size of a whale. But you were right, I do feel much better.'

'Good. Now, come on, birthday girl, let's get going. Leo, Luisa, you too!' The two kids jostled each other to see who could get out the front door first.

*

'This isn't the way to the pub,' said Rose, confused. Mark had turned the car right out of the Kalkari drive, not left towards Eumeralla.

'Oh, I wanted to stop by Trevelyn's on the way. Something got dropped off there for me by mistake.'

'But it's not really on the way. And I'm starving!' protested Rose. 'Can't it wait?'

'It'll only take five minutes.'

Rose knew something was up when they drove up to the restaurant and saw that the carpark was almost completely full, but it was only when she recognised Thommo's ute – with the numberplate CORK – that she twigged.

Mark pulled over outside Trevelyn's, beeped the horn, and the front door opened. People began to flood out. Thommo, Astrid and Max, Deano, Charlie, Angie, Jake holding hands with Cara, Dan, Bob, Mrs B, Officer Doyd and more, until about forty people were standing in the drive.

Rose gasped and looked at Mark. 'Really?'

'Uh-huh. We couldn't let you celebrate your birthday quietly, I'm afraid, darling,' he said, a note of triumph in his voice.

They scrambled out of the car, and Rose was swept up in a sea of hugs before being propelled into the dining room. Pink paper lanterns lit up the white walls, strings of pompoms hung from the ceiling and urns of roses gave off a sweet perfume. As she went out onto the verandah, she saw huge platters of cheese, salami and prosciutto, olives and dried fruits that had been placed at intervals on tables, together with salads, bread and bowls of fresh strawberries, raspberries and thick yellow cream. In pride of place was a large pink cake.

'Oh, I don't know what to say. How beautiful it all looks!' Rose was touched that they had gone to so much trouble for her. 'Was this you, Mattie?'

'Actually it was mainly Cara. I just helped out a bit.'

'Now Mattie's being far too modest. She designed this – what do you think?' Mark said with a flourish as he showed her the newly labelled rosé.

Rose gasped with pleasure. 'A wine, named after me? How gorgeous! Thank you, both – I love it! What a brilliant present.'

'Here, have a tiny sip,' said Mattie, handing her a glass.

Rose looked around the room and saw so many of her dear friends gathered there. She felt quite choked up. 'I'm so lucky to have such lovely people in my life. Thank you all for surprising me so thoroughly and completely. I can't believe I didn't have a clue!'

'I just heard,' Amanda stood in front of Mattie and Mark. 'Your proposal – the rezoning.'

Mark nodded. 'I only found out myself this morning, how on earth did you know?'

'Know what?' asked Thommo, who had been standing nearby.

Mark reached over for a knife and began to clink it against the glass he was holding, calling for silence. 'For those of you who haven't yet heard on the ever-efficient Shingle Valley grapevine, it would appear that our proposal to have the southern end of the valley rezoned for tourism use has passed its first hurdle. Jeremy Bell phoned me this morning to say that the wheels are in motion for a moratorium on any drilling or excavation in the valley while the rezoning is being considered.'

A loud cheer went up from the crowd.

'And we have your and Charlie's hard work to thank for it,' said Amanda.

More cheers.

Mark signalled for quiet. 'Thank you, Amanda, and yours too. But there's one more person to thank – someone who helped us pull together the proposal and, with her beautiful photographs, was instrumental in helping our case. She also stepped in at the last minute and helped to present the proposal to the committee. Mattie, come here.' Mattie moved to her brother's side, beaming at him. 'My sister, Matilda. I'm so proud of you and I know the rest of the valley is too.

'But I also wanted to share with you all some news of our own.' Mark looked over at Rose, as she beamed with joy. 'Rose and I are going to be parents – and of twins, no less!'

The guests erupted into cheers and claps again, but Mark tapped on his glass. 'I also have a question to ask Rose today, and I can think of no better way to do it than in the presence of our closest friends. Rose, darling ...' He took her hand. 'You have no idea how much you mean to me. You've become such a part of my life that I never want to live without you. Will you do me the honour of marrying me, my darling Rose?'

He looked at her with such love and tenderness that Rose felt her stomach flip-flop with delight. Everything seemed to be happening at once, and her head spun with it all. Was he really asking her, here, in front of everyone? There was only one possible answer.

'Yes,' she cried, spluttering. 'Of course!'

CHAPTER FORTY-SEVEN

'So whaddya think? Or are you too scared?'

Mattie and Charlie were saddling up for an early morning ride, the day after Rose's birthday party. It was only Mattie's second time on horse-back since her accident. 'Not scared, not scared at all,' she replied with false bravado. This was a test. She didn't want to fail it, didn't want her nerve to falter.

'Come on then, what are you waiting for?' Charlie said.

She took a deep breath and mounted Shakira. Together they trotted out of the stables. 'Let's go over towards Bob's Run – there's a track between the two vineyards that goes up to the top of the hill.'

'I think I know the one,' said Mattie as a memory surfaced of riding that way once with her brother, years before.

'Follow me then,' said Charlie, giving his horse a hefty kick to get it moving. He set off at a canter.

'Oh, Christ!' said Mattie. There was nothing for it but to follow him. The track was wide and dry and Shakira broke into a canter too, racing to catch Charlie's horse. They thundered along, scaring a flock of magpies sitting on a fenceline ahead of them. Mattie felt something within her release and she gave a great whoop of excitement. In that moment she was free, free of all cares, simply enjoying the ride. She wasn't scared any more. Not of this, not of anything. She let go of her nerves, discarding them like an old coat that no longer fitted her, and spurred Shakira on faster, ever faster. They reached an open paddock and Shakira began to gallop, Mattie holding onto the reins for dear life, not worrying that she might fall and hurt herself again, just loving every minute. She soon passed Charlie.

Charlie kicked his horse on again and gave chase.

Mattie pulled Shakira up as they reached the far end of the paddock and the track narrowed again. 'Whoa, girl. Easy there.' She heard Charlie coming up close behind her.

'I'd say you've earned back your nickname,' he said, gasping for breath.

'Oh yeah?'

'Fearless forever!' he shouted into the wind.

Mattie laughed, and tried to catch her breath. She felt on top of the world and thought back to the party the night before, to Rose's complete surprise and delight at Mark's proposal. She was thrilled for them both, and so happy to be gaining a sister – though in truth Rose already felt like the sister she'd never had. She could see that Mark and Rose's was a relationship founded not only on love, but also on trust and respect. That it could withstand all the challenges life threw at them.

She looked at Charlie, who had come alongside her.

'Charlie, there's something I need to tell you.' Her heart hammered in her chest.

'So it's true then.'

Mattie was astonished. 'What? What's true?'

'Amanda let it slip last night. I think she was quite pleased to be the bearer of the news actually.'

'How the *hell* does she know?' Mattie's hands tightened on the reins and Shakira gave a small buck.

Charlie shrugged. 'News travels in the valley. Cara told Jake, who told Thommo, who told Amanda ... or something like that. You know how it is.'

'Christ. Is nothing sacred around here?' Mattie was momentarily furious.

They slowed the horses to a walk. 'So when do you leave?' he asked, a resigned look on his face.

'This weekend. They don't know exactly what's wrong with her, but she's pretty sick.'

'Wait, what?'

'Mum. She's crook. Been having dizzy spells and then had a fall last week. I thought that was what we were talking about.'

A look of relief lightened Charlie's features. 'Oh, Mattie. I'm so sorry to hear about your mum. But I thought you were talking about going back to London – your incredible job offer?'

'How the hell did you know about that?'

'I told you – Cara told Jake, who told —'

'Okay, I get the picture.'

'And what about that?'

Seconds ticked by. Mattie looked him square in the eye. 'I'm not going.'

'What? I thought it was what you'd always wanted? The opportunity of a lifetime. That's what Amanda said.'

'Well, Amanda's a bloody nosy cow. As it happens, I've found other, better things to love. I've begun to think I might be able to make a go of photography. As a career. And I can think of nowhere else I want to take pictures than here,' she said, indicating the landscape. 'I've had a couple of calls since the exhibition, possibly even a commission. And now Mum's sick, I really want to be around for her, to be able to see her, not far away on the other side of the world.'

'So you're telling me that you're staying? For good?'

She grinned at him. 'Photography's not the only thing I've found to love.'

'Oh yeah?'

'Yeah. Looks like you're stuck with me, mate.'

Joy spread over Charlie's face and he reached for Shakira's reins, stilling the horses as he leaned over to kiss her. 'You won't regret it, I promise you that.' He looked suddenly serious. 'You know there was another reason things didn't work out with Marie-Claire.'

'Oh?'

'I told her that I'd started to have feelings for someone else. More than started, actually. Hook, line and sinker, if you must know.'

Her heart sang as she realised that he could only be talking about her. She couldn't imagine any sweeter words; they were the ones she'd wanted to hear for so long.

'It's you, Mattie,' he said. 'It's been you for years.'

She grinned and glanced sideways at him, a mischievous look on her face.

'What?' he said.

'Oh you'll see,' she said, urging Shakira forward towards a low fence at the end of the paddock.

She sailed over the jump, leaving him watching, open-mouthed, in admiration.

'Race you home, Charlie Drummond!' she cried, her words reaching him on the wind.

ACKNOWLEDGEMENTS

An enormous thanks to everyone who has been so supportive of first *Rose's Vintage*, and then this, *Angel's Share*. Andy, for his unquestioning loyalty and never complaining at the number of weekends I spent writing and rewriting; my agent, Margaret Connolly, for her unflagging enthusiasm and encouragement for my writing; my sister Becky for indulging me in numerous and wildly improbable plot discussions; Mercedes and Jane, my wonderfully positive early readers; Taryn, the most insightful critique partner a writer could hope for, and finally Black Inc., especially my editor, Jo Rosenberg, whose guidance, editorial smarts and good sense has been invaluable, expertly steering me away from unnecessary tangents and helping me to shine a light on the good parts.

To the enthusiastic, supportive readers of *Rose's Vintage*, especially those who have begged for a return to the Shingle Valley – I hope I haven't let you down and that you love this book as much as the first one.

Kayte Nunn is a freelance book, magazine and web editor and the former editor of *Gourmet Traveller WINE* magazine. Her first novel, *Rose's Vintage*, was published in 2016. She is a mother to two girls.

www.ingramcontent.com/pod-product-compliance
Lightning Source LLC
Chambersburg PA
CBHW030356030726
47497CB00002B/372